WHAT DOESN'T KILL YOU

WHAT DOESN'T KILL YOU

JAN GRAPE

FIVE STAR

A part of Gale, Cengage Learning

GALE
CENGAGE Learning™

Detroit • New York • San Francisco • New Haven, Conn • Waterville, Maine • London

GALE
CENGAGE Learning

LIBRARY OF CONGRESS CATALOGING-IN-PUBLICATION DATA

Grape, Jan.
    What doesn't kill you / Jan Grape. — 1st ed.
      p. cm.
    ISBN-13: 978-1-59414-888-0 (hardcover)
    ISBN-10: 1-59414-888-0 (hardcover)
    1. Young adults—Fiction. 2. Dead—Fiction. 3. Texas—Fiction.
I. Title. II. Title: What does not kill you.
PS3607.R373W47 2010
813'.6—dc22   2010019571

First Edition. First Printing: September 2010.
Published in 2010 in conjunction with Tekno Books and Ed Gorman.

To five of the most awesome young people I know: Riley, Jarred, Jackie, Cason, and Lucas. They all are witty, smart, funny and good-looking; the fact that they are related to me is immaterial.

ACKNOWLEDGEMENTS

It's absolutely impossible to thank everyone who helps a writer with their book. I still need to mention a few. Russ Hall, friend and fellow writer whose idea for this book is totally responsible for it being published. Your help was invaluable, Russ. My singer/songwriter pals at River City: Grille, Mike B., John G. and John Arthur, whose music each week helps keep me in a positive mood. And for always being there, Ed Gorman and Marty Greenberg. Last, but not least, Tiffany Schofield, editor extraordinaire. Thank you, all, thank you very much.

CHAPTER ONE

The ghost of young Sarah had haunted the Whalen place for the better part of the past hundred years and would kick up a moan and rattle every time a West Texas wind swept through the old abandoned Victorian home, or at the very least when anyone was fixing to try and move in. Its paint had long ago been sanded away where it stood stark and tall, with staring broken-glass eyes among the stubble of dried brush and bent yellow grass. No one had managed to live there since Sarah's time, and even a film crew from a college that had tried to stay there a night had clambered into their van before two A.M. and peeled out into the night leaving behind a pretty darn good camera.

Sarah's kin had all died of the fever when she was but fourteen, and she'd had the grit to go on living there alone until a drifter or peddler named Garcia came to live there and made her his common-law wife. Together they had a son, Estaban, but not long after that Garcia drifted on. Sarah ran the place as an inn for several years until a fellow named Coleman Burns came back from the gold fields with a poke of gold dust worth some sixteen hundred dollars. She heard a scream and found him a ways from the house in a pool of his blood with a man bent over him taking his gold.

The sheriff said it was a murder and robbery, and that Sarah Whalen was the last person to see him alive. She was tried, convicted, and jailed without her ever saying a word. Long after they'd hung her, the only friend she ever had admitted Sarah's secret. The friend was on her own deathbed and said the man Sarah had seen bending over the dead miner was Estaban, her son. Now they say she haunts the house while keeping a watch out for her son. To this day you might hear a scream now and then from the house that would make your blood turn to lumps. Plenty of people had said they'd heard it. Too many to doubt.

CHAPTER TWO

Cory Purvis stood with the wind tugging at her pale blond hair and stared at where the clouds formed dark clusters. She didn't know what had set her off thinking about the ghost. Some said it wasn't a ghost, that it was just a mountain lion; some folks even said it was parts of each, as if that was possible. Possible had nothing to do with anything out in these parts. Hard to tell if it wasn't all just wishful thinking, wishing for something, anything to happen out here. Most times when people heard something, or thought they did, were times like right now, with the sky darkening like a bruise spreading from the horizon into angry black fists of clouds shaking themselves toward the cowering, unhappy earth, flashes of lightning happening so deep inside the thick dark masses that you saw only flickers of blood red snapping on and off like a faulty lamp with a wire scraped bare.

Still and all, you stare at a stretch of rock-littered, yellow-gray-red sandy soil while feeling the relentless dry heat of the sun-baked ground as a storm creeps in, with its static electric crackle tingling the air until you jump at the slightest touch, and you're likely to see whatever you want, even a ghost that's part mountain lion. When your skin feels dry as parchment, each warm breath of gusting air feels like embers of a fire settling to the bottom of your lungs, and you wake in the morning feeling tired and useless before the day rightly gets a chance to begin. Then a passing semi truck, or a plane far off in the sky dragging its long spreading white contrail, or even a ghost might be a welcome sight.

Cory looked away from the threatening sky and approaching storm to watch an orange-brown ball of tumbleweed turn end over end, a basket-sized cluster of stiff tan dried sticks rolling faster in the breeze of the coming storm. It bounced off the edge of the raised wooden porch, curled along the edge of the flat one-story general store building. Cory stood staring at it as if it fascinated her, though it didn't. She was a thin young woman, sixteen years old, with far too much sense of inner dignity to want to be called a girl. She was a young lady now, with whole thoughts that were all her own. Cory wore a t-shirt bleached starkly white with her hands shoved down in her jeans pockets, and she stood on the store's porch watching the ball of dried sticks pass from one end of the town to the other, never stopping, nor sticking. It rolled out of sight, lost in a reddish gray swirl of dust.

You wish, she thought, for some little change, for something to be different. But it's the same old, same old day after day.

Time stretches out in a small Texas town, in any small town in America for all that. It had been eight very long, windy and dust-blown years since she'd arrived out here. She was still a year from being out of high school, and felt she had lived two or three lifetimes, each of them more like the first than before.

As far as she could see in either direction, the two-lane street through town looked deserted except for the pickup truck in front of the store shuddering to the purr of its engine's idle.

She didn't think much of Wesley Hargate, the fellow who leaned against the driver's side of the pickup, his forearms resting on the sill. He spoke to the driver but nodded over at the half-Indian who stood beside Cory.

"You might could ask TyTy over there." Wesley's eyes squinted against the growing wind. "He might fancy seeing a road-a-o." He said it with an unnecessarily hard emphasis on the "a." His glance swept Cory's and TyTy's faces.

Cory squinted back at him. In the hollow flatness of the wind, the four of them might as well be the only people in the world. The wind was a lifting and dropping hum vibrating in her ears. She could taste dust with every breath.

Cory and TyTy stood a dozen feet from the truck on the store's porch.

Wesley was speaking loud enough to be sure Cory and anyone else nearby heard. Cory's head swung to the disappearing tumbleweed, then back to him. Wesley nodded his head toward them, hollered over, "Yo, TyTy, you want to see some show where animals are roped and tied all up?"

"Aw, lay off," TyTy said. He looked up, one eye narrowed, the black iris of the open eye neither smiling nor frowning at Wesley. He was holding an empty Dr Pepper can. He began twisting it in his hands until it tore. A jagged piece of the exposed gray metal slid across his callus-crusted hand. Blood began to seep from an inch-long slit in his right palm. He stopped the bleeding by closing his hand into a fist.

"What's he talking about, TyTy?" Cory's voice was soft enough for just him to hear. She looked away from TyTy in case he wanted to tie his handkerchief around the cut or something.

Wesley leaned back slightly and turned his head to spit. The brown streak arched through the air and then trailed off, leaving a spot or two on the faded pale blue side of the truck. Farley frowned as Wesley reached and wiped at the spots with the sleeve of his shirt, the fake pearl buttons of his sleeve grating on the worn paint and metal. Not that a few more spots would matter—the low inside corners of the truck by its wheels and bed had long ago grown leprous with reddish brown rust.

Farley sat behind the wheel of the truck, staring at the two on the porch. His face was lightly tanned, the rough seams and sun squint marks not visible, smoothed for the moment. His eyes were blank; the lights were on but no one was at home. Cory thought Farley was made out of perfect Deputy Sheriff stuff. He had not had an original thought since . . . well, since never. It was why, she figured, he was always around a cowardly bully like Wesley.

Wesley was one of those fellows who hung around, figuring they were on the inner circle of some cluster of friends. Yet when he was not there, everyone wondered why he hung around at all. His comments were usually snide, his interests all narrow and self-absorbed. He liked to bully, but only when he had someone like Farley to back him up. He had never shared a warm, giving, or human moment in anyone's memory. But there he was, just the same.

Farley, though, was the kind of guy you would expect to find working on his day off, working like a coyote playing tug of war with its clenched teeth tight on a piece of loose rope. He had little life off the job as far as anyone knew, not that he was a good deputy. It was just what he did, was all he ever did.

Cory watched their faces. She wondered what the rodeo had to do with the missing girl Farley had driven to the store to ask about. The two young men seemed to share some secret smile between themselves, one not intended to embrace TyTy or her. She had not heard of any damn rodeo. Farley said he had picked up the squeal about the girl on his private police band radio and was being active off-duty, the way someone like him would.

The breeze from the coming storm tugged at the pale bangs of Cory's blond hair. She lifted a hand and ran her fingers through her hair, letting it tumble back where it might.

Behind Farley's pale blue sun-bleached truck, the sky was still almost half clear on the right, while a solid black line was lifting on the left, high like a wall or tidal wave. Flashes of short barbed lightning flickered in muffled red deep inside the black. Now and then a crackle of white flashed along the lower edges

of the thick dark clouds. Already the scrub mesquite an
pear cactus to the left of the short row of unpainted wooden
houses across the street was beginning to be lost in a hazy, then
engulfing, shadow.

"Best get inside," Wesley called to Farley. He stepped away
from the truck. The tires whirled dirt as they spun in the gravel
of the parking lot and the truck pulled back out onto the road.
Wesley moved in a brisk stride toward the General Store where
TyTy and Cory still leaned on the outside of the porch rail.
Drops began to fall. The first few were round and large, landing
with a hard splat. They came at a steep slant, the wind picking
up as the edge of the storm neared. As each of the first drops
fell, a small cloud of dust rose up around where the drop hit.

Wesley ran the rest of the way and went inside. He let the
store's screen door bang behind him. TyTy and Cory eased to
the back of the porch. They stood as far back as they could
under the eave. Rain speared down, slanted in their direction. It
increased in intensity until it was an incessant roar and they
could see only a few feet out into the thick sheaf of steel-colored
needles. They stood side by side, their backs to the wooden
wall. Rain splashed against their boots. They could hear loud
voices inside.

"What was it you came over to see me about?" Cory asked.
She moved her face closer to his, scanned every line of the face,
the high cheekbones, dark tan, the shock of thick black hair that
stuck out to the right from his forehead like a salute. He was
lean, six feet tall, and though he was young he looked as hard
and as weathered as a fence post. In the three years she had
known him, she had always admired his stoic sureness. Now he
seemed uncertain, hesitant. The stability of her own world
rocked for a moment. But instead of dismaying her, it made her
push harder to be more assertive. "Come on." She wondered
for a second how wise she was being. The first time he ever gave

15

her any ground, and she rushed to fill it.

It was Saturday, so TyTy had known to find Cory at the store. She had been whiling away the weekdays of summer doing odd chores at some of the area's spreads. On weekends she hung around the store, had a cold soda or two, did not have a taste for anything stronger.

TyTy pulled out his blue handkerchief, opened a palm that was a bloody smear by now, and began to wrap the cloth tightly around his hand. He lifted it over to Cory. "Here, tie that off, would you?"

Cory did. His head was bowed to watch. From her angle his face looked chiseled from red clay. His skin looked hard as stone, yet soft. She wasn't used to seeing him from this close.

For a few years he was just one of the young men who hung around the store, and there were enough of those. She hadn't paid him much mind one way or the other. Then one day he came in to buy first aid supplies to help a bird he'd found. She had gone out to his car to look at it . . . a fledgling osprey that had gotten out of its nest before it could fly well. TyTy had fixed a lightweight splint for its leg, and it had pecked at him the whole time.

"Do you think it's the spirit of one of your ancestors?" she'd asked.

"What kind of comic books you been readin'?" he had said. "It's just an osprey. You better get me a can of sardines too. They eat fish mostly."

She asked him about the bird two weeks later, when his scratches showed signs of healing. "How's it doing?"

"Well enough to fly away," he'd said. He was never going to be accused of being overly chatty.

She watched him now stare out into the rain and beyond it. "Tell me," she prodded again.

"I've been thinkin' 'bout that," he muttered. "I probably

shouldn't of said nothin'. I just gotta check on somethin'. You'd best stay here." His eyes flicked away from hers, unable to maintain contact.

"Come on. You've got to take me now."

His head turned to her; the black eyes flickered in sparks for a second. He said, "Sometimes you act like a grown woman; other times like you're sixteen."

"I am sixteen," she said, almost shouted it.

She wanted to grab him and shake him. But they had never touched, in all the time she had known him, and she didn't want the first time to be in anger or frustration. She had to look up at him. He was three years older. It was a big gap, but that didn't make him an adult or anything. He could not pull that parental need-to-know stuff on her. "We're better friends than that," she said. "Spill it."

"No. I mean it. I never shoulda said anythin'." His eyes swung back to hers.

"But you did. Now start talking before I grab you by the nostril hairs and start running figure eights out there through the rain with you."

"You know, that's not very romantic talk comin' from a young girl." He tried for a half-smile that he did not quite hit.

"Who says we're romantic?" She paused but got no reply. Her insides fluttered, surprised she'd said anything like that. "Quit hedging. This will go easier if you just talk." She folded her arms and stood close to him, looking up into his face. She was closer and knew that made him uncomfortable. He slid back half a step.

"It's just something I have to check on over at that Whalen place, like I said." His eyes could not stay locked with hers for long. He looked out into the rain.

"The Whalen place that's haunted?"

"Don't say it's haunted." His dark eyes were back in line with hers.

Man, she thought, what a set of eyes he's got. "How do you know it's not haunted?"

Cory did know that not that long ago, on one of those particularly harsh dark and stormy nights that happen out in this flat stretch of nowhere as if the sky was trying to make up for not visiting in such a long while, that a film crew of students with paranormal interests all the way from Texas Tech University had come here to stay overnight in the house, thinking they might get a good news piece for the media and show a bit of brave derring-do as well. They'd lasted until only a bit after one-thirty A.M. when the whole bunch had dashed for their van and rocketed off into the night, leaving behind a pretty good camera and tripod at that.

"Why would you want to go inside that old place?" Cory said.

"It don't matter. I just do."

Cory let out a hard breath of air. "Don't tease me. Give me more than that to go on."

"Look, you want to stay here? 'Cause that's fine with me. Simpler too."

"You talk, words come out, but you don't say anything. You're no different than those men who pass through here and won't ask for directions, even if it means driving for miles out of the way or running out of gas."

"You'd better get used to that if you intend to have anything to do with men for the rest of your life."

"No one says I have to."

"You don't believe in ghosts, do you?" TyTy asked. The corner of his mouth lifted.

"No. But I believe in rain." She looked into the sheets of it hammering down, bouncing up off the hard soil, muddy rivulets already rushing down the slight slope to the left.

"Look, it's nothin' to do with you. It's me that thinks I gotta go over there," TyTy insisted. "You stay here. I shouldn't have said anything." He looked like he wanted to reach and touch Cory's bare arm but knew better.

"But you did. Aw, I'll go. But . . ." She watched the rain shift from a nearly left horizontal angle to as steep a pitch from the right. ". . . in this?" Cory looked at TyTy with raised eyebrows.

"It don't bother me none," TyTy said. "I've been wet before."

"What could be so blamed important we have to get soaked over it?" Inside there was more hollering from Wesley, then some yelling back at him that settled into steady low cursing.

"Weather puts 'em in a mood, don't it?" TyTy said.

"What was that business about a rodeo?" Cory tried again.

"I can't say. It's too . . . Oh, nothin'."

"What's so special you can't even talk about it?"

"It's not that it's special."

"Tell me what Wesley was talking about, TyTy, why he thought a rodeo, or the ropes, would be so funny for you." It bothered Cory that there was something TyTy could have in common with a pond scum person like Wesley that he couldn't share with her.

"Just somethin' that slipped when we was talkin'. I don't usually chat with the likes of him and shouldn't have that time. Forget it. Lay off." TyTy stopped himself before what he said got too harsh to take back.

He looked away, out into the needles of the blur of rain that surrounded the porch. He pushed himself away from the porch wall and ran out into the rain. "C'mon," he yelled back over his shoulder.

Cory hesitated. She did and did not want to go all at the same time, but she leaped out anyway into the rain and was instantly soaked to the skin. Cory ran as hard as she could, slipping on the mud, but running as if chased. She got to the passenger side of TyTy's old Chevy Nova at the same time TyTy was sliding behind the wheel. As soon as she'd slammed her door, TyTy turned to her. She knew her eyebrows were beetled and her stare intense, but it was not enough to overcome the raw innocence of her face. She said, "Now, tell me everything. We're not moving from here until you do."

Around them, the raindrops hammered with a rattling intensity into the loose gravel of the parking lot beside the store.

CHAPTER THREE

"If you're going to chew, take it outside. You know the rules."
Giff Purvis leaned forward, arms resting on the counter pad
beside the old-time cash register.

The sound of the rain beat down on the store like an angry
corps of drummers, hard enough to make Giff wonder if there
was not a bit of hail mixed in with it.

Wesley looked at Giff, disbelief shifting to belief from
whatever he saw on Giff's face. He moved to the screen door,
stepped outside. In a moment he came back in, letting the
screen door slam behind him to regain whatever dignity he
could. "Place sure has a damn lot of rules for a general store,"
he muttered.

Wesley eased over to the small magazine rack, stood looking
at the covers. The sign on the rack said, "Buy them if you want
to read them." Wesley made more low mutterings to himself.

From his vantage point, Giff could see everyone in the store.
He tapped the counter in time to the scratchy classical music
coming from the old tube radio, a piece from "Prince Igor" by
Borodin. The sound came in and out, fading and swelling like
some barometer in tune with the storm, mixing with the sound
of the hammering against the tin roof of the store . . . a roof
Giff had crawled across sealing, so he knew it could take
whatever this storm could offer. The store and the living
quarters that connected behind it were on high ground. Giff
didn't have to worry about the flash floods that happened

whenever it rained like this. Most of the hard-baked soil in Texas could never absorb water as fast as it came down. Dry creeks and rivers became raging sluices. Up on the town's small rise, the buildings were safe. It was a good time to be inside and enjoy the sounds of the storm. The only thing better would be to be back in the house at evening with a fire going in the fireplace and a book in his hands.

Since quitting drinking, Giff listened more than talked and spent every moment reading when not in the store . . . books, newspapers, anything. He also drank too much coffee now and was thin. He often wandered around the house late at night, as he said, like the ghost of Hamlet's father. Hearing the soft breathing coming from Cory's room was the stabilizing force every time he wondered what had happened to the Giff Purvis he once knew.

Giff looked along the rows of cans, supplies, produce that lined the side walls. The center of the store was clear except for a low gondola of featured goods, packets of chips, a marked-down overstock of Spam. Over by the potbellied Franklin stove, Zoe and Shimmy both tilted back on straight-backed chairs. Shimmy put more of a strain on his chair, oozed over the sides a bit. Zoe looked as lean and made of the same stuff as the chair. Wesley glanced over at the two idlers, then eased over to stand near the front of the store.

Above the magazine rack was a framed front page of an old newspaper that always gave Giff a chuckle. The lead story described the experience of a woman named Emma Ferguson who decided to become a Baptist. The revivalist making the conversion didn't know she had a cork leg. Every time she was immersed she'd flip clear over and shoot out of the water. After three abortive tries the thoroughly soaked Mrs. Ferguson had stomped out onto the shore and said she'd had enough to decide her to become a Methodist instead. Wesley's bored eyes passed over the document without a pause.

Beside the magazine rack there was a stretch of wall where Giff let locals display crafts for sale. There were humane animal traps, quilts, and hand-carved wooden toys and walking sticks. Along the floor were two baskets filled with twisted lumps that, at first glance, looked like gilded balls of coral. Those were a contribution from old Mrs. Panderworthy. Giff didn't know where she'd got the idea, but she traipsed around looking for fire ant mounds. When she found them, she staked the spot and came back and poured hot molten metal down the hole. When it dried and cooled she'd lift it out, shake it off, and the metal would be in the exact shape of the inner tunnels of the ants, the catacombs usually forming a ball, but all of them different. She sprayed the end product silver or gold. If you looked close, you could see an ant leg here and there beneath the paint. Around them were other objects just as hard to figure out at the first glance of a tourist. Some of them had been on display long enough to gather a patina of dust.

"What's this thing up here?" Wesley pointed to a length of chain with a ring welded to one end and two short lengths of pipe welded to a longer piece like an arrowhead at the other end. It looked a lot like the universal symbol for the male, with a foot of chain down the middle.

"It's a deer cinch," Zoe said, without moving from where his straight-backed chair tilted against the wall. The potbellied Franklin stove beside him was not lit. "One of Shimmy's inventions." That should have been a sufficient warning to anyone who knew Shimmy.

When one of the locals came into the store and said, "Anyone know who might've put a potato up the tail pipe of my truck?" The universal group answer was a raised, then lowered chorused half-groan of "Shiiim-my."

Wesley stared at the thing, set himself up by saying, "How's it work?"

Giff put his hand across his mouth. Shimmy got up from his chair to go to the front screen and look out at the rain. He had his face away from Wesley so the boy could not see him suppressing a smile.

"Why, first of all you get behind a tree, and then you take that ring end there," Zoe pointed, "and you slip it over the stump of a sawed-off limb."

Wesley's forehead was bunching into a youthful and doubting V of wrinkles.

"When a deer comes by, you ram that other end up his butt, and it's a cinch—you got him."

Shimmy was laughing out loud. Giff looked away. When his face was composed he swung it back, saw the pink still fading from Wesley's face.

"Them two are still sittin' out in that car with the engine goin'," Shimmy said. He stood by the screen door looking out at the rain. He wore blue bib coveralls over a plaid flannel shirt, the sleeves cut off in jagged lines at the shoulders, revealing arms bigger than most men's legs. A round can of snuff showed beneath a front pocket of the coveralls. The denim showed a faded ring over the can. "What d'ya think . . ."

"Let it alone," Giff said. Whenever he thought of Cory when she wasn't here, he always pictured her as the fragile, pale, extremely skinny girl he'd first seen standing in the airport, as alone as any human can ever get, with expectant wide eyes and ears out like a taxi cab with its doors open.

Shimmy's eyes swung to where Giff leaned on the counter from the other side with the old-time cash register within easy reach to his left. Giff stared at him with a look that needed no words. Shimmy was six-foot-six and somewhere past three-fifty on the scales. Giff knew that to Shimmy he probably looked no bigger than an ax handle and probably seemed to have as much flexibility.

"Well, excuse me all to roller skate." Shimmy looked back out at the rain.

Giff's eyes narrowed as they trailed Wesley through the store. The boy was like constant fingernails on a chalkboard to Giff, and it seemed to most everyone else. The thing about customers in general, and Wesley in particular, that bothered Giff was their invading his space. It would be nice if he could run a store, make the money, and not have to deal with most people, especially ones like Wesley. At an earlier time Giff tried to befriend the boy. Seconds into the effort, Wesley opened his mouth and started to tell Giff how he ought to be running his store. Giff instantly had regrets, and he'd stopped the conversation. Since that time, Giff reached for, and almost achieved pity for, Wesley when he had anything at all to do with the boy, which was as infrequently as he could manage.

"There goes Cory with that TyTy," Shimmy said. His face was closer to the screen. "Hellish weather for goin' on a drive."

Wesley was bent at an odd angle, trying to see around Shimmy's bulk. From the corner of his curled-lip mouth he said to Giff, "You sure the two've them are not being in-ti-mate, or somethin'?" He purposely put the emphasis of "intimate" in the wrong place. Wesley gave a half-glance back toward Giff, to see if he was getting a rise. "They're probably gonna . . ." It was as far as he got.

"Out," Giff said. He took a half-step away from the register. A red haze formed in his vision. He felt his hands tighten into fists.

"But it's rainin', Giff . . . Mr. Purvis. You wouldn't . . ."

"Out." Louder this time. Giff felt his breath coming in short, quick jerks.

Given a chance to be apologetic, Wesley's face instead turned mean, spiteful. "Don't act like you don't know she's getting ripe. Even though she's a skinny little thing now, you oughtta be able to see the way that Indian looks at her."

One second Giff was behind the counter; the next, unaware of his actions, he had straightened, pulled himself around the end of the counter, and was rushing across the length of the store.

Zoe's chair dropped to the floor. He jumped to his feet and grabbed at Giff. "Careful there, Giff. That's Sherm Hargate's son."

Giff felt his heart pounding . . . a hand sledge smashing against the steel deck of a ship . . . his muscles in knots, and his feet hitting the store's floorboards. Zoe's hands slid off him, barely slowed him. Wesley moved in quick half-steps to the door, held it half open and stared back at Giff, his eyes widening as Giff pushed his way past Zoe.

Shimmy stepped in and put both bear-like arms around Giff.

Giff struggled, shouting, "I don't care if he's the lost Dauphin."

"Nobody's lost a fish this far inland," Shimmy said. He turned his frowning head over his shoulder and said to Wesley, "You might best move your snotty ass outdoors, and quick."

Wesley sulked the rest of the way out the door, let it slam shut. He broke into a sprint across the boards of the porch as he headed for his truck.

Shimmy loosened his grip on Giff. "You all right?"

Giff bent forward and took a couple of deep breaths. "Soon as I get my breath back," he wheezed. His hands clutched his own legs above the knees.

"Hey, Giff. I'm sorry." Shimmy leaned closer, held out a tentative hand.

Zoe was already headed back for his chair. "Don't be," he said. "Giff needs a good squeeze now and again. He's not a package of Charmin toilet tissue, after all."

Giff had one hand up on the counter. His head turned so he could look with a raised eyebrow at his friend.

Shimmy stood in place, his arms hanging down at his sides. He looked embarrassed, sorry to have had to hold Giff back. He said, "She's been with you a good while now, ain't she."

Zoe eased back onto his chair, tilted it back, took a couple of tries until he had it just right again. He said, "You should've been there to see Little Cory when Giff first picked her up at the airport. How old was she, Giff? Six, seven years old?"

"Eight."

"How'd you come to be there?" Shimmy asked.

"Had to drive Giff over now, didn't I?" Everyone knew that Giff no longer drove, that the car he had used to get to Bent Bell had long ago rusted to the ground behind the store.

Shimmy turned his head to look back outside.

"Her ears sure stuck straight out," Zoe said.

"They did indeed," Giff admitted. "Just a bit further, and she could have flown here instead of needing that plane."

"But her ears don't stick out none now," Shimmy said, turning back to them.

"There was an operation," Zoe said. "An expensive one."

Shimmy looked at Giff, knew he was not made of money, and he was right. The expense had set Giff back for most of the savings he had back then.

"You should have seen her when she was little, though, Shimmy." Zoe's eyes were focused far away. "She was sharp as a tack then and's been honin' up to an even brighter edge since. She may well end up smarter'n Giff here."

"That wouldn't be such a stretch," Giff said. "I was barely smart enough myself to know how little I knew. My brother, Cory's father, was the over-achiever, and he's the one who became successful."

"And dead," Zoe said.

"Through no fault of his," Giff said.

"Come on, Giff. You're the one always saying that something good always comes from everything, no matter what."

"I guess that was when Cory moved out here," Giff said.

"She's gettin' top grades at school and'll probably sail right into college," Zoe said.

"She does seem a bright little bug," Shimmy said.

"You always say that intelligence is the same as curiosity." Zoe nodded at Giff.

"I said that about being intellectual," Giff corrected.

"Same damn thing," Zoe said. "Anyway, Cory's as curious as a dozen cats."

"And as full of restless energy." Giff was still adjusting to the idea that he had scrimped and saved to send Cory to college some day, but it would mean sending her away, which came hard after coming to care for her as much as he did.

"Yeah," Zoe said. "She's gonna go outta here and make something of herself for a change."

Giff started to speak, but something was making his throat tighten. He stopped and reached for the water bottle he kept under the register, took a sip.

"You got something in your throat, there?" Zoe asked.

Giff looked up, said, "You prepare yourself your whole damn life to age into a grump and this is what you get instead." He sighed. "It's a damned embarrassment is what it is." But he knew he would not change a bit of what had happened if he could.

"We can sit here all afternoon," TyTy said, "but I've got nothin' to say. You can get out and stay if you want. I still think I've got a chore to do."

They sat that way for another five minutes, both with faces

forward watching the rain through the windshield that was beginning to steam over. Only the dim lights of the dash lit their faces. It was enough light to see each other, but not so much that it dispelled the eerie mood in the car. Cory's face looked small and delicate, TyTy's like something carved out of dark flint.

He glanced at her, saw she was staring ahead at the windshield. He abruptly shifted into gear. The car gave a lurch. The back end swung a bit in the mud as the car pulled out. TyTy straightened it out, bent forward toward the steering wheel. Cory turned her head enough to watch his shining intense face, an occasional drop of water oozing from his dark wet hair to drip down across his temple past a high cheekbone. His whole face was tense as he squinted to see the road. "Sure is a frog walloper, ain't it?" He tried for a more cheerful note. His handkerchief-wrapped hand clenched the wheel.

Cory crossed her arms across her chest, partly for the warmth. Her shirt was soaked and pressed tightly to her. She was almost flat-chested. But because of the "almost" she kept her arms folded until the shirt could dry. Usually she put out a lot of heat, but the damp denim of her jeans and the cotton of her white t-shirt were pulling heat from her instead of holding it in. In the clammy cool of the car, she huddled with a small shiver.

TyTy reached and turned on the car's heater. It would take a minute or two to warm the inside. Cory hunched a bit toward the vent when the warm air blew her way. She stared out her window at the wall of rain that surrounded the car. It was hard to believe that hours ago the open ranges out there were tan and sandy, with pale dust across the surfaces of the prickly pear cactus, sage and mesquite.

"Why can't you just tell me what you expect to find out there?"

"Maybe nothing."

"Or maybe something. What?"

"Remember what you and I were talking about last week?"

"About Miss Dumpsie?"

"No, it wasn't about your stupid paint horse."

"She's not stupid."

"Anyway, I wasn't talking about your horse. I meant about where you wanted to be, compared to your friends. That's what we were talking about."

"I didn't say they were my friends. I said I went to school with them." She turned her head and looked into the spider lines of rain trickling down her side window. The dim lights from the dash let her see some of her own reflection. She looked wet, and not all that happy.

"You were talking about what you hoped to accomplish, what you hoped to do."

"I only said I wanted to at least not be like Crystabelle, wanting to be a star, or Vickee with two Es, who's studying to be a nurse," she said.

"Right."

"You know, that Vickee is the one who's missing. She the one Farley was looking for," Cory said, not doing a very good job of keeping a bitter edge from creeping into her voice. The price of being a tomboy loner at school was that the other girls had let her.

"I know which Vickee," he said. "Yeah, those are the two."

"Are you sure you were listening right? The conversation wasn't about them. It was about me." She peered out into the blur of the rain, not looking his way. She was sorry she couldn't see what plants there were outside through the thick pounding rain. She felt she was like them, stubborn and scrawny, but able to grow in the toughness of the desert, even bloom sometimes. "One of the things I said was that I'd like to leave here some day, get away from living the way I do with Uncle Giff. I've always said that if I got half a chance to leave here, I'd be out of here like wings on a wildcat."

"That chicken killin' music he gets on that radio . . ."

"You mean the opera? That's only usually at nights it comes on the station. And it's not like what you say. You just haven't a taste for it. If you heard that scratchy classical station for as many years as I have, you could just tune it out." Only that wasn't entirely true. Sometimes, riding her horse out across the range or out under the stars by herself, she heard whole patches of the music in her head. It sounded better then. "Anyway, it's not about me leaving or staying. It was just that I wanted to fix on something to do that was good. When I leave here, that is."

"And Giff discourages you?"

"It has nothin' to do with Uncle Giff." She sighed. "He's been good to me, took me in, raised me when . . . when I didn't have parents anymore. It's just that he's . . . well, I'm . . ."

"I'm tryin' to talk about Crystabelle and Vickee here."

The topic was heating Cory up more than the car's heater. "What I said was that a lot of people aren't careful about how they put their lives together. I'm very careful, maybe too careful. Most people just seem to push off and sort things as they go along, see how they respond, try to figure out what to do next. I like to have a plan, to see steps through, to know I have a clear destination or goal, and that I'm not thrashing around. It hasn't always come that easy. Sometimes I have to pull myself aside and think what to do, what would be best. I said I've been doing a lot of that lately."

He squinted, trying to see the road ahead. The car was moving slowly through the thick rain. She would have pulled over and waited if it had been her driving.

"I don't know that people always get the luxury of planning everything," he said. "Some things just happen."

31

"That's kind of a lazy answer," Cory said. "A lot of people just keep showing up for life and are swept away by it. All I'm trying to do is clearly know what I'm doing and why, not get rushed into anything." She paused, said, "Let me ask you something."

"You're getting off the subject." A rare irritated edge had crept into his voice.

She ignored it and said, "There were other Indian boys at school. There was KipKip and TieYie, for instance. They were quiet, like you. But since they've gotten out of school, they went to other places. KipKip came back from that first year at Fort Hood with short hair and a jagged scar up one cheek . . . he claimed he got it from a pimp, though everyone else said the whore did it. But anyway, the others call him Boldfeather now. And TieYie, if he hadn't got shot and killed in the street up in Detroit where he went, he might've gotten a new name too. It's like white kids have childhood nicknames like Cubbie, Spanky, or Tommy. But they outgrow them. Folks still call you TyTy. Is it because you still live around here?"

She watched his face take a firmer set. He stared ahead into the rain pounding at the windshield. Now, she'd done it. She'd hurt his feelings without really meaning to. When her mouth got going . . . why couldn't she just shut up?

Cory hated not knowing things and seeming clumsy because of it. She didn't know if the name thing for Indian kids worked everywhere or whether it was a local thing among the kids with Indian blood at her school. Uncle Giff might know. He knew a lot of stuff, and the more esoteric and least likely it was ever to be needed, the more he knew about it. But he still didn't know where the pastern is on a horse, so she had a thing or two on him.

"I'm sorry. I shouldn't have gone there," she said. "I guess it bugs me sometimes that you hung around, stayed in Bent Bell when you didn't have to. I know that if I didn't have another year of high school I'd be out of here in half a tick. But that has nothing to do with you. What was it you were trying to remind me of?"

It took a few minutes, but when he spoke his voice was flatter. He said, "You were comparing your not staying in town, once you graduate, to Crystabelle and Vickee with two Es, who've both stayed around. Crystabelle's there at GALS and Vick's back here from nursing school for the summer."

"What about them?" she said.

"How come you think about them, talk about them so much," he said, "if they're not your best friends?"

She bit her lower lip. She'd almost said that he, TyTy, was her best friend. At school there would be a huge gulf between their ages. Since he was out, it didn't seem to matter as much, at least to her. But she didn't talk about that, or bring it up, like it would be bad luck. Instead, she said, "They don't treat me like one of them. But maybe that's good. It's funny that people say 'thick as thieves,' 'cause that's how it really turned out to be with Crystabelle and Vickee with two Es."

TyTy glanced her way but didn't comment, gave his attention back to the road that was barely visible past the rapidly flapping wipers and torrent of rain.

"I don't know if Crystabelle would've gone that route on her own, but Vickee would steal a fly from a blind spider. She's the one got them into that trouble where they had to get up in front of the whole school and talk about stealing."

"I didn't know about that."

"You were out of school by the time that happened. Uncle Giff was onto them early. They were both barred from his store. But they got caught twice in Carnicius, once at Walmart and another time at the 7-Eleven."

"Had to get up in front of the whole school?" TyTy said.

33

"That must've been embarrassing."

"I think it bothered Vickee more that her secret was out. Crystabelle was always getting up in front of everyone, craving attention. It's why she's a singer now, I think. Maybe I shouldn't talk about Vickee, though. You were seeing her, weren't you?"

"Only for a short spell. That was a while back, and it's over. You and I talked about all that."

"This rodeo, or rope thing, why don't you tell me about . . ."

"Leave it alone," TyTy said. Added, "Please?" But it did not take off the edge.

"Fine," Cory said. "Just fine."

The rest of the ride to the Whalen place was quiet, very quiet, just the sound of the rain hammering hard on the car's roof, and the whoosh of the tires pressing the soaked asphalt and ripping through puddles and small streams that stretched across the road.

Cory had only passed by the Whalen house before, not gone up to it. It was out of the way, and she had never had any reason to go near.

With the deluge, she could barely make out the tall steel poles that crisscrossed high above the gate and the cattle guard. TyTy swung the car off the pavement and through a muddy gap where someone had cut away a stretch of the barbed wire and pulled out one of the stakes.

Cory had heard that high school kids came out here to neck, that the spread, since being let run down, had become a kind of lover's lane. But that was about the time she had cropped her hair short and decided to ignore boys, and they had returned the favor.

The car bounced and slid a bit as it plowed through the mud and settled into only slightly easier going as TyTy steered it into the ruts of the long lane.

Cory bent closer to the windshield, peered through the needle sheets of rain. The house seemed to spring up ahead of them suddenly, dark and looming, three wooden stories high with Victorian lines.

When TyTy turned off the car's engine they sat for a moment in the unrelenting din of rain. The house hovered dark above them. The glass of the windows that hadn't been broken by thrown rocks seemed to glare into the storm.

"We gonna just sit here?" she asked.

"We might." TyTy seemed as snappish and tense as she had ever seen him.

She asked, "Why are we here? We could go over that if you plan to sit and talk."

"To check on something." He stared through the rain toward the house.

The heat in the car began to slowly seep away. Cory shuddered again. TyTy stirred, having come to a decision. He reached across to get a flashlight from the glove compartment, said, "Come on."

They sprinted over to the crumbling porch, slipping on the mud as they ran. Under the leaking porch roof they paused for only a moment. TyTy pushed open the front door and led the way inside. It felt odd to Cory to go in without knocking.

The inside of the house felt even stranger. The rooms were cluttered with small debris, crumpled food wrappers, pieces of broken furniture near a fireplace where a fire or two had been built using whatever could be found.

TyTy's light swept through the foyer that opened directly into a sprawling, large living room. A chain hung from the ceiling where a chandelier had once been.

The old house groaned under the weight of the rain. Gusts of wind whistled along the eaves in what did seem a scream at times, not loud enough to be a mountain lion but perhaps enough to be mistaken for a ghost. Boards squeaked with each step they made. TyTy led them along a path that was marked in the dust. He seemed to know where he was headed.

"What did you . . ." Cory started.

"Soon," he said.

Above the sound of the rain she could hear a hum. It became a buzz as they passed down the long hallway to a room off to the right with sliding wooden doors that were most of the way open. The buzz was louder now, and there was a smell. Cory moved closer to TyTy.

He took a few more steps into the room. She couldn't see for a moment. He stopped, and she came around to stand beside him. He held the flashlight pointed down at the worn wooden floor. Once she could see, he slowly swung the beam up from the floor. The light caught the buzzing, whirring black dots, flies thicker than she'd ever seen. In the center of the form was something pale. Cory gasped.

There, when the flies whirled wide for a moment, hanging from ropes, one end tied to the stairway newel, the other to a hook on the opposing wall, hung the body of a young woman, her arms bound at the wrists. Her head lolled over to one side. A crumpled skirt lay below her on the dirty floor. The woman's clothes had been pulled away from her chest, her bra was ripped at the center and hung open. Her youthful face and unblinking eyes were in sharp contrast to the knife slashes back and forth across her chest and throat where the blood had dried black, where the flies now swarmed. The light fixed on the woman's face. A horned frog at her feet scurried off into the night.

"This is what you wanted me to . . ." Cory said, then stuttered to a stop. "Oh, my God," she said. "It's Vickee."

"With two Es," TyTy said, too in shock to stop himself.

CHAPTER FOUR

Cory's head hung out into the rain. Her hands were on her knees and her toes were at the edge of the crumbly wood of the porch. The taut muscles of her back jerked beneath her wet shirt as she coughed and spat. The rain ran down across her hair and across her cheeks, taking away only some of the taste of bile.

TyTy reached out to hold her shoulders. She tried to shake off his hands with a hard shrug. This was the first time he had ever touched her. She was over-aware of that and reached with one hand to press against his hard chest, pushing him away. She did not want it to be like this. Her face turned toward his. She swept her forearm and the back of her hand across her mouth.

"How could you?" was the first she could manage.

"I didn't mean . . . I didn't know . . ."

"She's dead! Really dead. Vickee. Why didn't you call the law? Why not tell me that? Why bring me here?" Her voice was loud and a bit hysterical, she realized. But whom would she disturb?

"I didn't know she was . . ."

"Dead."

"You won't let me . . ."

"TyTy!" She stood upright and tried to punch him on the shoulder. But he was holding her and supporting her; that made it awkward. She was as mad as she ever remembered being. And worse, she was crying. She never cried. It was not about

37

Vickee, though. She gulped and struggled for control of herself.
But just when she wanted to be firmest, she felt herself relax in
a slump, almost leaning against TyTy, which she did not want to
do. It was just when she thought about what she had seen in
there, and that Vickee was never going to breathe again.

"You gonna let me talk?"

She gulped again, didn't want to answer him right away. She
struggled, not against him, but inside she felt still as mad as she
ever recalled being, and as hurt. She pushed her face out into
the rain again to wash it. He let her go, except kept his hand
holding hers. She couldn't tell right now if it was tears or the
rain that ran down her cheeks.

"I didn't know she would be here, or that she'd be dead."

"We've got to call . . ." Her words trailed off into the rain.

"We can't call the sheriff," he said slowly, giving her a chance
to absorb every word, "because the first person they go after in
any murder investigation is someone close to the victim."

"But you weren't close, were you?" She pulled her hand away.

"I was seeing her again some lately." His voice faded with the
confession. "And they'll have other reasons to want to talk to
me."

She did punch his shoulder this time, as hard as she could,
hard enough to hurt her fist. But it did not seem to register
with him. She said, "What does that mean?"

"Look, I don't mean to keep cutting you off, but let me finish. I came out here 'cause I was worried. But I didn't expect
nothin' like this. You gotta believe me, Cory."

"We've got to call."

"Couldn't we . . ."

"Couldn't we what?"

"Maybe if we can figure out first who . . ."

"You want us to try and solve this? Us? It's Vickee! How
could we? Even if we knew where to start."

She stood facing him on the porch, her face still leaning out in the rain a bit, her hair and shirt dripping.

"We know it wasn't me," he said. "Don't we?" When she didn't answer right away, he said again, "Don't we?"

"So they ask you questions. You answer them, say you didn't do it. What could happen to you?"

"A lot," he said. "You don't seem to understand. I'm in a serious jam here."

"More than you will be if you withhold information from them?"

He didn't answer, stood looking out into the downpour.

"What could you have possibly done that makes you think they'd focus on you?"

His head snapped to her. Their eyes locked. She could see some internal struggle. She had known him a long time. They had always been honest with each other. She didn't know what to make of what she saw now. She was beginning to shiver.

"Let's talk in the car," he said. He reached for her hand again, but she pulled it away.

As they ran she felt raindrops hitting her; but she was too numb to feel stung or cold from them this time. Their feet slipped in all of the same spots, but they got back to the car without falling outright.

They climbed inside and slammed their doors. TyTy fired up the engine. He reached to turn the heater on full.

He had said they would talk, but neither of them seemed to know where to start. After sitting like that only a few moments, TyTy put the car in gear, eased slowly around, and started to back out the long lane.

The shock of what she had seen was still getting through to Cory. She stared into the mirror that the darkened, rain-streaked passenger window had become. She had always thought of herself as tough, or at the least not a coward. How naive and helpless she seemed to herself now that something real had happened. You never know how insulated, how protected you are growing up until something like this.

Then it hit her that this was not just any dead girl, but Vickee, a girl she had known and gone to school with, however far apart they were on the local social scale. This was someone she had seen breathe, and laugh, and . . . Cory rubbed her small fist along her wet cheek and looked at TyTy, who showed no expression at all and seemed all stoic firmness behind the wheel.

Come on, TyTy, she thought, smile, frown, yell if you want. Just let me know you breathe and feel like the rest of us. But she did not say it out loud and knew it would do as much good to talk to one of those wooden cigar store Indians, though she could never say that either. Uncle Giff had lectured her sternly once for some accidental thing she'd said that she later found out was racist. But that's not what taught her the difference. She had gotten that from the suppressed hurt she had seen on the face of a young Hispanic girl in response to some of her own careless words at another time.

She rubbed both hands down the sides of her face, turned to look at TyTy. Why was her head so scattered when she needed to think?

"Just what was between you and Vickee anyway," she said suddenly. "You and the guys seem to have some sort of . . ."

"Please don't push me on that too much," he said. "It was all a big mistake that's getting bigger. You're going to have to . . ."

"I'm not going to have to do anything if you don't level with me."

He was wrestling with the steering wheel as the car jostled and slid on the mud of the lane's ruts. When he could, he swung his head to her. "Please," was all he said.

It was very unlike him. He had always been the one she had leaned on, counted on. She was trying to form another careful

40

question when she noticed the colors. Flashing lights, red and blue, were piercing the rain in front of them as they neared the gate. The lights made sparkling lines down the rain streaks of the windows.

She turned to TyTy.

"Oh," he said. He glanced her way. The car began to slow. "No matter what happens . . ."

"TyTy, what're you . . ."

There were two sheriff's vehicles coming up from the road into the lane.

"Whatever happens, Cory Lee," he said, pressing harder on the brake until the car was stopped. He turned off the engine. "I want you to know that you're the one I really care about."

CHAPTER FIVE

From his lean-back perch on the chair by the stove, Zoe watched Giff pick up a feather duster and start out from behind the register. Giff waved the duster in a slap-dash fashion across the tops of cans, not too concerned with what got dusted. Shimmy was spinning a yarn about something that happened at GALS, and Giff was not in his usual listening mode. GALS was a kicker-dancing honky tonk in a warehouse-shaped building halfway between Bent Bell and Carnicius—not much to look at by day, though its parking lot was jammed with trucks and cars each night. Giff eased around the counter and worked his way along one shelf of goods until he was closer to the front door. Without seeming to, he bent and peered, trying to see outside into the dark past the screen.

"What're you up to?" Zoe interrupted Shimmy's story.

"Who, me?" Giff said.

"In denial too?" Zoe shook his head. He had been around Giff long enough to catch any subtle change. Giff could be cranky with customers and friends, but Zoe was convinced that it was all bluff.

Zoe turned his attention back to Shimmy. "Sorry," he said. "You were sayin'?"

"So this guy don't know it, but he's got blue dye all over his face now, and no one tells him. He's far enough along in the evening to think everyone's laughing at his jokes. That is, until he goes to the can the next time and catches a glimmer of his face in the mirror. Whooee. You should'a seen him hop then."

Shimmy leaned his bulk against one of the counters. Earlier he had bought a box of saltines and a couple of cans of sardines from Giff. He reached to the counter where he'd opened them, draped a sardine across a cracker and put a squirt of mustard on top. He popped it into his mouth and chewed, then grinned and waved a hand to Zoe toward the open crackers and fish. Between a half-mouthful, he said, "You sure you don't want none?"

Zoe shook his head.

"Let me ask you, Shim," Zoe said. "You've been a practical joker long as I've known you. Hell, 'THE' practical joker 'round here since you moved out to these parts. What the hell ever got you started?"

There was something about the steady rain and it being dark at mid-day that contributed to an air of melancholy and dread. Zoe sought to keep the chatter light and sprightly.

Shimmy finished chewing and reached for his can of Diet Coke, which looked odd to Zoe, who knew Shimmy would prefer a beer if Giff allowed drinking inside the store.

Shimmy swept a shirtsleeve across his mouth. "I don't rightly know. I was always just handy that way. You know, started with doorknobs, pennying doors, room stuffing, that sort of thing. At weddings I'm the first person they call when they want to rig someone's car, though I had to learn the hard way that the car has to be able to run after the wedding."

Zoe felt his forehead wrinkle. "I know the doorknob trick with a jar of Vaseline. But what's pennying doors and room stuffing?"

"College tricks," Giff said. His voice carried back, hollow, the length of the store. He looked back at them from where he had been staring out through the screen door. "You get a steel door on a steel frame and you drop pennies down the crack until they jam. Anyone inside can't get out. The building janitor usually has to chisel them free. To stuff a room, you get a stack of old newspapers and crumple them. You start at the back of a room until you get to the door. When someone opens it, all they see is crumpled paper from floor to ceiling."

Zoe raised an eyebrow at him. "You seem to know damn all about some of this."

Giff ignored him. He was working his way back through the store with the duster until he could slip behind the register counter. He asked Shimmy, "What's the ultimate? What's the worst thing you ever did? Something you regretted."

Shimmy looked away. Zoe watched some color wash across the big man's cheeks. Shimmy took a moment. When he turned back, he had regained his composure. His usual silly grin was back in place. "Well, there was this once. Guy I knew lived across from me. We sneaked into his house during a winter snap."

"Who's this 'we?' " Zoe asked. "You got a mouse in your pocket?"

"Just a pal of mine. Anyway, the other guy . . ."

"Victim," Giff said.

". . . had one of those kitchens that you step down into half a step."

"What did he do to you?" Giff asked.

Shimmy ignored him. "We were in the middle of a cold snap, and I happened to have just bought about forty or fifty packages of raspberry Jello."

"Happens to almost all of us," Giff prodded.

"We opened all the windows and turned on the air conditioner, set it as low as it would go."

"You set up Jello on the man's linoleum floor?" Zoe asked.

Shimmy looked at him, then went on. "My place was across from his. When he came in, we waited until he was at his door.

Then we called him. His phone was in his kitchen. The windows were still wide open and we could see him rush across to get the phone. When he stepped down into the kitchen he hit the Jello. He slipped and went out of sight."

"And you regretted that? I don't see why," Zoe said.

"Well, not so much the Jello. We even helped pour hot water and scrape it out. But it got up in on the bottom inside of the refrigerator and the man had ants so bad the next summer that he finally moved out."

"Costing you a source of ongoing amusement, eh?" Zoe shook his head.

Shimmy said, "I suppose you never did anything like that."

"I did get in a jam once in Biology class in high school," Zoe said, "for offering to show a girl my Y chromosome. But I'm over all that by now. You still do this stuff, don't you, Shim?"

"I see a guy get out of his truck over in Carnicius. He's shoving change into the meter, and I see on the back of his belt he's got his name engraved. It says, 'Joe Bob.' So I wait until he turns around. Well, I don't know him from Adam's house cat. But I rush up to him and say, 'Joe Bob, how the hell you been?' He's pumpin' my hand and strainin' his eyes at me, like he must know me, but can't remember from where, like maybe he was drunk or somethin'. I say, 'How's the family?' 'Cause I figure everyone has one. He nods, real slow like. When I leave him he's starin' off at nothin' for the longest time tryin' hard as he can to remember where he met me. But he's never gonna get there."

Zoe shook his head at Shimmy. "What makes you do this stuff?"

"I don't know."

"Just a clown," Giff suggested, "laughing on the outside . . ."

"Hell," Zoe shook his head. "Maybe playin' tricks all the time is like crying, whether on the inside or not."

It was quiet and awkward in the store for a moment. Shimmy looked away. Giff rubbed at a spot on the countertop with his thumb.

Zoe looked up at his big friend. "Let's say someone crosses you now, Shimmy. What's the quickest and easiest way to get payback?"

"The easiest? Oh, that's not hard." Shimmy smiled to himself. "You just go to the Post Office, get you one of those 'Change-of-Address' cards. You put down the guy's address, then in the next section under 'new address' you put wherever you want his mail to go for a few weeks."

Giff tilted his head at Shimmy, as if looking for horns. "You know, Shim, you're pure evil. You're aware of that?"

The rain continued to hammer down. Giff stood up behind the register and stretched. He reached for the broom and went back up to the front of the store where he could peek out and look for TyTy's car without seeming to be waiting for Cory. He saw a pickup pull into the lot. The inside dome light came on, and he saw a woman reach up to twist the rearview mirror to check her makeup. He spun and started for the back of the store.

"Zoe, you mind watching the store for a bit?"

"What's got into you, refried beans for breakfast?"

"It's her." He was moving quickly through the store, heading toward the back.

"Mrs. . . ."

"You know. Just take over the command module until she's gone."

"Aw, be a man. What's she got that makes you nervous?"

"She has hungry eyes. We've talked about this before." Giff frowned at Zoe. He ignored Shimmy's nosy look. Giff passed the back counter and was through the doorway just as the front screen opened. He heard just a scrap of Shimmy's comment.

". . . never seen a grown man move like . . ."

"What can I do for you Sherrie? Yeah, it's me, Zoe. Giff had to step out a bit."

The voices faded as Giff passed through the hallway that led to the living quarters. He closed the connecting door behind him, passed the door to his bedroom. He had given the bigger bedroom to Cory when she hit her teens. All he really needed, after all, was a place to flop at night and read until he could sleep.

Giff could hear the rain on top of the house as he passed through the kitchen and slipped out the screen door that led back toward the stable. A carport top allowed him to stay dry getting to the stable, but he had to slip around the dusty tarp-covered car that had been allowed to slowly become unusable. He opened the door, and Miss Dumpsie heard him. She gave a whinny.

"I thought you'd have sense to come in out of the storm," Giff said. She tossed her head, turned it to one side so one of her big eyes could watch him cross to the stall.

He took a deep breath. Fresh bales of hay were stacked up along one wall. The rain heightened the smells of the room— the leather of the saddle stretched across a wooden sawhorse and the strong animal smell of Miss Dumpsie, her wet hide glistening in the light from the bulb that hung from a cord above.

The back of the stall opened out into the small pasture behind the buildings. Giff could see the rain slanting down through the dark outside the door. It was filling the tank at the far corner of the pasture—a Texas-style tank, dug in the earth as a small triangular pond with a dam along one side to catch water when it rained like this.

Giff had seen Miss Dumpsie up to her knees in the tank pulling clumps of moss from the bottom and eating it the way Popeye ate spinach. "That stuff won't hurt her," Cory had told him. "Standing in the water like that's good for her hooves too, keeps 'em from drying out and splitting in the heat." But Cory was more careful about other plants in the pasture. Giff had seen her little body working to a sweat in the sun pulling weeds and taking them to a pile on the other side of the fence to be burned later. "There're lots of plants could make her sick," Cory'd explained. "If she eats the fallen berries from a Chinaberry tree, or mistletoe, or the tender mesquite leaves, she could get colic. The beans from mountain laurel, mescal beans really, could make her worse. Then there's snakeroot, nightshade, and lots of other plants that aren't good for her either." Giff had asked how horses in the wild ever managed to survive. She'd beetled her usually smooth forehead at him and had said that sometimes they didn't. She sure went the extra mile for her horse. It made Giff wonder sometimes if he'd put as much effort and concern into raising Cory.

"Well, old girl. Looks like it's just us," he said. The horse swung her head until she could focus one big eye on Giff. He felt a bit awkward around Cory's horse, and worse, he thought the horse sensed it. Miss Dumpsie was fifteen hands high, according to Cory, was bay with four white socks, a white blaze down her nose, and irregular patches of white on both sides. She had a long gentle face, but looked at Giff, he thought, with apprehension.

"You know me. Don't act like you don't. I'm the one pays for all that expensive worming." He held out a hand slowly.

Miss Dumpsie backed a step in the stall. She tossed her head toward her feed trough. Giff looked over the top of her stall, saw the trough was empty. He had better not feed her. Cory would want to do that when she came home. He grabbed a double-handful of hay from the top green bale against the wall. The smell was mowed-field rich the second the clump came loose from the bale. It was a wonderful and rich country smell, better by far than manure spread across a field, though he had gotten used to that as well. He moved closer and held the hay out to her. She shuffled her feet, turned her head sideways so she could still look at him.

"Cory's not home yet," he said. "Here. Have a snack." The paint horse looked at him, stamped a foot, but did not come closer.

"You know, you're part of what cost me the chance to head back to Austin." Miss Dumpsie shook her head, tossing her bay and white mane. "Well, not really. But I was thinking about it."

When she came no closer, he dropped the hay in the trough and stepped back. She moved forward to take an eager bite.

While she chewed and moved her head for another bite, Giff moved closer, rested his arms on the top of the stall, lowered his head to tilt sideways along his forearm. He watched her. She seemed to accept him now, looked up at him with those big soulful eyes, the same as Cory's, not begging or saying a word when Giff had buckled up his own needs and bought her the paint pony.

"You know, old girl, I'm scared." The words surprised Giff as he heard them spill out of his own mouth. But he went on. "Hell, it's just us out here. I can admit that to you. I never felt this way before in my life, never expected to." She lifted her head, tossed it and looked at him with that one eye—an eye that he felt looked understanding, though it may have been that he craved understanding, even from himself. "I was doing fine by myself, just fine. Now I think I'm going to be alone again soon, only I'm not as fit or eager for it as I was. You'll probably be gone as well. What do you care?"

The mare looked up from her chewing. Her long head tilted to one side, and she looked at him in a way he had to consciously dismiss as understanding. She took a couple of haltering horse steps closer, lifted her long neck and brought her head up and over the top of the stall. Giff nearly took a step back. Instead he lifted a hand and reached out slowly. It was the first time she had ever let him approach her.

Miss Dumpsie held still and let Giff run his hand down the length of her nose. She felt more vibrant and alive to him as soon as he was touching her. The white blaze went all the way down to the end of her nose, widening so that the hair was white, the nostrils pink and moist. The soft flesh of her nostrils opened wide, then narrowed with each breath. Warm air from her breathing steamed up toward his hand. Her hair felt smooth as he stroked downward. She held still, let him get some comfort from petting her.

"You're all right, old girl," he said.

She lifted her head, shook it. His hand fell away.

He grinned. "Hell, I ought to be getting back inside anyway. But . . . well, thanks."

Giff stuck his head into the store, hissed at Zoe. "Is the coast clear?" he whispered, loud enough to travel half the length of the store.

The look on Zoe's face told him all he needed to know, but too late.

A face popped around the corner inches from his own. His head snapped, and he forced himself not to reel a step back.

"Mrs. Easton."

"Sherrie."

"Um. What're you doing behind the counter?"

"Looking for you, silly." Her voice had dropped to a sultry whisper. She was close enough for Giff to know her breath was minty fresh and that she wore a touch of some musk-based perfume. Giff's eyes flicked over to Zoe, who was staring in amusement.

Sherrie Easton was by no means an unattractive woman. When Giff looked back to her, she was an inch or two closer, quite a way into invading his space. Her Liz Taylor eyes and smooth skin combined with a sensuousness that made Giff uncomfortable when seeing her from a distance. This close, he was not at his best.

"You should . . . you should . . ."

"I had a dream about you," she whispered, "about us."

Giff eased through the doorway, slid past her, getting close to her but not touching. He moved quickly along the back of the counter until he could come out onto the store floor.

Sherrie gave him a pouting look, then chuckled to herself. She shrugged and went to Zoe, took the paper bag he was holding out.

"Did you get everything you were after?" Zoe said, fighting in an obvious way to hold back laughter.

"No," she said, "but I'll be back." She walked slowly to the front door, her hips straining each side of her skirt from the inside with every step.

As soon as she was out the door, both Zoe and Shimmy broke into hysterical laughter. Shimmy was doubled over, slapping a thick knee. Every time Zoe stopped, he would look at Giff and start laughing again in spite of himself.

"Why me?" Giff said, when they finally trailed off enough to allow him to speak. "What can she see in an old rawhide string like me?"

"Chemistry," Zoe said. "There's no accounting for it. God knows I would never expect to see you on the cover of *GQ* or *Esquire,* but you're sure just the right pollen for that queen bee."

"Well, I wish she would find someone else to favor with her attentions."

"What's wrong with you?" Shimmy said. "She's offering you

what every man wants, with the possible exception of seeing two women go at it."

"Hey," Giff said. His eyes clicked to the back door in spite of himself. Shimmy knew that kind of talk in the store made Giff nervous, even when Cory was not around.

"Sorry." Shimmy blushed, the contrition temporary, but genuine. He glanced down at his watch. "Anyway, it's time I headed over to GALS. The afternoon has gotten away from us again."

"Let me ask you," Zoe said, "have you ever missed a night of going over there?"

"I didn't miss a single night last year, was even there on Christmas."

"You ever tell Giff here that you did your Christmas shopping at a truck stop once?"

"That true?" Giff asked.

"I was out of time. Besides, some people like getting fuzzy dice and all that for the holidays."

"You go over to GALS every night," Zoe would not let it alone, "a dance hall, and yet you don't dance a lick."

"Just got two things goin' against me. My feet." Shimmy looked down at the tips of his size thirteen boots. "But I don't go there for the dancin', just to see a few women. I like to see 'em breathe, especially if they have nice lungs."

Zoe glanced at Giff. "You never been there, right?"

Giff shook his head.

"They bring women all the way over from Carnicius," Shimmy said. "Some of 'em have even had a silicon job." He paused, perhaps to see if he had gone too far with Giff.

Giff said nothing, over-aware that he had snapped at Shimmy a short while ago.

"You ever get tired of just lookin'?" Zoe asked Shimmy, "get to thinking you might like having one around?"

"Sure." Shimmy shrugged. "Doesn't everyone? But I look at myself in the mirror and say, who'd have me. Then I go over to GALS and just look."

"Looking but never touching doesn't bother you?"

"Tell you the truth," Shimmy's voice had lowered to a conspiratorial, even confessional level. "I sent off for a couple of them silicon breasts and nailed 'em up on the wall at my place by where I come in. So whenever I come in or go out I cop a feel."

Giff blinked. His eyes locked with Zoe's; both held the same graphic image. "Is he kidding? Tell me he is," he said.

"Don't know," Zoe admitted. "I haven't been over to his place in a long while. But if I go, and if they're really there, I may give 'em a squeeze myself."

Shimmy shook his head at both of them and started for the door.

Giff walked Shimmy to the front of the store. Shimmy scampered through the rain and across the sweeping rivers of mud the street had become. However he moved, Shimmy seemed to shamble. He always reminded Giff of the bear at the circus that rides the tiny unicycle or tries to dance the ballet, being awkward and elegant at the same time, somehow turning its bumptiousness into an occasional second or two of real grace.

Giff looked out across the street and up and down each way, but saw no sign of Cory.

"That Shim's sure drawn to that place like a moth to a flame," Giff said.

"Shimmy's a social creature, needs to eyeball and mingle with others. You've just convinced yourself you ain't, is all." He had been watching Giff's stiff movements around the store.

When Giff had walked all the way back to the stove, Zoe said, "You know, you don't seem yourself lately, Giff."

"Oh? Who do I seem like?" Giff stood looking at the chairs

but not sitting. He reached up to fiddle with the antique fountain pen in his pocket. It no longer worked, but he always carried it. The thick sides were smooth and comforting.

"I mean, you're all kind of jangly and uptight at the same time."

"Sorry if that troubles you."

"Is it that woman, Sherrie Easton, coming around that does it? Or are you still antsing around about the day coming when Cory's gonna leave here?"

Giff didn't answer.

Zoe said, "If I didn't know better, I'd have said that giving up drinking's made you scared of women?"

"Or a misogynist. A woman-hater?"

"Whatever. Tell me the truth, do they just give you the creeping willies nowadays, or what?"

"It's not that." Giff reached up to rub the sides of his nose.

"Well, then?"

Giff hesitated. He looked up and saw Zoe waiting. "I'm lousy about intimacy when I'm sober. I tighten up. It's why I really moved out here, to live alone, and why I was so worried when Cory came to live with me."

"But you made it through that."

Giff said, "I was so busy with her little problems at first, getting her ears fixed, helping her adjust to losing her parents . . . I looked up and there wasn't anything to adjust to after all. Somewhere during all the hard work, everything emptied out into her needs. I'd lost that part of what made me afraid."

"You ever think," Zoe said, "that that might be the way it is for a lot of men with women?"

Chapter Six

The patrol car was the only car on the road. Its headlights speared through the black and silver slanting lines of the rain. Sheriff Michael Sparrow looked over at the girl in the passenger seat. She huddled beneath his cold weather jacket, even though he was running the patrol car's heater warmer than he liked. She had draped his jacket from under her chin down across the tops of her legs like a small blanket. Her frowning face beneath the blond hair stuck out over the olive drab of the jacket. She had been silent so far.

Even slumped in the seat like that there was a lot he could read from her demeanor—that and watching her at the station as they had booked her young friend. She had the confidence of youth that comes from a sheltered life. He had been surprised to hear from her that her parents were deceased and that she lived with her uncle because she had the manner of someone nurtured in a close and loving home. He was anxious to meet this uncle.

He looked out across the surrounding terrain. In this far corner of the county, Texas sprawled across a ripple of hills that flatten for stretches only to lift again in sharper hills the closer they got to Bent Bell. In the summer, the steamy heat rises from the land in wavelets. It always reminded him of films he had seen of African savannahs, except the brush in Texas ranged from the dull green lavender of sage to the dust-covered mesquite and the darker green of the sprawling live oak trees.

"Do you think he'll be all right in there?" Her voice seemed small. It wavered with a bit of uncertainty. Matched against her earlier glimmers of confidence, it made for a healthier contrast, endearing her to him a bit more.

He glanced at her. She was sixteen, had a round young unblemished face on top of a slender, almost gawky frame. The half-Indian boy was nineteen, but strong, built like a man. Kids these days. They discover the basics—eating, sleeping, the mechanics of mating—and think they are in on the secret handshake of life. In spite of her off-and-on self-confidence, he could not attribute cockiness to Cory or to the Indian boy for that matter. She seemed more stunned than jealous. Maybe they were just friends, as she'd insisted. He glanced at her, said, "He would be better off if he just would say something."

When she did not respond, he said, "But I understand the type. We have lots of folks here with Indian blood in them. And they are all alike enough you could bank on them. Laconic, taciturn, call it what you like. There isn't one of them who you could say has their tongue hung in the middle and is over-fond of talking."

Cory's head swung to him. Her eyes were half-hooded. It was hard to tell what was going on in there.

Sparrow had no delusions about getting much from her on the ride. His white hair and sixty-year-old features made him a geez, an old fogie to anyone under thirty. Not that he expected to get much from her or TyTy. If the boy had not talked in the first two or three hours, they were in for the long stretch with him. It was apparent from talking with the girl that she knew nothing. Oh, she had some suspicions about TyTy. She had made a special effort not to share them, which had only made it all that much easier for Sparrow to read. *But TyTy, he may or may not be involved. But he knows something.*

He glanced over at the girl. She reminded him of his ex-wife

Elizabeth. He didn't know what made him think of her. Both she and the young girl had fine blond hair. But Elizabeth had been tall, haughty—oh, she could be haughty. She'd had a lot of aspirations and expectations, and when she'd left, she had let him know he'd failed her in all of them. Maybe it was the intelligence behind the pale blue eyes in Cory's youthful face that brought all that back.

"You know," he said, "Bent Bell, the town where you live, never really had a physical bell that I know of. It's not like Old Dime Box, Texas, which is actually named after a small wooden box at the center of town where locals dropped a dime to pay for a carrier to bring them their mail from Giddings. Bent Bell was just a spot along a cattle trail near a bit of water that grew into a small town on its own." His own scratchy voice echoed inside the car over the sounds of the engine and the tires on the wet road. "Oh, maybe there was a bell once, and if the cattle ran over it, it sure enough would have been bent. But no one knows that there ever was a bell."

"My uncle would enjoy that. He collects stories." Her voice was flat with forced politeness.

"I've heard that said about him." He glanced at her. The gibbering on any old inane topic had been to calm her. Her face was turned to the mirror that the passenger window had become against the backdrop of the rainy night outside. He could not make out her expression in the reflection.

"Your uncle runs a store, that right?"

Her head bobbed, but she did not look his way.

"He's lucky Bent Bell is way over here in the corner of the county, not near anything in particular. It's not likely some chain of convenience stores is going to throw up any competition."

She sank an inch lower on her side of the seat, pulled the back collar of the jacket up higher under her chin.

"There's another interesting thing about this little corner of the county," he said. He gave her a quick glance, then looked back to the rain-blurred road. The steering wheel was not warming to his hands as it usually did. It stayed cool and clammy. "When they took the census, they found that this corner was throwing the whole county statistics off. The demographics out here, if the census can be believed, tells us that seventy-five percent of all people in this corner of the county are male. Does that seem credible to you?"

She did not answer at first. He turned his head, saw she was nodding.

Her small voice was muffled by the collar of the sheriff's jacket, "And most of them," she said, "hang out at my uncle's store."

Crystabelle leaned closer to the mirror and peered, as if she could see clear into her own pores. The circle of lights that framed the mirror let her see every beginning wrinkle on her face, though there was little to see at eighteen years of age. She had lied, said she was twenty-one to get the job, though they had to know otherwise. She pulled at the skin of her face. It snapped back in place with a resilience it would not show in a few minutes after she had layered on makeup thick enough to give her features against the harsh lights of the stage.

"Yeah, you sure got it," the voice from the corner of the room said.

She glanced over. Sherm Hargate was tilted back in the straight-backed chair, the heels of his cowboy boots up on the corner of her trunk. He had taken off his cowboy hat. It rested on the floor beside him. A small spray of peacock and pheasant feathers in some kind of design was on the front of it. The harsh lights of the dressing room made the skin of his rounded pate so shiny it almost hurt to look at it. But with the hubcap-sized silver belt buckle centered in the rise of a stomach almost as big as the rest of him, he was not that much to look at in the first place.

"Why don't you go out and mingle with some of your beer-guzzlin' buds," she snapped. "I'm on in a few minutes, and I wouldn't mind a little time alone."

"You know," he said, making no move to spring to his feet, "when you're up on that stage singing, the pale baby spot outlining your face against that darkened back of the stage, I look at you and I think, 'Whooee.' I'll tell you. I get a shudder. You are something else, something magical, something desirable and far out of reach." His voice had a pronounced twang he seemed to enjoy and emphasize. She glanced at him in the mirror. A broad smile stretched across his pudgy face. He looked away from her at some blank spot on the wall where he was playing the video of his memory. "It's hard to believe then that you're human, someone who needs to eat, sleep, hell, fart just like other people. But then I see you in here where your true bitchiness has learned to grow and prosper, to show you can be just like us ordinary people."

Her mouth pressed together tight. She wondered if he could read the glare she was giving him in the mirror, or if he was simply too dense for that. His hands rose and he crossed them over the bulge of his stomach. The lights caught the glitter of the two gold pinkie rings, the huge gold Rolex watch that hung loosely from its oversized wristband. He really would turn the stomach if it were not for all that money. He insisted on telling her he was only thirty-five, yet she had gone to school with his son, Farley, who was her age. She figured him for fifteen, even twenty years more than he'd said.

She took a deep breath, waited until her voice was as under control as she could get it. "You really do look thirsty, Sherm. Why don't you go out and dip your bill while I finish wrestling into the war paint."

He unwove his fingers, stretched both arms, and lowered the front legs of the chair to the floor, reaching for his hat as he did. He rose heavily to his feet, lifted the hat and dropped it in place, bent to look over her shoulder at himself in the mirror.

She looked at the reflection. In contrast to her own face, she could see every pore and seam in his as well as the light glisten of sweat already across his forehead. She repressed a shudder.

"Yeah," he said, still leaning over her shoulder and looking into the mirror, "I still got it too." He bent and gave her a sloppy kiss on the side of her neck, turned and headed for the door.

She reached and grabbed a tissue, rubbed hard at the moisture she felt in cold and exaggerated gooeyness on her neck, not caring if he looked back and saw or not.

Giff stood by the screen door, trying to glance out into the dark rain without seeming to do so.

"Oh, give her a rest," Zoe said. "She'll be fine. You don't usually worry this much about her."

"Only because I try to respect her. She's going through a . . ."

"Rough time?" Zoe had the paper folded open to the crossword puzzle. He was at the stage where he spent more time licking the end of the pencil than filling in clues. "Well, hell, Giff. It's so long since either of us been that age, I doubt we could . . ."

"Zoe," Giff interrupted. He was leaning closer to the screen door. "You mind slipping into the back for a sec?"

"Who . . ."

"Just go. Okay?"

Zoe rose from his chair, moved stiff and slow, but headed for the door that led back to the living quarters.

Giff straightened the stock as he moved back toward the

register where his comfort zone was greatest. The screen door creaked as it opened slowly. Giff turned, acted surprised to see Saris McFeeny leaning through the door to peer in and make sure no one else was in the store. Water dripped from his jacket, making a small puddle inside the doorway.

"Coast is clear," Giff said. He had seen Saris stand around the corner of the building across the street several times and watch until every other customer or hang-out had left before he would scurry across and buy the supplies he needed.

Though Bent Bell was itself a tiny town out in the corner of the county, McFeeny lived out in the hills as far from it as he could get. The mini-trailer where he resided had long since lost the option of mobility. It was painted a flat green and tilted on cement blocks with one corner settling. It was near enough to a spring for Saris to get water. But it was all scorpions and rattlers for miles in an area not even fit to graze cattle, and that included the years when ranchers go out and burn the needles off prickly pear cactus so the steers will have that to eat.

"What'll it be?" Giff asked.

Instead of picking the items he needed off the shelves, as he usually did, McFeeny sidled around the center gondola, still looking for other people. It had taken all of his nerve, Giff figured, for him to make it inside the store the first time some years back. Giff had him pegged as a reclusive hermit in the extreme. Over the years it came through that Saris had more fear than hate of his fellow man. It made Giff feel a bond.

Giff was all the way around the counter, in place behind the register. McFeeny came up to the counter and stood across from Giff. Some inner emotion was wrestling its way to the surface.

McFeeny had a gray, grizzled beard with pronounced sideburns. A worn baseball cap, with its St. Louis logo barely legible, was twisted and pulled down tight on the bushy hair that came to the shoulders of his frayed safari jacket.

He started twice to say something, his eyes dropping only to lift with his dark tanned face and connect again with Giff's. There was visible pain in the watery blue eyes that were surrounded by the kind of wrinkles caused by being in the sun all day.

"What?" Giff asked. He did not know how to go about making it easier for Saris.

After two false starts, McFeeny reached up with gnarled and dirty fingers. He undid the buttoned flap of his left shirt pocket. He reached in and drew out a bit of rock. There was a tremor to his hand as he rubbed it on his jeans, then put it on the counter in front of Giff. "Been short," he said, "lately. Can you . . ." He let the end of the sentence hang.

Giff picked up the rock, brought it up to his eye. It looked like a dirty lump of glass, the kind you might find in the cinders at some glass foundry. The exterior had a slight frost to it except on one corner where a clean facet let him see the clear interior with its blue tinge. He put the edge of the stone to the glass counter, pressed and made a half-inch mark in the glass. He looked up, saw Saris wincing at the sound of the rock scratching the glass.

"Nice one," Giff said. It was not quartz, which is a seven on the hardness scale. Topaz is at least an eight. The deep, clear cut on the countertop told Giff that he was holding a gem. "Cut down and faceted, it could go forty carats," he said. "Topaz is going for about fifty bucks a carat these days, retail."

Saris stared at him.

"What do you . . ." Giff started to say.

McFeeny made a vague wave with one hand to the goods on the shelves around him. He also worked in a quick glance toward the front door, anxious to get his business over with before anyone else came into the store.

"Go ahead," Giff said. "You get whatever you need." He picked up the gem and reached out to drop it back in Mc-Feeny's pocket. "I'll carry your tab. But you hang onto the rock. You want to get it cut and sell it, that's another thing, Saris. I'll trust you for the money you need for supplies."

The look on Saris's face was almost worth the tab. His bloodshot eyes misted over, and he turned away, began to gather up cans and a new blanket since winter was coming on. Giff watched the man scurry as if there was a deadline. He wondered what it was like to live out there with no heat in the winter and not even a fan in the summer, no electricity to run it if he had one. As he brought each handful of goods over to the counter, he gave Giff a smile that was both shy and bursting with excited gratitude.

Giff helped put what he gathered into the cloth rucksack Mc-Feeny had brought in with him. They had just finished and totaled the bill when the screen door opened. Sheriff Michael Sparrow came in, and with him Cory, the uniform jacket still wrapped over her shoulders.

McFeeny's eyes snapped open wide. He had the bag and blanket to his shoulder in one motion. He sidled around to the front of the store on the far side of the room from the sheriff, was slipping out the screen door by the time Sparrow and Cory reached the back counter.

Cory slipped off the coat, handed it to the sheriff. She gave Giff a short glance as she went around the counter and headed toward the back living area.

"You okay?" Giff said, trying to keep the emotion out of his voice.

"Fine," she said. "Just fine." Then she was gone, out of sight after a final toss of blond hair.

"I don't get as many hugs as I used to," Giff said, "now that she's in her teens."

63

"You don't need to tell me." Sparrow had watched Saris all the way to the door as he left. Now he was glancing around inside the store. "Got a couple of nieces and nephews myself back East, all grown and married now. I'm just now back to a hug status with some of them, though I get plenty from their kids when I'm ever around to see the little squirts."

Giff read Sparrow's uniform insignia and the gold nameplate. "Did those kids have a wreck? Where's TyTy? Is he okay?"

"I'll get to that."

Zoe came out of the back. He nodded to the sheriff. "Michael," he said.

"Well, Zoe Albrick. How the hell have you been keeping?"

"Can't rightly complain, and no one listens when I do."

"You two know each other?" Giff looked back and forth between them.

"Not professionally," Sparrow said. "Zoe's father and I used to do a bit of dove hunting when I first came out here." He turned to Giff. "I've heard a bit about you. First chance I've ever had to run into you." His head cocked. He was catching the scratchy music coming from Giff's radio. "Is that Wagner's overture to Tannhäuser?"

"It is. And you're the first person I've ever heard around here come close to pronouncing the umlaut."

Zoe's head was snapping between them. He stopped at Giff. "What the hell's an umlaut?"

"The two little dots above the A." Giff's eyes stayed locked with Sparrow's. He was getting sized up right back.

"Where the hell're you guys seeing dots?" Zoe's head swung back and forth between them. "When you start talkin' like that, it's time for me to bug out with the buffalo." He took a couple of steps toward the front of the store.

"Stick around," Sparrow said, and there was enough firmness in it to snap Zoe's head back. "I want to have a talk with the both of you."

Giff glanced toward the back of the store. Cory was probably back feeding Miss Dumpsie, maybe brushing her with a currycomb. He had watched her before, taking hours to brush the horse, talking, telling Miss Dumpsie the tribulations of her teenage life. Giff had always stayed far enough back not to hear her actual words and eavesdrop. What she told the horse was between the two of them.

The sheriff was looking at Giff. "You know, I was telling your daughter Cory . . ."

"Niece."

"Your niece Cory on the way here that this little corner of the county has one demographic oddity, a characteristic, so distinctive, that you must have noticed it by now. It's that seventy, maybe as high as seventy-five percent of the population here is male."

"That explains why it's so hard to get a dance partner at GALS, I guess." Zoe gave Giff a half wink.

"GALS, I take it, is what the locals call the Grand American Lone Star Dance Emporium?"

"You would be right about that," Giff said.

"The only watering hole in this neck of the woods," Zoe said. "Open all day for beer and pool. Closes at five to open again at seven as the only two-stepping dance hall."

"You sell beer and a little wine," Sparrow said to Giff.

"But allows no drinkin' inside the store," Zoe said. "So you can't rightly call it a night spot."

"I see you don't sell lottery tickets either," the sheriff noted, looking at the goods within reach of the register. His eyes swept the canned goods, the produce.

"The world's got enough false hope without me fueling the fire," Giff said. He kept his voice dry and factual. His head tilted a bit to the right.

"This place takes me back," Sparrow said. "Real old-timey feel you've got to it. Guys swapping lies around the potbellied stove."

"Potbellied guys . . ." Zoe started to say.

Sparrow held up a hand. "You've got just a vestigial touch of East Coast accent left," he said to Giff. "Ivy League?"

Giff nodded slowly, with reluctance. Without seeming to, he tried to get a better look at the ring he had seen on Sparrow's finger.

"I thought so," the sheriff said.

"What're you?" Giff said. "Harvard?"

Sparrow's mouth spread wide in a smile. "Veritas," he said. "And let me guess. You're a Yalie."

Giff nodded, even slower than before.

"Skull and Bones?"

Giff said nothing.

"And here you are running a tiny general store in this corner of nowhere."

"And you a big-time sheriff in this cow flop of a county," Giff said.

"Touché."

Zoe said, "Any chance either of you're gonna speak English soon if I gotta hang around?"

Sparrow ignored him, but by his body language made it clear Zoe should stay.

"Let's cut through one thing," Giff said. "You didn't apply on-the-spot detective skills about my background. You did some checking before you came out here. Why?"

"And you got lucky because I'm vain enough to still wear this school ring. But I didn't check all that deeply." He glanced at Zoe, then swung his head back to Giff. "You ever married?" he asked.

"Nope."

"Well, just want to say you seem to be doing all right by way of raising the girl. She's got spirit, but manners with it."

"Thanks."

Zoe's head moved with the social patter. He glanced toward the stove, as if wondering if he could sit in his chair if he was required to stay.

"If you fellas are gonna drag this reunion out a spell," he said, "I might as well set." He ambled over and eased into his usual chair, the one he had occupied most of the day. "Hell, Giff. I guess I knew you'd went to college, but not this."

Sheriff Sparrow eyed the chairs around the stove with unabashed longing. "I remember raconteurs who traded yarns around a campfire," he said. "But I didn't know it could become a way of life."

"I didn't plan things this way," Giff said.

"So you never married. We got that far. Did you move out here because of that? Or was moving out here the cause?"

"Both."

Sparrow looked over at Zoe, to see if he was being patient. Tilted back in his chair and comfortable now, Zoe looked like patience itself.

"I hope our exchanging schools doesn't mean I'm supposed to come out and play chess with you now," Sparrow said.

"He don't play chess with other people," Zoe said, missing any double meaning Sparrow had intended. "He prefers to play with himself."

"I'm sure that's just how you intended to say that," the sheriff muttered.

"Well," Zoe said, "he says he's been playing some guy . . . Cappuccino . . ."

"Capablanca," Giff corrected.

"Guy who's been dead since before W.W. II."

"Right now I'm in Havana, and it's 1913. But enough about

67

my late-night frolics." Giff gave Zoe a look, one that warned he was talking too much.

"You mind if I take the weight off?" Sparrow asked Giff.

"Let's both."

The two of them sat down on the other chairs. Giff watched Sparrow's careful movements, the way he was at home as soon as he was settled in one of the chairs. If he had a stick, he would have whittled. The sheriff had a country way about him that fit in easily. It was a manner that it had taken Giff quite a while to acquire.

Sparrow looked at Giff. "I understand you collect stories."

"I'm a listener," Giff admitted.

"It was coming on to Thanksgiving," Sparrow said, "and we had a family there in an East Coast county I worked at, before coming to Carnicius, that had been at odds with each other for half a dozen years. I don't even recall what got it going. But the two boys, Blake and Tuttley, were at the center of it."

Sparrow gave them each a glance, found them both rapt and not ready to interrupt. Giff noticed that Sparrow could mimic some of the local rhythms and grammar, but that the long Massachusetts "a" sounds and the occasional "r" on the end of a word ending in a vowel surfaced in a way that was at odds with the way locals spoke.

"Well, Blake, he was the peacemaker of them. He decided to reconcile the family. It had been years since they had been together on Christmas or Thanksgiving, so just before Thanksgiving he took in Tuttley's obituary to the local paper. Of course, Tuttley wasn't dead. But the folks at the local newspaper didn't know that. They'd never had anyone turn in a fake obituary on a family member before."

It was quiet in the store. Giff was usually closed by now. The rain beat down in a regular and comforting patter. A new bit of music began on the scratchy radio—Villa-Lobos's "Bachianas

Brasileiras." Sparrow tilted his head that way, but did not stop his tale.

"Well, you can probably see this coming. But everything didn't turn out as well as Blake hoped. The incident involved knives, guns, and a broken coffee table. Tuttley ended up seriously wounded. Blake was killed in the fracas."

"Damn," Zoe said. "Did they reconcile at his funeral?"

"No, they didn't," Sparrow said. He seemed to be watching Giff for a reaction.

Giff had heard a lot of stories that meandered and did not seem to have a point. He usually wrote them down, let them stew a bit. Some of them came around for him later. Other stories never did. But he was tired, and restless. He wanted to go back and talk with Cory. He pressed Sparrow: "Which gives us some sort of segue as to why you're among us tonight, I hope?"

The sheriff sighed. "As much as I would enjoy this sort of cracker-barrel repartee on a regular basis, I should cut to the chase this once. I'm faced with a conundrum."

"Good lord," Zoe said. "Did you get it from a machine?"

"A dilemma?" Giff suggested.

"Maybe even a rubric?" Zoe volunteered.

Sparrow gave Zoe a look. "Not too likely," he said.

"I'm gonna leave if you guys're gonna speak some other language I don't know." Zoe made no effort to climb out of his chair.

"The reason I'm out here, to this corner of the county, is to investigate a death."

"Who?" Zoe tottered on his chair for a second.

"A young girl, lives out here, bused in to Carnicius like everyone else when she went to school. She just graduated this past year."

"Who?" Zoe pressed again, sounded even more interested.

"It was Vickee Allen, nursing student, back here on a summer holiday."

"How did she die?" Zoe lowered his chair and leaned closer.

"I'll wait on an autopsy report to be official about that. But she sure enough didn't tie herself up over at the old Whalen place and cut herself with a knife that's not there. Looks like there was some sex involved too. I'll have to wait on the M.E.'s report before I know more about that."

"So, she was stabbed," Zoe said.

Sparrow's eyes narrowed to irritated squints. "No. I didn't say that. I said I'll wait on an autopsy before I know anything. There're lots of things could've happened to her. She could've been poisoned, or strangled, or O.D.ed, and then cut up later. The point is I've got an eighteen-year-old girl who at the least has been murdered. By morning I'm going to have everyone from the media to Junior League to the local NRA all whipped up into a vigilante frenzy. The sooner I get a hook on this one, the better."

"What's this have to do with Cory?" Giff asked. "And TyTy?"

"They found the body."

"How'd you find them? Rainy night like this, it's hard to see across the road, much less all the way from Carnicius to the Whalen place." Giff was watching Sparrow closely, felt Zoe almost holding his breath as he waited for an answer too.

"You know Perk Tillus, lives in the spread next to the Whalen place?"

"First rate grouch," Zoe said.

"He's that and some more," Sparrow admitted. "He's supposed to be watching the Whalen place for a development firm over to Austin. The damned place has turned into a lover's lane."

"That's what worried me about Cory being there," Giff said.

"Well, Tillus ran a few of the kids off. But they just came

back another time. So he decided to call the law next time. We had a car or two over here anyway in our search for the girl. She'd been missing three days."

"And Cory and TyTy just happened to be the ones your troops landed on?" Giff said. He tried to keep any emotion out of his voice, but he felt his face flush.

"We got a string of calls from Tillus. He said there'd been regular activity at the house all week. But we had a slateful ourselves, ranging from sixteen domestic flare-ups, a grass fire followed directly by a small flash flood, not to mention Mrs. Groat who called in to say her husband had climbed up a phone pole and wouldn't come down, then she says, 'Oh, never mind he just turned into an eagle and flew away.' "

"Every town has a Mrs. Groat," Zoe said.

"We have a dozen varieties of her." Sparrow was looking at Giff. "But you see what I mean. When a couple of our units did break clear, the first people we found at the scene were the two kids, Cory and TyTy."

Giff fought to keep his brow from knotting. Sparrow was an interesting piece of work. There was more he didn't say than he did. Why send two patrol cars to scare off parkers in a lover's lane, if that was what the call had been about. The other thing that bothered Giff was the sheriff's Harvard ring. When it turned on Sparrow's finger, there was tan beneath it. It was not something the man wore all the time. After he'd checked on Giff's background, more thoroughly than Giff thought was possible, he must've slipped on the ring hoping to do a little Ivy League bonding. But why? The sheriff had clearly worked to camouflage himself in the local setting, picking up as much of the regional patois and manner of speech as possible for someone with a native Massachusetts accent. Now he was stepping from behind that mask with what—another mask?

Sparrow was looking around the quiet store again, enjoying

the sound of the rain outside and the dry interior. "What an idyllic life you've carved out for yourself," he said. "Like kids perpetually sitting around the campfire trading yarns. God, I wish all life was that simple and good again. I don't get in many old-time stores like this."

Zoe started to say something, but Giff beat him. He said, "There is storytelling, and there is storytelling. All kinds get shared in here. Some stories are told to satisfy the teller, others, of the higher order, to entertain, inform, enlighten, even educate the listeners."

Sparrow's head swung back to Giff, locked there. His eyes seemed to throw sparks from beneath the shaggy white eyebrows. "Among kin of mine," he said, the localized sound of his voice suspended for the moment, "I number a Scottish great aunt who's something of a master storyteller herself. She always told me that the very best stories, in fact the only ones worth giving a listen, are those where the teller gives up his or her co-nyach, lets the feeling flow from deep inside. It's all about deep emotion, tapping the core of what troubles you, motivates you, or makes you feel attached in any way."

Sparrow stopped speaking abruptly. He looked away, let whatever was on his face fade until a smile eased back into place.

"That isn't what brought you out here tonight, is it?" Giff said.

"No. I wanted to ask if you could bring Cory back in, come tomorrow morning. I'm not getting anything out of the young half-breed, and I hope she can help, that she'll be willing to help."

"I'll do what I can," Giff said.

Sparrow nodded slowly, "Still and all, what a grand place to be, sitting among friends day after day and sharing fresh tales."

"Some aren't all that damned fresh," Zoe said.

"Even so," Sparrow stood, helping himself upright by pushing on his own upper legs, "I envy you all for the camaraderie, the trust among yourselves."

He turned and started for the door. Giff watched the hunched shoulders. It occurred to him for the first time how alone someone like Sparrow must feel having come to settle out in a contrasting culture like this, having to deal with people every day. It did not surprise Giff to find loneliness in others, as well as in himself. But how each one of them dealt with it, wrestled with it, he felt, was some measure of inner hope in triumph over common sense.

Chapter Seven

The cell was a holding cell, not as big as the bullpen down the hall where most of the weekend drunks and regular jail visitors were lodged. Metal cots hung from thick chains on both walls. The floors were concrete and the walls cinder block. At the end of the small room was a stripped-down toilet. The jail seemed quiet to TyTy, even though there were occasional echoing shouts from down the hall.

He had never been in a jail cell before, had never planned to be, so he had never prepared. He didn't know what to expect next. He'd used his phone call to let his mother know he wouldn't be home, but there wasn't even a bail set yet. So it looked like he was here for the night.

When he closed his eyes, all he could see was Vickee, hanging there, dead. He tried to imagine her any other way and could only see her naked. That didn't help, especially knowing she was dead. He thought of Cory, but the expression on her face stopped him. She'd been surprised, hurt, disappointed, all things he'd not seen in her before, and ones he'd caused. He hadn't been able to see his mother's face over the phone, but her voice had sounded the way Cory's face had looked. All his life he had never been in trouble before. But he sure enough was this time, and even more with all the people he cared about.

For now he sat on the bare metal of the cot and stared out at the hallway. He would be all right, he told himself, if nothing went more wrong than already had. Then he heard the voices coming down the hall.

Farley led the way, wearing his deputy sheriff uniform. If what was on his face was a smile, TyTy didn't want to know what amused him. Farley looked right at TyTy. They had gone to school together, had been in some of the same study halls with Vickee. But there was only faint recognition in the look.

"Got you some company," Farley said. The man behind him was quite a bit taller, and wider. He moved into the cell with a sullen scowl. His face was full of rough, thick features and a three-day beard. He looked and smelled like he'd been put in to sober up and perhaps for some kind of violence. TyTy had seen that kind of battered, belligerent, and bigoted face before, and had always avoided it.

Farley slammed the cell door shut. The big man just stood there. Farley started back down the hall, then stopped. He called back into the cell, "Oh, by the way, the Indian there likes young white girls."

CHAPTER EIGHT

Cory didn't see Giff come into the stable. She was carrying another pitchfork of hay over to the stall and saw Miss Dumpsie look away, pretending to be disinterested. Cory looked back toward the door and saw Giff leaning against the wall watching her.

She didn't say anything, hung the pitchfork back up on the wall, and took the currycomb from its shelf again. Cory had already given Miss Dumpsie one good currying. She got into the stall with the mare, who had turned her nose to the trough. Cory rubbed a flank with her hand, then started in with the comb. She watched Miss Dumpsie's hide quiver in a ripple of pleasure.

Giff's leaning against the wall watching, though, made her uncomfortable. She wished he'd just say what he came to say.

Miss Dumpsie's long head turned back to look his way. Her big eye gave him a distant look, letting him know everything was all right now that Cory was here.

"Anything you'd like to talk about?" Giff said.

"No."

"Come on, Cory. I'm not pushing. It's not every night the sheriff brings you home from some lover's lane."

"Is that what you think's between TyTy and me?" she said.

"You're going to feel urges. That's normal. But . . . but you . . ." This sure didn't seem easy for him. But she didn't help.

"I'm not doing anything with TyTy, if that's what you're hemming and hawing about."

"Look, Cory, I'm feeling guilty. We should have had a talk a long time ago. It's just . . . well, I don't . . . you've got to . . ."

"Oh, I know where you're heading with all that. You don't need to worry. All me and TyTy've been are friends." She could do little to hide the bit of chagrin in her voice about that. "Our lips haven't even locked in anything like a Hollywood snarl of wet slurping sounds, if that's what's bugging you."

"Well, uh . . . look, Cory, what you do, um, that way, is . . ."

"I just wish people wouldn't act so smug and smart about being able to do something that the lowest farm animal knows how to do," she snapped, dragging the currycomb hard enough across Miss Dumpsie's rump to make the horse whinny and move her hind legs restlessly. *Sorry, girl,* Cory thought, and eased up with the comb.

"If this is the birds and bees talk, there's one thing they have in common that you haven't mentioned yet," Cory said. Damned if she would make this easy for him.

"What?" He seemed tired, resigned, a little beaten.

"They have wings."

"They do indeed," he said. "But the day comes you're ready to leave here, you know I won't stand in your way."

"Can't," she said.

"Can't," he repeated. His head hung an inch lower, though it was not his way to pout or act hurt. She wanted to go to him, give him a hug like old times. But she did not let herself.

"That's the first sure thing you've said." She realized she was done combing her horse, had been for some time but had kept her hand moving just to be doing something.

Giff was silent. She turned and looked at him. It was hard to mistake the raw affection on his face. She looked away, put the comb back up on its shelf. "Well, I'm glad we had this little chat," she said. "It's been helpful. See you at breakfast." She turned and bolted out of the barn.

Giff lay on his hard cot of a bed staring up at hazy shadows on the ceiling of the darkened room. He rolled his head to one side, looked at the clock. Four A.M.

Oh, what the hell. He pushed back his cover, climbed out of bed. If he hadn't gotten to sleep by now he was never going to make it.

He had a quiet shower and got dressed, then went out into the store and started a pot of coffee. He felt tired but as awake as a mouse gnawing on an electric cord. He could hear his own soft steps in the surreal quiet.

At six A.M. he went up through the store, opened the door to step outside, and bring in the plastic-wrapped bundle of Sunday newspapers the truck had dropped off. It had stopped raining. A battered black pickup was parked out front. Giff grinned to himself. He pushed the door the rest of the way open and went out to the truck, rapped on the window.

Zoe's head lifted off the back of the seat. He looked over at Giff, then reached to roll down the window. "Wasn't asleep, just resting my eyes," he said, half unintelligibly. A wavering hand went over to the heaped ashtray and lifted a smoldering cigarette. An open can of beer rested between his legs.

Giff looked him over. "A fine mess you are. I was gonna ask you to watch the store 'til I get back."

"It's why I'm here," Zoe said. He dropped the cigarette into the beer can. It made a soft "spuft" as it hit bottom and went out. "I only had the one breakfast beer, wasn't out on a hoot all night." He stretched his arms and yawned. He reached for the door handle.

Giff was relieved to see that Zoe was wearing different clothes as he stepped out of the truck.

"You're up before the chickens yourself," Zoe observed.

"Just a bit restless."

The two of them went back inside the store. Giff headed toward the pot of coffee on its burner.

"How do you want your coffee?"

"You know darned well. Black, if it's good. If it's not, with cream."

"How's that?"

"Better get me some cream."

Giff watched him open it and pour in the milk to swirl into the dark coffee. "Didn't know my coffee wasn't acceptable to all," he said.

"It's not bad." Zoe looked up. "It's just the coffee I get over to the café is too weak to defend itself. This stuff is so strong it barely needs a cup."

"Runnin' the store's not going to be a problem for you?"

"Except for some of your customers. Aren't there any normal people around here? That Rod Harmon came in asking if you had any of that nicotine gum. I told him, 'Rod, you've tried patches and every other damn thing. You can't pick up a habit that way. Why don't you just buy a cigar, or some cigarettes, hell, any ol' real tobacco product?' He says, 'Can't abide the stuff. Wish it was that easy for me.' I told him, 'Get some other habit, then. Get an ax and be a serial killer for all I care.' He says, 'Don't like cereal neither. Ate a prize was in the package once, damn near died.' So I says . . .'"

Zoe stopped when they both heard the front screen door open. He glanced toward the front door. "Oh, Jeez. I better go. Here come Dewey and Louie." Then he remembered he couldn't since he had promised to cover the store. He sighed and waited.

Two tiny figures with white hair pushed in through the door. The woman's voice—Lou, though the guys called her Louie behind her back—was shrill enough to carry to the back of the store.

"... to know something's rotten in Detroit." Giff caught the tail end of her sentence, doubted if it would have made more sense if he'd heard the whole thing.

"The way she talks drives me crazy," Zoe said in a loud whisper. "That and they're always fighting. Man, if they're a Christian role model of the perfect marriage, I know why I'm single."

"Come on," Giff nudged Zoe, said quietly to him, "Lighten up. They shouldn't bug you."

"They just seem a little sanctimonious to me," Zoe muttered.

"Do you even know how to spell that?"

"No. But I know the smell of it."

"Give them a break. They're in their eighties."

"You're too nice to 'em. It only encourages them."

"Shhh."

"Oh, they're both deaf as posts. Anyway, why aren't you as nice to that Sherrie Easton?"

"Mrs. Easton, you mean. Be nice to her how?"

"Oh, jump her bones or something."

"I think I'll go with the something, or whatever's behind door number three." Giff straightened from his lean on the counter and called out, "Kind of early for you two." He walked toward them. His voice boomed in the store as he sought to be loud enough for them to hear. "Never had you in on a Sunday before. What brings you out this early?"

Dewey wore a dark suit with a white shirt and string bolo tie. Lou had on one of her Sunday dresses and three strings of costume jewelry beads.

Lou gave Dewey a shove in Giff's direction. He snapped a frowning look back at her, then came a few steps closer and stood near enough for Giff to see a spot of egg yolk on Dewey's shirt collar.

"We saw, in the mornin' paper," Dewey said, his eye contact coming and going with Giff's, " 'bout your little Cory being . . ."

"You could have knocked me over into a cocked hat," Lou said, pushing past Dewey, impatient to get to whatever was on their minds. She crowded closer to Giff, looked up at him with her very pruney pale face, her perfume almost knocking him back a step. "You ought to see that girl gets to church now and again," she said, "gets a look at the Good Book instead of, God knows what she's . . ."

"Now Lou," Zoe's voice was loud and stern. He had come closer to them. "Is this any business of . . ."

"Oh, I've thrown in the trowel on you, Zoe Albrick. Anything you say is so much wallow over the dam."

Dewey and Lou's heads both turned back from Zoe and fixed on Giff.

"Why don't you ask her, talk directly to her?" Giff said. His voice was softer. They were close enough he didn't need to shout now. "After all, respect is a two-way street."

"It's your place to raise her up right, make her do what she should. Put your foot down. She has to do what you say." Lou's lips pressed together tight, she frowned up at Giff.

"You've got to give her instruction," Dewey said.

"I do."

"Like what?" Lou snapped.

Giff hesitated, then said, "That it's not necessary to disrespect someone just because they disrespect you."

Lou rocked back as if he'd punched her. "I don't know what makes you mean all of a sudden, Mr. Giff Purvis. It's always been the bilk of human kindness between us." She spun away before he could reply. She went over to a counter, pretended to look over the goods as if they had really come in this early to buy something.

Giff glanced at Zoe. They both still shuddered from hearing her talk. When Giff looked back to Dewey, he saw a glimmer of understanding, if not compassion in his eyes. His small thinning white head leaned closer to Giff and he said in a lowered voice. "It gets to me, too. You should have heard her going on the other night about Jason and his golden fleas."

He moved away too, left Giff and Zoe to go back and add more coffee to their cups. Dewey and Lou spent another couple of moments, their heads together near one of the counters.

When they did speak again, Giff heard Lou first, "Dewey, you stupid idiot."

"Well, I guess we shoulda brought the coffee table with us."

"Now why in land's sake would we want to do that?"

" 'Cause your purse was on it when I saw it last."

"We have to go back, and it's all your brick-headed fault."

"How can it be . . ."

"Oh, shut up, Dewey, and just get moving." She gave him a shove.

They headed for the door. Giff had mixed feelings. The only time they weren't fighting in a mean-spirited way with each other was when they were off on a crusade together against someone else.

Just before they were out the door, he heard Lou say, "Needles to say, I let him know he was casting his burls before twine."

Zoe was pulling one of the papers loose from the bundle Giff had brought in. He opened to the story about the murder. "So, just who was this Whalen, anyway?"

"All I ever hear about him," Giff said, "was that he was a hard worker."

Zoe looked up, nodded. "Well, he's long dead now."

★　★　★　★　★

Giff turned the key. Zoe's truck lurched, and Cory covered her mouth but was not able to suppress the laugh. She saw his frustrated frown and his effort not to look at her. She thought of how smooth TyTy was with a car.

"It's been a while," Giff said.

"I guess it has. You want me to drive? I can, you know."

He started to say something, stopped himself. "Sure," he said. "Go ahead." He got out of the truck and went around to slide into the passenger seat.

She waited, let him see she was grinning. "Thanks," she said and turned the key. The truck started smoothly; she shifted and eased out onto the road. She was feeling better, and a little contrite. His letting her drive, trusting her in a way that reminded her he had not asked where she learned when he had signed so she could get a license. It might as well have been a license to drive a space ship as far as he seemed concerned. His thoughts had long ago left driving a car and the mobility it offered him. Now all that seemed less of a difference between them and more something they could share.

She drove a few miles in quiet, watched him peer out the window in fascination at every ordinary thing along the road. She realized for the first time that he hadn't left the store in years, that he was practically a fish out of water.

She glanced at him, knew he had probably not slept all night. She had heard him get up a couple of times and roam out into the store.

He knew her as well as anyone could, she figured, that she was restless, a busybody, and impatient on top of that—just about the last sort of thing the sheriff would want. There was a lot Uncle Giff knew but found hard to say.

"I want to do what I can for TyTy," she said. "He's my best friend. So go ahead with the lecture about how I ought to stay in the wings, let the law handle this."

"Are you planning to be detective on this? Because you know what they say about people who act as their own lawyer—they have a fool for a client."

"I don't care if I do seem foolish. I'm gonna do what I can. It may not be a whole he . . . heck of a lot. But I aim to do what I can."

She waited, expecting a lecture of some kind to start any minute. This was serious stuff. She knew that. A girl had been killed, in an ugly way, and the killer was unidentified, and he must be roaming around their town. She finally glanced at her uncle and saw him looking out across the bend of a river that ran along beside the road for a stretch. It was brown with frothing white caps of rapids after the storm. In summer that riverbed was most often dry.

When Giff finally did speak, his words were slow and careful. "Don't be afraid to make mistakes. I've spent a lot of my life sorting through my own regrets, of which there're a regrettable many."

"Not about me, I hope."

"No. Most of mine were about opportunities I didn't pursue when the moment was right."

"How do you know when the moment's right?"

"That's the main problem. If it's any consolation, all this plays better in hindsight. When I was making my mistakes, I couldn't tell a blunder from doing the right thing."

"Like what?"

"On a simple level, sometimes saying no when I should have said yes, and vice versa. Pushed when I should have pulled; pulled when I should have pushed. Who knows? Maybe I did make some right choices but just don't know how everything would've turned out."

"You make life seem confusing." She slowed at a crossroad.

"Good," he said, looking both ways, though she could see clear road as far as she could see. "Because it is."

She didn't say anything for the next mile or two.

"You'd do anything for TyTy?"

"Yeah."

"Even if it affects your going to college or being able to keep Miss Dumpsie?"

"What's she have to do with anything?"

"I just want you to be thinking it through, Cory. Everything has a price. Everything."

For a good twenty minutes Giff and Cory sat in two worn captain's chairs in Sheriff Sparrow's office while he was elsewhere, attending to the law and order needs of a county almost too small in population to need a sheriff. Cory's stare was fixed on a length of stained rope coiled in a plastic bag on Sparrow's desk. Giff felt sure he knew what it was, which made it the one thing he didn't want to look at in this room. Instead, he looked at the spines of forensic pathology texts, books on crime scene investigation, stacks of magazines, many of which were still in their plastic mailing sleeves. His eyes skipped lightly over the scrap of bad Latin on the aging wooden sign and the other college mementoes, intended to make their own statement. The room had the clutter of a busy professional person's office, and Giff supposed that was how Sparrow intended it to look since he didn't seem the kind of person to leave things to accident or chance.

When Sparrow bustled into the room, he barely glanced at the two of them, just gave a brisk wave of one hand for them to follow and headed back out of the office. While he was leading the way to the interrogation room, Giff held out a hand and grabbed Cory's bony shoulder. She turned to look at him. He felt the tremble in her small frame, knew she was rattled enough not to feel angry with him, just nervous in general. He said, "Just remember, Cory, there will probably be a recording made of what you say."

Her eyes flicked over to the sheriff, saw him frowning at Giff. She tried for a smile for Giff, but it was a feeble one. She let herself be softly nudged into the room.

When Sparrow closed the door behind her, he turned to Giff. "This way," he said, and led them to an adjacent room where they could look through the two-way mirror.

Giff stood beside Sparrow and watched. He didn't feel good about peering in on Cory this way, had always respected her privacy. But he wanted to be near this time in case her impetuous young mouth got her into trouble. That nearly outweighed his concerns about her privacy.

The two-way mirror was as large as a big television screen. The interrogation room's furnishings were Spartan—a small steel table fastened to the wall, flat green paint on the walls with height markings for lineups, and two chairs, one with a bright red cushion and the other canary yellow. Giff watched Cory walk across the room, break into a run when she saw the red puffy swell over TyTy's eye. She rushed forward to where he sat with his handcuffs linked by a chain to a ring on the wall.

Giff looked over at Sparrow. The sheriff's lips tightened, but he didn't explain TyTy's bruises.

"What'd they do to you?" Giff heard Cory's voice through the speakers. She reached out her hands, held his. Giff started, but then noticed that TyTy looked as surprised as Giff felt.

"I guess I'm supposed to say I fell down, or something."

"Did they beat you?"

"No. Farley was on duty last night. He switched some redneck to my cell, made sure I was in with someone who thinks it's still the Wild West."

Giff glanced at Sparrow, saw a red flushed line of anger creeping up to the white sideburns. Voices from the speakers turned his face back to the two-way mirror.

"The sheriff tells me you haven't said anything, not even if it could get you off the hook."

"You know how it is."

"No. No, I don't. I've never been a guy," Cory said.

TyTy shrugged.

"How come they're keeping you? The paper says she was dead a day before we found her."

"Did it say anything about me being a material witness? That's all they'll tell me I'm being held for."

"You might be out right now if you'd just have cooperated. Do you have any idea who killed her?"

"No. Just that it wasn't me."

"Tell me about that."

"Oh, Cory. I shouldn't have to explain to you."

"You wanted to go out there, have a look around. Wesley was ragging you about ropes, tying things up. Then we find her that way. You knew something, TyTy. What was it?"

TyTy shook his head, looked down.

"Do you want me to leave?"

"No." He looked up. His voice held the first emotion Giff had heard from him.

Cory waited.

"This isn't easy," TyTy said.

"I didn't expect it to be."

"What I told you back there, when they . . . when the sheriff's cars came, that no matter what happens, you're the one I care about."

"I heard you then," she said. Giff saw her glance at the mirror.

"What I'm tryin' to say . . . what I need to confess is that I'd gone back to seeing Vickee some. I know. I know. It doesn't make sense if I care about you."

"We never had anything official. We were friends. That's all. You didn't owe me any reports on what you do in all your time." She got the words out but nearly choked on them.

Giff knew she was just sixteen. But that didn't mean she didn't feel things as intensely, or more intensely, than he did.

"That business about the ropes, and the rodeo and all . . ." TyTy looked away.

"Yeah?"

"She . . . Vickee liked to be tied up—when she did it, I mean."

"Why?"

"I don't know for sure. Maybe it got her over the guilt about doing it."

"Doing what?" Cory gave him no time to answer. "Oh, forget about that. How'd you find out about her being like that?"

"You know."

"No. How?"

"She told me. It's what she liked. The way she . . ."

"I get it." There was more snap in her voice than she probably intended. But Giff thought she was holding up pretty well so far, considering.

This would have been fascinating for Giff if he were not so tense. The girl he thought he knew, who'd grown up under his roof, knew a lot more than he knew she knew. But she also had her own moral code, one that was apparently stronger than that of the other kids at school, and even that of her best friend. Giff couldn't help the swell of pride he felt about that, though there was still a twinge at not having more detailed talks with her. Still, she was at an age where the opinions of her peers weighed far more than that of a parent or anyone older than herself. So he reckoned she had done quite well on her own.

"When was the last time . . . the most recent time you two were together?"

His head lifted to stare at her again. She was calm and looking back without a flinch.

"It was a couple of weeks ago. I was supposed to see her again later, but she didn't show. I knew I wasn't the only one who knew about her . . . what she liked."

"The locker room?"

"No. You know. I said earlier I'd been drinking. Well, lots of the other guys knew."

"Farley, Wesley, swell pals of yours like that?"

"They're not my friends. You know that."

"That's not really better, TyTy. So you told guys you don't even like?"

"No. It wasn't like that. They knew from somewhere else. The only thing to slip out was about me seeing her."

"Why? Why did you feel you had to tell them?"

"Because they were giving me a hard time about you, calling you a skinny young thing, asking if . . . if I'd . . ."

"What?"

"If I'd ever poked you. I denied it. Come on, Cory. I just told them about Vickee to get them off my back about you."

"You can't imagine how much better this is making me feel."

"I don't get it. I try to do everything right by you, and . . ."

Cory stood up. Her chair fell back onto the floor. Giff could see she was breathing hard and struggling to stay in control. Giff glanced at Sparrow, saw he was as mesmerized as Giff.

"You liked me, wanted to be with me, but in honor to that you went out and shacked up with another woman, one who is, who was perverted enough to want to be tied up?"

Giff didn't know whether to blush or laugh at her calling herself a woman. But he did know that there was no right answer for TyTy. He watched the young man's mouth open, then close.

It took Cory a minute or two to compose herself. Giff watched her in amazement, saw how her confidence came and went, but that she always wrestled it back into place.

She took her time picking the chair up and setting it upright. She sat back down. When she was calmer, she leaned forward on her elbows, looked up close into his face, "How did you know to look at the Whalen place?"

" 'Cause that's where . . . well, we were there before, together."

"And what'd you do that time?"

"What she wanted. Aw, come on, Cory. You're not making this any easier."

"I know. Look, I'm not trying to be cruel. You're a young man with needs. It's not like I don't have biological needs myself, however I've chosen to ignore them. But you say you're trying to respect me. So, why didn't you just get you some of those magazines, the kind Uncle Giff won't stock for you fellas in the store?"

"I made a mistake. A horrible mistake. This came along, was right in my face and was tempting and easy. But, Cory, you've got to believe me. I had nothin' to do with Vickee's death. I knew the pattern of her wants and knew that other guys did too. Sometimes she wanted me to leave her there overnight, come back in the morning and . . . have my way with her again. The whole thing was part of some giant turn-on, a fantasy for her." Giff could see Cory fighting to show no emotion, and not succeeding very well. "I had fantasies too, about you. But I forced myself not to act on them."

"It's beginning to look," Cory said, "as if it might have been better if you had."

He hesitated, looked down and then up. "Are we still the friends we were?"

"No." She stood slowly to look down at him. "We're not the friends we were. But we're still friends. I'm here, aren't I?"

While she left the interrogation room, Giff turned to the

sheriff. "Do you have enough now to let the boy go?"

"I'm going to need to keep him for a few more questions." Sparrow saw something in Giff's eyes. "But he'll be in a cell by himself."

"I'm glad to hear that. I'd feel personal about it if he gets any more bruises while he's in here."

CHAPTER NINE

Sparrow looked in through the glass door at the three small tables centered among the clutter of items offered at Moleen's Gifts & Stuff Shoppe, the kind of boutique that epitomized mainstream culture in Carnicius, the kind that tried to do two or three things at once to get by. Walls of tiny Hummel figures, crystal figurines, and collector plates surrounded cases full of the kind of bric-a-brac Sparrow always hoped he wouldn't get at Christmas time. Only one person sat at one of the tables—a tall man, whose straight back was rigid enough to have a poker shoved up inside him. He sat holding a magazine folded open in one hand and a raised bone-white demitasse cup in the other. Sparrow eased open the front door and went inside.

He'd never had occasion to come into the little downtown shop, but he'd met the small white-haired woman bustling out of a back room.

"Sheriff Sparrow." Her face was trying unsuccessfully to wrestle itself into a smile, though she gave the tall man at the table a quick glance. He looked up too, the small half-sized cup still poised in the air.

The sheriff held up the flat of his hand to Moleen Petralia. "Just a few words with Reverend Falcone here, if you don't mind."

"I don't, and I'm sure Brother Clayton doesn't," she said. Sparrow watched her nervous hands twist and tug at the middle of her stained short apron before she spun and hurried toward the back room again. She paused, turned back, and waved toward the big hammered copper cappuccino machine that sat one the counter nearest the tables, and said, "Coffee? Espresso? Or I have calzone or canolli, if you like?"

"No. Thanks." The abruptness of the words made her blink and sent her scurrying into the back.

Clayton Falcone lowered his magazine and cup at the same time, with the same precise and erect movements that marked his upright, stiff bearing. He waved the thick long fingers of a pale hand toward a chair at the table. He seemed unsurprised that his habits were so well known that someone knew to tell the sheriff where to find him.

"Please do sit. You should really try the fare here. This is about as cosmopolitan as Carnicius gets."

Sparrow pulled out a chair, eased into it, noticing that the open magazine was *The Economist*. It was the first copy he'd seen in a long time. He looked up at Falcone, a tall man, six-three or -four, who had the posture of a military lifer, though Sparrow knew he'd never been in any of the armed forces. The demitasse cup was half full of the black espresso, and two small smiles of lemon rind and a single espresso bean rested on the matching saucer beside it.

"You should really come in here more, Sheriff." He waved a hand over to a small magazine rack that held covers Sparrow hadn't known were available in town; there was even a regional literary journal. "It's a quiet haven, a respite from the madness outside. It's a pity the earlier pioneers wrested this bit of Texas from the savages only to have it populated by philistines, and worse."

"Do you talk that way to your congregation?"

"Oh, heavens no. They . . ."

"Don't like being patronized?" Sparrow interrupted.

Clayton pursed his lips, then covered the frown by lifting his cup and taking a sip. Sparrow watched the slow movement, wondered if that was a very good toupee Clayton was wearing. Falcone's long face was pale beneath the short, gray, carefully parted hair.

He put the cup back down and looked at Sparrow. "Is this about the unpleasantness of poor dear young Vickee's death?"

"Your niece."

"That's right. My sister's child. It was a horrible, horrible thing. But why bother with me?"

"Routine." Sparrow thought about pulling a small note pad from his pocket and glancing through the notes but decided he wanted to concentrate on the face of this one.

"Good heavens, I don't suppose you'll want an alibi, because I have a corker. I was with my congregation that evening, and immediately after that spent the night with Moleen and her husband, Renzo. He was doing poorly, as they like to say out here, and I was at their side, and then on their sofa for the night offering what spiritual comfort I could." He tilted his head an inch or two to the right and peered at the sheriff. "Do you know God yourself, Sheriff?"

"That's good. Counter-attack."

"I have nothing to hide. I don't know why you think I might."

"Did you stay with the couple more than the one night?"

"No, it just seemed like it." The preacher didn't seem to care if his voice carried to the back room or not. His lips twitched again, this time in a half-hearted attempt at a smile. "I really wish we could be on better terms. There are so few people with whom I can discuss matters other than the plebeian interests of the community."

"We all have our little crosses to bear," Sparrow said. The smell in the room was a tangle of roasted coffee beans, scented candles, and a touch of dust.

"You can imagine, can't you, what it's like where people are more concerned about Blue Heeler dogs than with the healing of souls."

"At this point in an investigation, my concern begins to be about the soles of my boots I'm starting to wear thin." Sparrow had come in with not much reason to like this man of the cloth and would really have liked to know how accurate his hunches were. He watched him slowly lift and empty the small cup, then slowly put it precisely back down on the saucer.

"I'm curious," Sparrow said. "You preach at a Methodist church, yet your sister and her family attend the First Baptist. Why is that? Didn't your sister grow up attending the Methodist church too; and doesn't the woman usually end up being the one to select the church for a family?"

"I can't begin to imagine what this has to do with your case."

"Just curious."

"There is far, far too much idle curiosity in the community as it is."

"But I'm a professional busybody. Humor me."

Clayton started to sigh, but suppressed it.

"The fact is, my brother-in-law and I don't get along. Never have." He looked back down at his empty cup.

"That's not quite the scriptural truth according to what I've learned so far," Sparrow said. "When Vickee was still an early teenager, didn't your sister and her husband make the abrupt move to another congregation? Isn't it true that neither of them speak to you yet?"

"It would be wonderful if all the brothers and sisters under God could abide together in peace. But, as we all sooner or later learn, that is not the way of the world. Surely you have noticed that, haven't you?"

"I've noticed a lot of things. But none of them so far have helped me much with this case. You interest me, though. Why don't you tell me all about you and the girl."

The preacher's back got even stiffer, if that was possible, and he nearly sputtered. "I refuse to answer any questions on that subject. Sheriff, surely you don't intend to dishonor that tragically deceased child?"

"You know that's not who I'm dishonoring here."

"This interview is at an end." Clayton looked away, then down at his spoon, which he straightened with a finger that trembled until the spoon was symmetrical to the saucer.

"Your wish to decline to talk doesn't preclude my need to know. Talk here, or you can talk in my office."

"I still refuse." Clayton looked up and stared right at Sparrow, unflinching in his intensity now. "You drag in a clergyman, and you'll begin to understand in earnest the perils of being in an elected office." There was a touch of real emotion in the preacher's voice this time, perhaps fear.

Okay, Sparrow thought. *What do I really have here? Both parents have blue eyes, the daughter had brown eyes. The wife's brother here has brown eyes. I run DNA tests, and who knows what I might confirm. But, even if this pompous and sanctimonious preacher was the one tying up his niece and abusing her when she was a little girl, the one who taught her to like the ropes and sex like that, and much worse, if it turns out she was really his biological daughter through his sister, unknown to Spencer Allen—let's say I could prove all that—would it help the case? No. It'd be background color, very colorful, at that, but I'd still be looking for a killer.*

Sparrow rose slowly, not sorry to be done talking to Clayton. "I intend to keep an eye on you. Anyone who volunteers an alibi before they're asked always worries me, and I think there's a lot more between you and your niece that you're not telling me."

Clayton looked up, with the first shadow of uncertainty in his expression. "Sheriff, I encourage you to judge not, lest ye be judged."

Farley came in the door, looked over at Sparrow behind the desk, his nose in a pile of folders. The sheriff looked up. "Take a seat." He went back to the papers.

When he looked up again, Farley was rigid in his chair, trying not to squirm. His uniform had fit him five pounds or so ago and was struggling now. But it was pressed and impeccably clean.

"It's always been my rule," Sparrow said, "that someone who makes a mistake and learns from it is worth more to me than someone who stays too busy trying never to make mistakes."

Farley didn't respond but had bent forward in his chair. He caught himself and sat up straight.

"What do you know about the young girl, this Vickee Allen?"

"Just what you know now. She had a thing about being tied up, sometimes liked to be knocked around a bit."

"You think it was because of some guilt she had about having sex?"

"I couldn't say."

"You never . . . She never shared her favors with you?"

"No, sir."

"You ever ask?"

"Well, a time or two. But she said no."

"Yet she would spend time with someone you knew to be part-Indian. That bother you?"

"No, I . . ."

"Shoot straight with me."

"Well, it did seem unnatural."

"But it was perfectly natural and normal for her to be tied up by white guys?"

"What she did was kind of her business. It was a little kinky.

But I've heard of stranger."

"Let's leave what happens over at Chunky Pearson's sheep spread out of this. You knew something about the woman, the victim, and you didn't share it."

"I wasn't really on duty when you brought in TyTy, sir."

"But you were when you did a little cell switching."

"That was wrong, and I'm . . ."

"Do you realize that if he wanted to make a stink about it he damn well could? It would be one that would come back on me. People don't talk about it much, and out here in the sticks they don't have all the same bleeding heart concerns as left-wing city folk about how we all got this land from the Indians once. But if someone litigious gets hold of this, they could cost the county money and give this department a reputation it doesn't need. Am I getting through to you at all in there." He looked at Farley's eyes, which had closed to beady slits.

"I'm suspended, aren't I?"

"Just ten days, enough time for you to think."

"Will there be a desk job for me?" Farley asked. "Sir? While I'm suspended."

"I'm afraid I don't have anything that needs done at a desk, son."

Farley stood more quickly than he needed to, spun, and started a crisp walk toward the office door.

"Son?"

Farley slowed and turned.

"Stay away from this case too, while you're off. Take the time. You could stand the vacation. How long have you been with us?"

"Three and a half years, sir."

"Without ever taking a day off or missing a sick day, though you did give half the department the flu once. Take the time. Try to kick back. It'll feel a bit alien at first. But if anyone could use it, you could. Are you with me?"

"Yes, sir." If ever words sounded insincere, they were Farley's. He spun again and took crisp steps to the door.

Specks of red light whirled across Shimmy's beaming face, then flickers of yellow, green, and blue. The balls of mirrors out over the dance floor twirled in slow time to the country swing music filling the wide hall from hidden speakers throughout the darkened ceiling beams. Sherm's head was tilted back to look up at the big fellow.

"Why don't you ask some of these young fillies to dance, 'stead of standin' there with your tongue hangin' out each night."

Shimmy raised his longneck bottle of Shiner Bock to his lips, took a thoughtful sip. "I don't have your touch with the young 'uns," he said. "You still got that Crystabelle singled out of the herd?"

Sherm lowered his head, knew his hat brim would cast his face into shadows. "She's the entertainment of the moment, Shimmy, but you know how that is."

"Can't rightly say I do."

"Well, you should. Big fella like you. Women see those size thirteen boots a' yours and they're just natural gonna start to think. You know where I'm going with that?"

The music grew louder in a swell. The song's words drowned them out for a moment:

Loved me like a dog in the bed of your pickup truck;

Left me and I can only wish you all the very best of luck.

The couples two-stepped by, all headed in pairs going the same direction around the oval dance floor. The men slid their roper and cowboy boots along finished hardwood floor now dusted with sawdust; the women followed the male lead, some twirling with flared skirts and with smiles you could hang a hat on.

"Not as many people as usual," Shimmy said.

"Maybe they got outta the mood after spending time talkin' to the sheriff or one of his men today." Sherm's eyes followed a young girl who had a large "X" on the back of her hand—a mark the doorman had put there to confirm she was too young to be buying or drinking beer. "Did they stop by your place?"

Shimmy nodded, took another drink. "I 'spect they visited everyone from Bent Bell to Carnicius. Damned shame about that young girl."

"Sure enough was. There aren't nearly enough pretty ones as it is. What'd you have to say to 'em?"

"Hell, you know where I was." Shimmy looked down at Sherm. "We was at your place playin' cards. Do you disremember your trying to convince me that a straight beats a full house?"

Sherm let out a sigh that was lost in all the dance hall noise. "It's not that I didn't know the rank of poker hands. It's just I thought you might could be thick enough to go for it." His eyes locked on the young girl again.

"Don't disrespect me, Sherm." But Shimmy laughed as he finished off what was left in his bottle. He turned to go and get another but looked out to the floor, said to Sherm, "Hey, now. That son of yours can sure enough dance like one of them T.V. stars." Wesley was with one of the young girls.

"Where do you think he got that gift? Like maybe it's in the genes."

"His jeans or yours."

"Hell, I've always been the Fred-damned-Astaire of this family. How d'you think someone looks like me landed Sue Beth?"

"I supposed you used a net." Shimmy pushed off through the crowd after another beer.

When Shimmy came back, Sherm hadn't stirred from his

spot on the rail. The way a Texas honky tonk works is that the dancers fill the floor for whatever song fits their mood, whether it's a two-stepper, a waltz, a swing dance, or every once and again the "Cotton-Eyed Joe." The couples go around and around, in a circle the same direction. The women usually go backward, though the men can switch and the good ones always do. Those with the least bit of experience can manage a twirl at the turns and a few other fancy twists. A man with a strong lead is much desired since the women dance with a variety of partners and need good direction. Every man has a slightly different dance style. Those not dancing line up along the rail and talk or watch, some leaning against the rail, others sitting at tables. A few, like Shimmy, never do make it onto the dance floor. If someone leaves a spot along the rail it is usually quickly filled. Though when someone of Shimmy's bulk came up and tried to squeeze in, room was often found for him.

The dance playing ended, the music shifting to signal a new dance but never letting up. Pairs of dancers headed for the gaps in the railing while others went out onto the floor. Wesley and the young girl passed by Sherm and Shimmy. Wesley glanced at Sherm, then looked away.

"Kids these days," Shimmy said.

"Yeah, can't live with them; can't live with them." But Sherm was glancing toward the stage at one end of the floor. It wouldn't be long before the lights would dim and Crystabelle would come out to sing.

"You shoulda had a girl, 'stead of a boy. Girls don't seem like so much bother."

"I don't think I could take it, knowin' what goes through my mind when I look at other people's young girls."

"Oh, hell, Sherm. You're just like a dog chasin' after cars. You go after every one, but you don't really want to catch one."

"That woman there at that corner table's got her eye on you, Shimmy."

"She don't neither."

"Does too. I can just tell she's the kind likes a man to be big and land on her hard." Sherm watched Shimmy. The lights weren't right to see if the big guy flushed, but he looked away. "Oh, she's still lookin', Shim. Her eyes are bright as mesquite coals with all the ashes blowed off. I think she's got the hots for you, sure enough."

Shimmy looked back down at him. "How come I don't never see your wife come out here with you anymore, Sherm? And don't say it's 'cause you don't take a sandwich to a banquet."

Sherm took a drink from his beer he didn't really need. He stared out at the people swirling by in step to the music. "She's took up with karaoke, Shimmy. Damnedest thing you ever saw. She got one a' them laser disk machines and practices all the time at the house, goes out to a place in Carnicius where she competes Tuesdays and Thursdays. Hell, I was the one almost made it as a singer once—those record folks said I wasn't a complete package, whatever the hell they meant by that. But Sue Beth works this thing harder'n I ever gave it. Power to her, I say. She's outta the house more'n in. I'm a karaoke widower, Shim." He sighed, tried to put some feeling in it.

"We've all got our little crosses to bear."

"Speakin' of which, Shim, that woman's undressing you with her eyes. And I think she likes what her imagination's finding."

"To hell with her."

"What's the matter. Big fella like you. Women don't care about your face, your build, whether your clothes are all dry cleaned and you're wearing smellum like most the guys here, any of the stuff like that. They just like a bulge on the front and back of your jeans—the back being the wallet. You don't have a problem, do you, less you're hung like a stud field mouse or somethin'."

Shimmy turned to Sherm slowly, leaned down close, almost whispered, "What say we just drop the damned subject, eh?" Then he straightened.

Sherm stood stiff and uncomfortable, taking steady pulls on his beer. Shimmy finally relaxed, turned back to him and tried out a grin. He said, "You think they'll catch that guy?"

"What guy?"

"The one what done it to that girl. You know, Vickee. The one in the papers."

"Shimmy, sometimes I can barely follow you. You're like the cowboy who hopped on his horse and rode off in all directions."

"What're you sayin' 'bout me and horses? I like 'em fine, and they like me." Shimmy leaned closer to glare down at Sherm.

Probably glad to see you're not climbing into their saddle, Sherm thought. But he said, "Hey, calm down. I didn't mean nothin' at all by it." Hell, Shimmy was just as steamed up as before, and over nothing. "Oh, check it out. They're dimmin' the lights. Crystabelle'll be comin' out to sing."

The lights slowly went out, and the baby spots on the stage grew brighter. Sherm watched Shimmy turn his bulk toward the stage, the flickers of his irrational anger soon fading from his face. "Damn," Sherm said. "She can sing to soothe the savage beast."

Sheriff Sparrow stepped out of the patrol car. His boots crunched across the dark parking lot until he opened the door to the lit interior. The new man, Winslow, sat in the department squad room at a desk. He had a file open and was reading.

When he heard the sheriff, he looked up and slowly closed the file. He started to stand up. Sparrow was still in uniform, though it was long after his day shift. He had hoped the uniform would cut him an edge with the men he'd just left. Though it hadn't been one of those old time "smoke-filled" rooms, the tension had been as high, particularly since Spencer Allen, the girl's father was one of them. His uniform had made little difference. They figured that when they'd lured him to Carnicius they'd bought him, fancy buttons and all.

"Um, Winslow," Sparrow said. He waved the deputy to stay seated. He was trying to recall the new deputy's first name. Bert, or something like that.

"Yeah?" The deputy eased back into his seat, looked at the sheriff without flinching or showing any emotion. He was a tall deputy, a good six-foot-five or so. He had the hard lean kind of body Sparrow ran into so often out in this part of Texas, like the men were made of all gristle or beef jerky. When you shake hands with one of them, it's like they're ringing a bell, the hand a claw clenching in iron grip at your own hand. Cowboy stock, Sparrow figured, lean and as hard as barbed wire. The man had one brown eye and the other pale blue. It was a bit disconcerting at first, made him seem like he was winking if you looked at him quick. But the expression on his face was usually serious, though he was not above a smile or laughter.

"Winslow."

"Yeah?" It was even more of a question this time.

"I'm switching your schedule. I want you working with me on this." He was looking down at the file Winslow had been poring over—it was the one about the death of the Allen girl, Vickee.

Winslow's brown eye squinted back at Sparrow. It made the blue eye seem wider and more piercing. "Haven't some of the other deputies been around longer?"

"But you have a background in C.I.D. and a degree in criminology." He nodded down toward the closed file. "And this case interests you, doesn't it?"

"I did a six-month internship after college, if that's what you mean."

"It's more exposure than the rest of these men have."

"You could call in the Texas Rangers on this. Fact is, I'm surprised they aren't already swarming around trying to solve this for you."

"I told them I thought we could handle it on our own."

"And?"

"And what?"

"Can we?"

"That's why I'm talking to you. It's important to me that I solve this one myself. Now, are you up to it?"

"Sure, I guess."

"What do you think so far?" Sparrow glanced down at the closed file folder again.

"Local." Winslow relaxed, leaning his back against his chair for the first time. He looked up at Sparrow. His rough hands smoothed the front of his uniform, the calluses making a rasping sound across the brown cloth. The hands settled on either side of the folder. "Girl might've been a willing partner, probably was. Things got out of hand."

"Think you can get anything on her movements?"

"Probably not. She's home for summer and is staying with her parents, probably lied to them. They're a mess besides. She was their only child."

"She's pals with a local girl, Crystabelle," Sparrow said, his speech starting to relax and resemble Winslow's slow drawl. He also didn't mention that he'd just taken a tongue-lashing from the father, Spencer Allen. "She's a singer, and part-time hooker from what I figure."

"And Crystabelle has harder edges than most the men around here. If she runs true to form," Winslow said, "I doubt she'd give us anything we could use."

"She wouldn't want the killer found and stopped? Hell, she might be next."

"I doubt she thinks that way. But we can push that envelope and see what we get." Winslow's eyes had narrowed. He looked off at nothing but was calculating. He looked back at Sparrow. "You mind if I ask you something personal, sir?"

"Go ahead."

"You're a man of considerable education. How did you come to be in law enforcement?"

"That was politely put. But don't let that old sign fool you," Sparrow said.

He had a worn wooden sign on his office wall that had been his father's. It read: "ILLEGITIMI NON CARBORUNDUM." It was a bit of fake Latin gibberish that his father had said went back to World War II and General "Vinegar Joe" Stillwell, though some said he got it all the way back from General Burnside of Civil War fame. Its mock Latin was intended to mean, "don't let the bastards grind you down," and the advice was something he thought of in respect to the local powers-that-be rather than the criminal element. Most of the deputies thought it had something to do with his Ivy League background, a thing they held in mute awe. He had not been moved to correct their confusion.

Sparrow was tired. He felt the bones of his shoulders sagging and aching as he went over and sat on the corner of the desk beside where Winslow sat. "Fact is," Sparrow said, looking away at nothing, "I was headed for law school when my parents were killed. They surprised a burglar, and my father was killed with his own gun, then my mother. The police never found who had done it. I was young and well intentioned, and it rocked me. That's what motivated me to go to the Police Academy in Massachusetts. Later, I worked my way up to Chief in a small East Coast fishing town, was elected County Sheriff and came out here to Texas when I was more or less recruited." He left out the part about the small cloud that had caused him to be willing to leave that first sheriff's position in New England or his second job as sheriff in Ohio. A case collapsed on him in New England—not enough hard evidence once the case got to trial. In Ohio it was the over-zealous handling of a witness, and a deputy who was too friendly with the press. All the movement could look good if packaged well on a resume, but his own feeling was that being sheriff of Carnicius County was his third strike. He had come as far west as he intended to be pushed. Working as a sheriff made moving harder because it was an elected position. Someone had to make it happen, and when you came in from outside you ended up owing someone. It was almost enough to make a lesser person bitter.

"That's what put a fire in your belly?" Winslow asked.

"Oh, it wouldn't toast a marshmallow some days," Sparrow chuckled. "Other days it flares up quite nice."

"This girl's murder stir it up some?"

"Her murder and the father who wants it solved yesterday," Sparrow admitted.

For a few moments it was quiet again in the station, just the soft squawking of the radio from the dispatch room down the hall. Then the P.A. system crackled, "Winslow."

The deputy stood up, and at the same time Moll stuck part of her truck driver build around the hallway corner and called over to him, "Got another domestic out to the Brancher place. You want me to call city for backup?"

"No," Winslow sighed. He reached for his hat. "It's mostly yelling and a bit a' chair throwing with that bunch." He took his usual big strides toward the door.

When he was gone and Moll had gone back into her room to her junk food and tabloids while she kept a finger on the night pulse of the county, such as it was, the room was even quieter than before. Sparrow still sat on the corner of the desk looking around.

Back in Cambridge, Massachusetts, when he'd been an impressionable freshman and had moved into the big city from a small New England town, he had thought that while in the midst of millions of people—all walking on sidewalks filled with a sea of varied types, most avoiding eye contact and all with no-nonsense faces—he had been lonely, and that he would never be as lonely again. But he had been wrong. He was far lonelier now.

CHAPTER TEN

Cory stepped out onto the store's porch just as Shimmy pulled up along the street in his truck. He climbed out and grinned at her, looking as large and playful as a walrus out of the water.

"How're you doin', Little Cory?"

"Just fine, Mr. Chism." She hated it when anyone called her little, although next to Shimmy that was more true than not. His late afternoon shadow spread across to the store like a zeppelin nosing toward the door as he walked closer.

She didn't know how he could always stay so cheerful, no matter what was going on. But maybe she was thinking too much about her own mood. She didn't mean to rain on his parade.

"Call me Shimmy. Mr. Chism reminds me too much of my pa." He stood and looked down at her. "I hear TyTy's still in jail."

"We'll see how long that lasts," she said.

"Not much we can do about it, though."

She was about to tell him that she was off right then to do something about it. But there was nothing to gain by spouting off to the likes of an easygoing guy like Shimmy. The town could burn down, and he would be likely to find something funny in it.

She started to walk around him, then stopped. "Hey, Mr. . . . uh, Shimmy?"

"What?" He turned, smiled.

"I was talking with the sheriff—well, listening's more like it—and he was going on about there being so few women around here in proportion to the men. I was just wondering what motivates men to stay around here."

She felt okay talking to him, safer, maybe because he'd always seemed a bit mentally slow, like the "special" kids they had at school. It could be he wasn't really all that dense, but compared to her uncle he sure seemed to be hiding his light under a bushel.

"If you're talkin' 'bout TyTy, it's 'cause he's in jail," Shimmy said, chuckled even when she didn't join him.

"Come on," she said. "I mean it. What motivates you? You haven't always lived around here."

He started to laugh it off, keep going inside. But the look on her face made him stop. He tilted his head and thought. "I knew some people here," he said, "like Zoe. And I was able to get a job here. That counts."

"That's it?"

"Well, folks here don't laugh at me."

"Why would they do that?"

" 'Cause I'm big and not as smart as a lot of guys." His face beamed the open honesty she'd expected of him. He laughed loud and shot straight because that's the only way he knew.

"Oh, you're just saying that. You're as good as anyone. You know that," she said.

She saw the clever like a fox look he was giving her, showing a bit of cunning he'd let slip a time or two before. She was never sure if he was as dull as he seemed, or if it was some defensive posture that made him feel good. But she had places to go and people to see—no time to dwell on that now.

"I've got to be going," she said.

"Be careful and don't get a sunburn, and try to get home before dark, else Giff'll get all worried again about you."

She started down the street, and Shimmy went inside the store.

The sun slanted through the screen door the way it always did on a late Monday afternoon at this time of year. Swirls of dust lifted up from the road outside with the least breath of wind, and a fly buzzed against the inside of the screen in a futile effort to reach the fading yellow glitter of the sun. Giff stood behind the counter and Zoe and Shimmy both had settled and tilted back on their chairs beside the potbellied stove. Everything was the way it had been for the past few years, but it all felt different to Giff now.

He could step outside and see the row of buildings and the mesquite trees and scrub bushes at the edge of town and not be able to tell a storm had passed through. It was all dried and back to Texas normal. But none of that was going to bring back that young girl who had died. Her death seemed to have cast a pall over the community, one it could feel past the banter and the going on with life.

Giff was having a hard time thinking about Vickee as a young girl. She was a female murder victim in a crime involving sex instead of the little girl who used to come into his store. He had a contrasting hard time in thinking of sixteen-year-old Cory as an adult. But he knew how Cory wanted to be treated. There was no mistaking that.

"Well, I'm glad the thick of summer's behind us now," Shimmy was saying. "And I can't wait for our first cold snap, a chance to see my breath come morning." He scratched at the front of his coveralls.

Giff had been hearing but not listening for the past couple of hours since the guys had arrived after work. The day had dragged along and now seemed even slower.

"I saw little Cory when I come inside," Shimmy said. "Where

111

was she headed?" He had to repeat the question before Giff looked up and answered.

"Out asking a few questions," Giff said. "TyTy's supposed to be let loose today. But until he is, she seems intent on nosing around."

"And you let her?" Shimmy said.

"Don't start sounding like Dewey and Louie," Giff said. "She's old enough to have her own notions and stick to them."

"Doesn't seem the sheriff is getting anywhere too damn quick," Zoe said. "You know, she used to come in here, that Vickee, but after Giff kicked her out for stealing, she stopped." He gave Giff an accusing glance.

"Heard she was a little light-fingered," Shimmy said.

"That Vickee was sure a sexy little thing, though," Zoe said. "She didn't mind lettin' everyone know it. She could sway those little hips."

"Makes me uncomfortable to talk about the dead that way," Giff said.

Shimmy shifted in his seat. He looked over at Giff. "What's the sexiest woman you ever saw in your life, then?"

"That's a tough one," Zoe said.

"Let him answer." Shimmy could see Giff was giving it serious thought.

Giff was looking off into a corner of the store. His head swung back to them. "It would have to be a woman I worked out with at a gym, later ran behind her in a 10K back when I used to jog."

"You never even saw her face?" Shimmy said.

"No. But she was an athletic woman, about my age, with long reddish brown hair. She kept it tied back in a pony tail. When she was on the StairMaster, or running, that long hair swung back and forth like a metronome."

"A what?" Shimmy frowned.

"A windshield wiper, then."

"And that was sexy?"

"Sure was."

Zoe reached up and scratched under his chin. "Giff, old friend, we need to get you out more often."

The front screen banged, and they all looked that way. It was Sheriff Michael Sparrow, in uniform, his face all busy trying to turn a scowl into a smile. A deputy was with him—a tall fellow Giff had not seen before. The deputy peeled off and hung up by the front of the store while Sparrow walked back toward them.

"Thought I'd find you fellas here," he said once he was through the store and standing among them. Though he still tried for the local accent, his buried Massachusetts background made him say "fellars."

"Making any progress on that murder?" Zoe asked.

Sparrow was looking at Giff. "I've talked with most everyone, though I was hoping for more help from some of the locals."

"With what?" Giff asked.

"Some folks are windy, and others are clams. But no one really seems to know much of anything. Been over to the young girl's college room. She has more sets of handcuffs than my department. But that still doesn't excuse her being dead. Seems someone—the killer, we think—tried to start a fire at the back of the building on the Whalen place. Probably on the day of the murder. Storm put it out. Someone—them or someone else— came back after the storm and tried again, had more luck this time. That old place was dry as tinder."

"Burnt down to the ground?" Zoe said.

"Nothing but a scorched spot out there. Sure, I could have left a deputy there, sitting around on taxpayer dollars. But who'd have thought . . ."

"Was there evidence still out there?" Giff asked.

"Not that we know of. We dusted in the first go-round, didn't find a single latent. We didn't have cloth samples, bite marks, anything else we could use on the body. It doesn't really make much sense."

"What other kind of help do you think you're not getting?" Giff wasn't going to back down. All that mumbo-jumbo earlier about trading school names still did not set well with him. He trusted the sheriff about as far as he could throw one of Sparrow's patrol cars.

"Well, there's your pal, Saris McFeeny, for one."

"What about him?"

"Went out to see him, and I saw the man light out into the scrub. I waited there all afternoon, through half a tank of gas keeping the air conditioner going in the car. But I didn't see any more of him."

"You probably scared him half to death," Giff said. He didn't worry about the edge to his voice showing. "What makes you pick on an old recluse like that, anyway?"

"I'm not picking on anyone," Sparrow snapped, just as unhappy with Giff. "Everyone has a duty to at least be questioned."

"You must know that old man lives off apart from everyone for a reason. He's skittish as the dickens around people."

"That's what interests me in him."

"Oh, right. A crusty old, unbathed codger like that is going to somehow meet a young girl like Vickee and lure her out to the Whalen place?"

"What's wrong with that? Screwier things have happened, and it's usually someone just like Saris when all is settled. What's the matter? Why are you looking at me like that?"

"You're trying to get a rise out of someone. I'm just trying to figure if it's me."

"I think the whole bunch of you is beginning to feel a little precious." Sparrow took off his hat and ran the fingers of one hand through his thick white hair that was matted down in the shape of his hat. He slid the hat back on, looked wistfully at one of the empty chairs by the stove, then turned a frown to Giff.

"Something brought you out here," Giff said. "You didn't come to see our cheery faces and trade lies, did you?"

"Someone beat the living bejesus out of Sherm Hargate in the GALS parking lot last night," Sparrow said.

Shimmy's chair tottered to the floor. "I was with him for quite a spell last night."

"So I'm given to understand." Giff had watched the sheriff glancing down at Shimmy's knuckles.

Sparrow looked up. Shimmy's knuckles were same as they always were, a bit dirty, but with no signs of a recent battle.

Sparrow said, "I'm not saying that parking lot isn't littered with broken teeth and dreams dating back through several years, but it sure seems I'm over to this previously quiet end of the county a lot lately."

"Do you think the beating's in any way connected with Vickee's death?" Giff asked.

"I haven't the foggiest at this point in time."

"You're nowhere closer to solving this thing, are you."

"I've narrowed the field a bit, but I'm still scoping half the males in this area."

"What's the worst-case scenario?" Giff asked.

"That it was someone not from here, someone just passing through."

"What chance is there it was that?"

"Almost none."

"This murder has a lot of folks 'round here actin' like it was a full moon," Zoe said. "Fightin' among themselves. Hell, we're gettin' to be a regular community full of Deweys and Louies."

"Now there's a fine pair," Sparrow said. "Don't get me started on those two. They not only stonewalled me but

115

threatened to sue."

"Join the club there," Zoe said. "You might feel unique if they didn't. They don't have the money to sue and wouldn't know where to start if they did. But they love to draw the idea of a lawyer like a cheap gun."

"It's going to backfire on them some day," Sparrow grumbled.

"Maybe you could appoint them county marriage counselors, or something," Zoe said. "That'd keep 'em out of mischief."

Shimmy snorted. "That'd be as dumb as giving whoever invented dynamite a Nobel Prize."

"It sure would," Giff agreed, though he fought back a grin.

Sparrow nodded to Giff and walked over closer, easing to the far end of the register counter, away from the stove. When Giff sidled closer, Sparrow lowered his head, mumbled, "You getting anything from your end?"

It took all Giff had to suppress a laugh. The whole manner seemed so Junior G-man.

"Well," Sparrow said. "Do you intend to help, or not?"

"If you want, I'll go out and talk with Saris, see if he has anything to say, though I doubt it. Will that help you?"

"It would check that off my list, if you can determine he has nothing to do with the murder."

"I can vouch for him now, but I'll go out and rattle his tree, see what nuts fall to the ground."

"Something else," Sparrow said.

"What?"

"Why's everyone out here treating me the way they do, yourself included? It's like I came here straight from New York City or something."

"You ever see a prickly pear leaf that's dropped into a river?" Giff asked.

"Yeah. It'll soak up water, swell until it's the shape of a football." Sparrow's voice got louder. "You saying I'm all puffed up over this case?"

"Just speaking for myself," Giff said back in a low voice, "I keep waiting for you to say one positive word about this part of the county. Your words and body language suggest you were dragged out here like this was the land of the unclean and you can't wait to get back out."

"Truth is, that's how I feel."

"Well, you might try showing it less."

Zoe watched Sparrow go out the door. When the sheriff was gone, Zoe looked over at Giff, who still had a bit of color in his cheeks. "If it's all the same with you, do you mind telling me what it is about him gets under your skin and starts a slow crawl?"

"It's probably just my instincts acting up." Giff shrugged it off.

"It's more than that." The sheriff seemed to rub Giff the way Sherm Hargate's kid Wesley did. But the two of them seemed worlds apart. "Is it that business about where you did your colleging?"

Giff looked thoughtful. Zoe listened to the low drone of an announcer's mumble coming from the scratchy radio, then a song started, something mournful, with a bunch of hunting horns going soft and moaning at first. "I mean, you've got a vocabulary that's snapped our heads back once or twice. But I never figured you for one of them egghead fellows before. Are you?"

"Am I what? Oh, never mind. I guess what bugs me about Sparrow is something in myself."

"Come again."

"I mean, there are things in him that remind me of me in a way I don't like to think about."

"You see some sort of reflection of yourself in him?"

117

"Just the parts I'm not happiest about."

"I don't know why you're so down on yourself sometimes, Giff. And even more important, I hope you don't think being out here with the likes of us is some kind of punishment."

"You know better than that, and if you don't, you should."

Zoe tilted his head at Giff. "You might could explain that better."

Giff took a deep breath, and looked back at Zoe. "Look, I don't know what Sparrow's background is like. I suspect he grew up in Massachusetts and may have had rich folks like most of the other students I knew in those days. But I came from a small town in Ohio, went on a full scholarship or I wouldn't have been there."

"You musta been smart to get that."

"The point is that I was surrounded by people my age who'd grown up quite differently from me. They had privilege. I had opportunity. That's what the American Dream is supposed to be—people who get to better themselves from where they start out. But I had the kind of head then that made me worry about all the others who weren't getting the same chance as me, while my classrooms were filled with a good proportion of bored young prigs who mostly wondered what I was even doing there."

"Were the kids like Sherm Hargate? His spread of eleven or twelve thousand acres has been in that family for eight or nine generations. It looks likely it'll all be Wesley's some day."

"No. The kids had more polish than Sherm, and you've got to realize that their folks were a lot richer, most of them anyway."

"You're always talking about prejudice. Sounds like you're kind of down on the rich here. Is that it?"

"No. I know I should have appreciated getting an opportunity others didn't, but it always made me feel I was living a lie. Still, I thought I'd try to make the most of it. I struggled for a while to do all I could, to use all the education I could to make things better for others. I worked jobs that tried to share better primary and secondary learning, and I helped with foundations. I tried to make some small difference but was only beating my head against a brick wall and wasting time. The truth is, that's not what the rich want at all. All of the stumbling blocks I ever faced, and the ones that finally tripped me and sent me stumbling, came from people who didn't really want the way things are to change."

"So you switched to chasing women, drinking, and finally come out here to while away the dregs of your days?"

"That's not the way I'd have put it, but that's about it."

"But you're saving up to put Cory through college. I've heard you on that often enough. Why set her up for what you went through?"

"I kept hoping college is what someone makes of it. Cory has a sharp and engaging mind, one she didn't inherit from me, but from my brother. I'll give her every chance."

"You think she'll handle it different from you?"

"You know," there was the first ray of hope in Giff's voice, "I believe she will. She's still young, but in her way I think she's smarter than I ever had hopes of being."

"What were you, one of them over-achiever types?" Zoe asked.

"I like to think not."

"What about Cory? She does real well in school."

"That feisty little gal does well because she attacks things. A lot of kids these days think all they have to do in life to make it is show up. High school's set them up for that lie by passing a lot of them it shouldn't have. But Cory doesn't have that problem."

"That attacking's a good thing, I guess," Zoe said, and looked a bit concerned, "just as long as life doesn't attack her back. Like what's happened to that Vickee."

CHAPTER ELEVEN

The area behind GALS that was built up to be a stage and dressing rooms was little better than a large shed added to the warehouse that comprised the bulk of the building. Cory had expected an exotic backstage and a plush dressing room. What she found instead was plain to the point of being rustic. She came to a door where someone, most likely as a joke, had marked a big star with a felt-tipped pen. She rapped, then heard Crystabelle's voice calling to come in.

Cory leaned through the door, hesitant to enter. Crystabelle was bent over a small bag from which she drew her makeup kit. She recognized Cory and said, "Good lord, Cory, you were about the last person I expected to see. You're all sweaty. Did you hike all the way here?"

Cory nodded, went the rest of the way inside and closed the door behind her. "Well, not exactly. I started to hike this way, then got a ride from Dewey and Louie. But they got on a preaching jag and drove me all the way to Carnicius. So when I got out of their car at the grocery I had to hike back here from there."

"I suppose it's only fair you get a turn at being the black sheep. God knows I got enough lip from those two old goats about everything I was doing and everything they thought I might be up to. Go ahead, sit down in that chair over there." She waved to a chair that sat against the wall.

"They mean well, I suppose," Cory said. "But it's real hard

to believe what they say when they interrupt each other to fight all the time while preaching to you. And I have to fight to keep from laughing most of the time."

"I think there're quite a few people around here would pay good hard money to see those two in a mud wrestling match. They could turn the money over to charity and maybe do some good for a change instead of just buggin' everyone."

Cory nodded. She sat stiff and polite in the chair, watched Crystabelle look over the jeans, t-shirt, boots, and denim jacket she wore. Crystabelle eased herself down onto the stool in front of her makeup mirror.

"Are you thinking of getting into this line of work, Cory? I'm hard pressed to think why else you'd visit. We were never close." Even without her makeup on yet, Crystabelle had a hard edge to her face. It was the look of someone who grew up too fast, knew way more than she should at her age.

"No. I don't have your voice, or looks, or build," Cory said. She gave a demure head dip to dispel any suspicion of sarcasm.

Crystabelle laughed. "Well, whether you mean it or not, it's good to hear. And it's true. I've never heard you sing, but you don't really have the build GALS requires."

"I'm a late bloomer."

"Let's hope, for your sake." She chuckled. "Now really, Cory, what is it?"

"It's about Vickee. She was your good friend."

"She was," Crystabelle said. She looked away thoughtfully. Whatever emotion was there she put out like dumping water on a small fire. Her face had hardened again by the time she looked back at Cory. "You thinking of playing the little lady detective here? Why?"

"They've got a friend of mine locked up. TyTy. You know him. I promised to do what I could."

"You aren't letting the young warrior play, are you?"

"What do you mean?"

"Are you having sex with him?"

"Good grief, no."

"Why is that such an obvious thing? Most girls your age have played a little Russian roulette with their bodies by now. I know I had, and Vickee. Whoee. She was humping coming out of the cradle, practically."

Cory felt herself blush. It made her mad and made her feel unsophisticated. She said, "You think sex is pretty neat, don't you?"

Crystabelle turned slowly away from Cory, stared back at her in the mirror. "Yeah, right. Is that what you think? Well, I guess you wouldn't know any better. Picture this: your neck is bent 'cause your head's jammed back into the headboard; he's over you, jamming it in, pounding away; a single drop of sweat keeps falling right in your eye, as soon as you wipe it away another hits you. Oh, yeah, Cory. It's one goddamn whoopee roller coaster ride." Her mouth puckered and for a moment Cory thought Crystabelle was going to spit.

"But . . . but . . . why?"

Crystabelle gave another of her low throaty chuckles. "Why do I do it? Well, I don't as often as I can avoid it. But when I do, I make sure I always end up with more than I gave. It's how I earned enough for my truck. You think I get paid squat for singing?"

"Are you trying to confuse me?" Cory felt her forehead wrinkle.

"You're way ahead of me there, honey."

Again Cory had the feeling that somehow Crystabelle had leaped ahead of Cory by ten or twenty years of living.

"I just don't understand. If you don't like it, why do you do it?" Cory said. "Just for money?"

"Sometimes I do like it, but not nearly as often as guys think, and not the way they think, either. I like slow, dreamy, intense and lingering. What I get most often is a day at the races."

"But you seem like . . . I would have thought you did it because you enjoyed it so much. You always seemed to ooze a pretty obvious sexuality. Why do that if you're not after the romp?"

"A man gets horny, he can't think. That's how you want to keep it. They get calmed down, they aren't worth much for a spell. You've got to give it up every once in a while, or it's all tease. But hang in there. Biology kicks in again, and the odds're our way. The little head always out-votes the big head."

Cory felt herself blushing to the roots of her blond hair. Damn. She wasn't as in control of the conversation as she had wanted. She said, "But Vickee. What was her . . . Why'd she do what she did?"

"Oh, Vickee liked it. Don't let me confuse you about that. She tried to be manipulative, get something back. But her drive ruled her. She was like a man that way. She had an eye for the studs, and didn't mind being a little forward about asking for what she wanted. You know what I mean?"

"The night she died," Cory said. "Did you notice her being around anyone in particular?"

Crystabelle tilted her head at Cory and smirked. "You better save that line of questioning for the sheriff. But I will tell you what I told him enough times. I didn't even see Vickee that night. I was here working, like I am most of my damn life. I'm working here now when I should be paying my respects over where they've got her laid out at the funeral home."

Cory took a deep breath. This was harder than she had thought, and Crystabelle was someone she knew at least as from the same school. "What about Sherm Hargate? Weren't you two . . ."

"Oh, I heard he got beat up. I had to get another ride home

last night. One of the bouncers, Bryce, found him and got an ambulance. Bryce says it looked like a couple guys worked him over."

"How did Bryce figure that?"

"Sherm wasn't as drunk as all that. It'd take a couple to do what was done to him. They stomped up and down on his . . . Are you sure you wanna hear this? You're lookin' kinda pale."

"Won't you . . . won't you miss him?"

"Hell, it's a vacation for me, not having him drooling over my shoulder half the time. He was help with the rent, but I didn't give him as much sugar as he let on. One, he couldn't handle it, and two, he wouldn't have kept coming back as hard if I had."

"Oh." Cory didn't know if she'd accomplished enough to compensate for the long hike here, and the coming one home again. "Do you have any idea who killed Vickee?"

"Honey, I wish I did. I'd have told the sheriff during one of his half dozen visits, and he's a damn sight better at this detective business than you're likely to be."

Winslow pulled the patrol car up into the Meadow Parke Funeral Home's parking lot, even though their business was semi-official. He'd noticed on the ride over that Sparrow had added a couple of extra merit ribbons to his uniform and had even shined the buttons a bit. The sheriff had also been quiet all the way here. Winslow climbed out his side and stretched, wondering again if the contemplative quiet had anything to do with Spencer Allen being one of the commissioners and the late Vickee being his daughter.

"Take a look around," Sparrow said, just as they were near the door. "See if anyone's hanging around who looks a little out of sorts. You know the drill."

Winslow knew the drill all right. It was the one where Sparrow didn't want to make an entrance with his deputy towering over him. Well, checking the place wasn't a bad idea. He'd known killers who couldn't stay away from the funeral of a victim, just like pyromaniacs who had to hang close and see the fire trucks come to the conflagration. But there'd been nothing fetish about this killing that Winslow had spotted yet, other than the tying up with ropes and all that.

By the door that led into the funeral home from the other side of the parking lot, a young man stood sucking on a cigarette as if he was trying to swallow it. The tip glowed to a tapered hot point and the kid's cheeks were sucked in by the force of his inhaling. The boy looked up at Winslow, caught the uniform but didn't otherwise react or act guilty. He might not have been old enough to be smoking, but what the hell, it was at a funeral home, and there was bound to be a lot of stress in there. The kid's suit hung on him in a loose fit, as if he'd either lost weight or the suit had been bought in anticipation of him growing more. But he wasn't going to grow much if he smoked every cigarette like that. The boy lowered his hand and let go of what was left of the cigarette, which was little more than the filter. He stepped on that, twisted his foot half a turn, and spun and went back inside. Other butts littered the asphalt by this door, and like many buildings in a no-smoking-inside era, the doorway smelled like an ashtray. Winslow glanced through the parking lot again, saw no one sitting in any of the vehicles, then turned and went inside himself.

The casket was down the hallway and in the center of a smaller room, now partially filled with people in different stages of grief. When it's a young person, there are always more students, many caught up in their own first sense of mortality. There was also always a sense of waste. Why a person this young? That sense was heightened now, since everyone present also knew this hadn't just been an auto accident.

Though he'd been born in the adjacent county, Winslow

didn't know anyone in the room. That made it easier to sweep the faces, and on most he saw genuine grief and shock.

Sheriff Sparrow was on the far side of the room, standing close to a man with red hair who was almost as tall as Winslow. Well, there'd been no help for Sparrow having to look small standing and looking up like that, Winslow figured. That would be Spencer Allen, the father of the victim. Clear on the other side of the room stood Mrs. Allen's brother, Clayton, the bachelor preacher. His long face looked as pale as the undertaker's, and he stared off through the crowd, looking neither toward the casket nor at his brother's family. Winslow had heard the brothers hadn't talked in years. That wasn't so odd in his experience, but Sparrow had said that it started in Vickee's early teenage years. Sparrow had done the interviewing of Clayton himself. The file entries had been brief, too brief. But Sparrow had asked Winslow to double-check the man's alibi, and that had held up. It seemed noteworthy to Winslow, though, that another preacher was scheduled to deliver the funeral services.

Sparrow had to tilt his head back to talk to Spencer Allen. Beside them stood a woman in black, half-turned and staring at the face in the casket. Another woman came up and touched her arm, but the staring woman seemed not to notice. After a minute, the other woman turned and eased away, shaking her head slowly.

As Winslow eased up, he caught Allen's voice, which had slipped up a notch in volume as more emotion crept into whatever he was saying. "I don't care what you have to do. I want results. The commission wants . . ." He looked up, saw Winslow, and stopped. The word "results" had been loudest. The woman in black, who Winslow had figured for Mrs. Allen now, didn't seem to notice. The boy who'd been smoking outside did, though. He had moved closer to his mother and now looked at Mr. Allen with the kind of disdain only a son can share.

"This is Deputy Winslow," Sparrow said. "I've brought him in on this. He has the most background of anyone in the department, and I've asked him to focus his efforts . . ."

Allen didn't wait for the sheriff to finish. He took a step closer and reached out a hand, shook Winslow's in one of those tests of strength that went along with the piercing intensity of his look. Eyes open and staring with the kind of determination that said he'd steamroll over anyone he had to, and could. It must've been pretty much in line with his parenting style, Winslow figured. The man seemed to demand respect, not be willing to earn it. You go to any small community and you'll find a man of Allen's intensity somehow involved in running the place.

"Do you have anything to report?" Allen leaned closer, in case Winslow wanted to say anything. But he didn't. He looked at Sparrow, who was glancing uncomfortably at Mrs. Allen. "You do, you let Sherm, me, or any of the other commissioners know right away, you hear?"

There it was. He laid it right on the table, in case Winslow didn't already have a whiff of the local power structure. He hadn't turned once to look at his daughter, lying in the coffin. But he had time to be puffing around like a rooster. Winslow pried his hand free and tried to step around Spencer to get to Mrs. Allen. But the husband turned and put an arm around her shoulder to turn her toward the two lawmen. She winced, and Allen frowned and dropped his hand off her shoulders. "You men, you do all you can for Letitia and me, won't you?"

Winslow nearly said he'd do what he could for Vickee. But Letitia had turned back around to fix on the coffin again, and Sparrow stepped in to nod Spencer Allen over to a corner where they could talk with their heads closer together. It left Winslow with a moment or two to mull over mention of Sherm Hargate's name as one of the local political muscles. Owning a spread the size of the one he did drew a lot of water around here. But, somehow, mention of his name had made Spencer's interest seem less personal.

Winslow glanced over at the coffin, where three schoolgirls nearly the same age had just burst into loud tears and were clutching each other. He swept the room again, noticing who was here, who wasn't. The girl's pal Crystabelle wasn't here. But she was probably working. There was an undercurrent here in the room, as if more than a few of those present had some idea of how Vickee had been spending her evenings making extra money for college. It was nothing Winslow wanted to bring up with the girl's father just now. He saw Sparrow and Allen talking heatedly, the taller man bending closer now. He also saw the boy ease toward the door again.

When Winslow pushed the door open, the heat of the day was just beginning to let up and the sun ease off. The boy was getting another cigarette going. He glanced at Winslow but didn't stop lighting his smoke.

"Your dad's a real box of cream puffs, isn't he," Winslow said.

The boy looked up at him. A quiver of a smile formed, then flitted away. "It didn't take you long to figure him out, did it?" His cheeks hollowed as he drew hard, and the lit tip glowed to a red point.

Kid's gonna be in a cancer ward before he's forty, Winslow figured. But he said, "What's the matter with your mother?"

The boy's face snapped back to him, then tilted an inch. Maybe he saw something there that made him feel he was being spoken to man-to-man. Winslow didn't know. The boy had a weak mouth, and his eyes didn't show much character either. He seemed to get most of his strength from the act of smoking.

His eyes showed a flicker of sadness, then went back to trying to be indifferent. "She's just upset over how Vickee turned out. I know I was pretty bummed too the first time I heard she'd turned a trick or two."

"I meant her back," Winslow said.

"Oh." The boy looked away.

Winslow watched the twin beams of smoke shoot out in angry spears from the boy's nose while he squinted at the asphalt.

"Did your parents ever beat you—you and Vickee?"

"What makes you say that? My name's Mark, by the way."

"Did they beat you?"

He dropped his butt and was pulling another cigarette from a pack inside his jacket. He was doing his best to look tough, or disinterested. "Again, why?"

"You get someone likes to be tied up, abused a bit, sometimes it goes back to the way they were brought up. Did Vickee ever want you to tie her up?"

Mark looked at the door, then out at the parking lot, as if deciding whether to leave or stay and talk. Winslow figured he wanted to talk. Something was inside that really wanted to vent, to come out.

Mark lit his cigarette and squinted one eye around the smoke as he stared up at Winslow in a penetrating look that was close to an imitation of his father's piercing stare. "Mom's the religious one. Dad isn't."

"And?"

"Don't you see. They never beat us. But Mom would beat herself—sometimes in front of us."

"Spencer . . . uh your father . . . uh . . . allowed that?"

"He didn't want her to, tried to get her to stop. But she even did it because of stuff between them sometimes."

"Her back's a little tender right now?"

Mark looked away. "It's a wonder she can stand in there."

Up in a tree across the parking lot, a mockingbird perched high on the peak of a residence and began to make a repetitive cry.

"Did you ever tie up Vickee?" Winslow repeated.

"Once or twice, a long time ago. I stopped. I thought it . . . something seemed sick about it."

"But she liked that sort of thing, didn't she?"

"Of course she did. It's what got her killed."

"Do you have any idea . . ."

"Not a clue," Mark interrupted. He threw his half-finished cigarette out into the lot without smashing it this time. He glared at Winslow, hating him at the same time he'd been glad to let some of his demons loose. Then he spun and rushed back inside where his dead sister lay.

Winslow walked slowly over to the glowing butt and crushed it under a twist of his heel.

The sun was slipping over the horizon. It would be dark in earnest soon. Cory walked along beside the road with her head down, thinking and a bit weary from the hiking. She wished she could have borrowed Zoe's truck or ridden Miss Dumpsie or almost anything. She fought against the feeling but began to feel the metallic twist inside of an old grudge against Giff for having never kept a car up so she could drive.

Then something else swept over her, a hurting emotion of loss and sorrow. It was for Vickee, and not because she had liked her or been close to her, but because people like Crystabelle who had been close weren't more touched by what had happened or hurt. Crystabelle was just plodding on with her life, no matter how cool she thought she was. That bothered Cory for reasons she did not understand, and she felt as bad as she could about the little girl Vickee who had breathed, played, laughed, and been someone's daughter.

It was getting dark. She almost didn't hear the sound of a truck slowing beside her. She rubbed hard at any moisture on her cheeks and looked up. Wesley sat behind the wheel of his white Ranger. He grinned in a way that did not make her feel more comfortable.

"You want a ride, Cory?"

"Which way you going?"

The question caught him off guard. He glanced up. "North, I guess."

"Well, say hello to the Eskimos," she said, and kept walking.

She heard him curse and then heard the gears of his truck being abused. He popped forward and swept off the road in front of her, was opening the door.

"Uh-oh," she said. She knew she should have said nothing. TyTy wasn't handy and she could see the skinned knuckles on Wesley's hand as he slammed the door and started stalking back toward her. He had some temper on him.

A truck heading the other direction swung across the road in a U-turn. It slowed and eased up beside her. She glanced and saw Shimmy's bulk behind the wheel. His window was open. "Hop in," he called. "Giff said you were still out. Didn't know you were out here on the highway. I was headin' over to GALS. But I'll be glad to drop you home first."

Cory rushed for the door and got inside. She watched Wesley climb back into his truck and slam the door. The truck peeled out, leaving a long streak of black rubber behind each rear tire.

"Young man oughta get more vegetables in his diet. Calm him down a bit." Shimmy was chuckling to himself.

Cory sank back into the seat as Shimmy turned the truck around and headed back for the store.

"It must be nice," she said, "to never be afraid of anyone."

"Why?" he said. "You mean 'cause of my size?"

"Yeah."

131

"You'd be surprised. Ever once in a while some young rooster gets liquored up enough to think he'll have a go at me, and for no damn reason, except maybe he's got some young fill . . . female he wants to show off for."

"But none of them can beat you, can they?"

"None have. But that's no brag. I'd as soon never lift a fist."

"You don't seem like a mean person."

"I'm not. Though when I was your age I had a temper and a half."

"That's hard to believe. But you outgrew it?"

"I ate my way out of it." He laughed.

They rode in quiet for a mile or so, then Shimmy said, "Giff says you're nosing around about that girl's murder. The sheriff dropped by and says he isn't any closer to wrapping it up. What do you think, so far?"

"I don't know what to think. Uncle Giff said I'd end up more mixed up than before, and it's starting to look like he was right. He told me one of his stories—well, it was by Aesop, really."

"Oh."

"It was the one about the mouse who comes back from having his first adventure in the world and he tells his mother that the terrifying voice of the fierce and evil-looking rooster frightened him away from approaching and hearing the murmured kind words of the friendly, smiling cat."

"Your Uncle Giff is sure a piece of work, isn't he? I don't know what to make of half his stories. He doesn't share them all that often, likes being the quiet type and listening all the time."

Cory said, "That shows how little you really know him."

It was past closing time, but Giff had kept the store open and the lights on until Cory got home. All the worrying he had done about her in the past few days was going to be the death of him, he figured.

The screen opened and slammed shut. He looked up from his spot behind the register, hoping to see Cory. But it was Sherrie Easton.

She wore tight jeans, cowboy boots, and her blouse was unbuttoned far enough down to remove any doubt about a bra. She swished and swayed all the way back to his counter until she was close enough for a wave of her musk perfume to sweep over him.

Her voice was low and husky. She said, "Fella comes into a grocery and says, 'A dollar twenty for eggs. Why that's a dime each.' Grocer tells him, 'For a hen, that's a whole day's work.' " She chuckled softly to herself, leaned forward on the counter, let her blouse fall open more, and seemed to enjoy seeing his eyes open wider.

Giff blinked and looked up at her face. Those Liz Taylor eyes weren't much better than the sweeping flesh he had yanked his eyes away from. He felt himself swallow in spite of trying not to.

"That was a little general store humor," she said. "Supposed to relax you."

He nodded.

"Husband's off on a poker night," she said. "Where's your little Cory?"

"Due any second," Giff said. "In fact, I thought that was her coming in. I'm only staying open until she . . . gets back. She's due any second."

"You're starting to repeat yourself. Do I make you nervous?"

"No. Well, yes."

"Why don't you just talk, then. Tell me what it is about me that bugs you."

He nodded down toward the wedding and diamond ring on her left hand. "You're married."

"That usually doesn't weigh so much these days."

"It does to me. People say men are skittish around commitment. Well, I'm not. I honor my own as well as those of other people."

"You always been this . . ."

"Sanctimonious and uptight?" He chuckled. "I guess I'm not trying to be. I was a little defensive there. But it does relax me a bit to get that out into the open."

"That's good." She reached across the counter and patted his arm. Her hand, even in the brief contact, felt very soft and warm.

"Tell you the truth," she said. "My husband's probably not playing poker. He's been slipping over and singing karaoke in Carnicius. I think he might be seeing Sherm Hargate's wife."

"Small world, isn't it."

"It seems so around here. But maybe that's what he meant by 'poker'."

"I hope you don't think . . ."

"No. I'm not trying to get back at him through you. Though that would be icing on the cake."

"I'm surprised you said cake instead of buns. You kind of like a provocative edge to your conversation." He leaned forward on the counter the way he did when talking with the fellows, getting more comfortable around her as they just talked.

She leaned forward too, and the blouse fell open and the wave of musk perfume swept over him again. But he was calm enough to ignore that by now.

"I'm glad we're able to at least communicate," she said. "I was beginning to wonder if you were human. Is there anything I can do to make us better friends?"

"You could button up your blouse a bit."

She did, but that only made the silk material stretch tighter over her flesh.

"I don't think that's helping. Better go back the way it was."

She laughed and put the buttons back the way they were.

Her fiddling with her blouse buttons in front of him seemed intimate to him. It had been a long time since he was near a woman like her.

"I'm glad you were open late," she said. "I thought I might have missed you."

"I was waiting on Cory, like I said."

"You care a lot about her, don't you."

He had been scratching away in his journal late one night and had written: "The measure of how much you care about a thing is often proportional to how difficult it was to get." It didn't sound right. He scratched "thing" out, wrote in "person," then changed "difficult to get" to "difficult to raise." But Cory hadn't been any of that. She had presented small obstacles and challenges that he had been glad to overcome—adjusting to Cory's presence at first, the cost of bringing her up, having the operation on her ears, even getting and maintaining Miss Dumpsie. All those years of emptying out and being there for her needs had made a bond that gave him understanding he would never have had as a bachelor recluse. He had scratched out the entry and been done with it.

Giff said, "I've been worrying for quite a while that she was in her teens and maybe I should be expecting a rebel phase about now, a 'question authority' trend. But Cory has always been a polite little thing, and she's stayed that way."

"Your brand of authority isn't all that threatening," she said. "It's one of the things I find attractive about you."

"You never had kids?"

"I wanted to, but my OB-GYN said I had a swell playground but I was missing a swingset, or something."

"I'll have to take your word on that."

"You don't have to."

"Now, Sherrie."

She giggled and patted his arm. "See, that's the first time

135

you've used my first name, and it wasn't as hard as all that, was it."

The screen door sounded and Giff stood up. Sherrie straightened from the counter more languidly. Giff peered past her nicely rounded shoulder and saw Cory coming through the store.

"I hope I didn't interrupt anything," Cory said.

"Mrs. Easton was just leaving," Giff said.

Sherrie looked back at him and winked. She sauntered through the store, cutting down on the hip swing a little since she knew the girl would be watching her retreat too.

"I was worried about you," Giff said.

"I could tell."

"Let's lock up and you can tell me all. The sheriff was by. They're letting TyTy out. Sparrow says it was protective custody more than anything."

"That's why TyTy got beat up?"

"Sparrow said they had a crowd lynch an Indian where he was once before, and for all the wrong reasons."

"TyTy's only part-Indian."

"Maybe they'd have only partly hung him."

"It sounds like an excuse to me. He just needed someone locked up a while to take the heat off himself, and if it was someone like TyTy, all the better."

"That's the way I saw it too."

"Oh, come on, Uncle Giff. I'll get the front door. You do the lights." She started toward the front of the store, mumbling, "Arrested for all the wrong reasons. Sounds about right."

CHAPTER TWELVE

They sat at the small dining table in the kitchen. Giff got up and poured another cup of hot water over a spoonful of Sanka crystals in his cup. He stirred as he went back to sit down.

"That's all I got," Cory said.

"With TyTy out now, are you . . ."

"Am I going to stop? I should, as if anyone around here cares."

"They care. They're in a bit of shock. It's not every week we have a young girl die, much less to have one murdered. And in that fashion."

"It's like there's some kind of bad seed in the community, the suspicion. Everyone's looking at each other and fighting more than usual, except maybe that Mrs. Easton."

Giff looked up from stirring his Sanka. Cory was looking at him with knowing, hooded eyes.

"You think I've got a little something going on the side?"

"You'd only be human if you did, it seems."

"Oh, come on, Cory. The world's not as corrupt as all that. You turned over a rock, and you're just seeing what you'd expect to see on the other side." He couldn't very well tell her that he had given up sex and drinking on the day Cory moved in. It would be too much for her. At the time, he had figured that if pregnant women can give up both, so could he for a while. He hadn't known then that the while would last at least eight years.

When Cory didn't respond, he said, "At least you haven't seen or heard anything new and earth shattering about the fellows who hang around the store."

"Uncle Giff," she hesitated, "a lot of folks kind of think of them as a collection of losers."

"What do you mean?"

"I . . . well, they don't really do much but sit around and talk a lot, when they're not off at their day jobs. Do they?"

"That's all I do too."

"I didn't mean . . ."

Giff took a deep breath, looked away. When he looked back at Cory, he said, "Just because someone hasn't achieved a lot in the conventional sense, in those things that other people value, doesn't mean he's a loser. It might be he's picked the right path. Think back to when men were hunter-gatherers. They spent a lot of time doing what we would call loafing, enjoying what there was to their lives. Maybe they didn't have television, but they watched birds fly, rivers flow . . ."

"Grass grow." Cory's face could barely hide a suppressed giggle.

"You know where I was headed with that." Giff smiled. "One trick of life is to align yourself with those who accept you as you are and think you're a winner. That's what these guys are to me."

"I didn't mean to insult you or your friends."

"I know you didn't. You're harder on yourself than I am on you. You want to rise above what you consider mediocrity, keep stopping and reappraising yourself like you're doing. That may be enough in itself."

"You mind telling me something?"

"Anything you want."

"Is there anything between you and Mrs. Easton?"

Giff tossed his head back laughing. When he slowed, he grinned at Cory. "She wishes there was. But, no. There isn't. I don't know what there is about me, but she seems to feel some magnetic attraction to me."

"I understand how that can work," Cory said. Giff had to imagine she meant her feelings about TyTy.

They were silent a moment before she spoke again.

"What do you think I should do about TyTy? Should I ever be around him again after the way he went behind my back and was seeing Vickee?"

Giff looked into Cory's face, the round expectant face beneath the soft tousled, short blond hair. She seemed as innocent as the day she had arrived. But he knew a lot was going on in that tiny head. "I thought I heard you say to his face that you were only friends."

"We are. But I . . . I always thought . . ."

"When I was not too far from TyTy's age," Giff said, "it would have embarrassed a girl with your high moral stamp to know me."

"Oh, do tell me a bedtime story," she giggled. "It's been a long while."

"When I was TyTy's age," he repeated, "I was going through that jerk phase that I sincerely believe most young men go through. I wasn't aware at the time of what a jerk I was being—just thought of myself as opportunistic and the young ladies as there for the picking. Testosterone was surging through me like adrenaline, and I went through those young ladies like a sickle through wheat."

He held up the flat of his hand to keep Cory from interrupting. She didn't seem to know whether to laugh or not. But at least this was no story about bread being a nickel a loaf.

"I don't say that to be proud. I'm embarrassed by it. It's funny now, but it wasn't then. I was out to cut notches on the bedpost until there was no post."

Cory covered her mouth with her hand, wrestling to hold back a giggle.

"It was an obsession. I don't mean to glamorize it, or make it silly enough to discount."

"Some of that drive is biology, Uncle Giff."

"But during all that time I never once thought about procreation, about nesting down some day, though I know some of the women did, and I played on that."

"It doesn't sound like you liked yourself much in those days."

"Well, those days've had their payback."

"But you're anything but that now," Cory said, once she had gotten over his use of so many clichés, something he usually avoided. This was all better than she had expected.

"It took me a while to learn it," Giff said, "but I found that I can abstain better than I can moderate. That's not to let me off the hook for the way I was."

"You've sure changed since then."

Giff nodded. "I think if I'd have been a girl back then, I'd be the kind you call a slut. Easy, and in it for my own pleasure."

"Like Vickee."

"Exactly, except for the tying up part. That's her own twist. But as far as the type goes, I was as bad or worse."

"Why are you telling me this?" Cory tilted her head at him. "You never confessed this kind of stuff before."

"I didn't want to send you the wrong signals before. I don't want to now. What I'm trying to do, since I think you're old enough and in the only way I know how, is to let you know I'm human—which I always mean as capable of error."

"Am I an error in your life?" Her voice was almost a whisper.

"If you mean having you move out here, no. Not at all." He rubbed his forehead, looked away, and then turned back to her. "There are always at least a couple of ways you can go about anything. For instance, you can confront it or run from it. For a long time after I came out here, I thought I'd picked the savvy path. That other people, like my brother, your father, were beating themselves up with false hopes and dream ambitions. Trying to get rich or to keep up with the Joneses. But, about the time you came out here I was beginning to wonder if I wasn't just frittering my whole life away."

"Was I just something you couldn't escape from?"

"As soon as I first saw you, and you were a pitiful little specimen in those early days, I knew that every decision I'd made that way wasn't necessarily right. I was kind of glad for another chance. But I had a couple of directions I could take about raising you, and I wasn't sure which was right. You'd lost or misplaced the instruction manual that was probably meant to come with you . . ."

Cory giggled, couldn't help herself.

". . . but I muddled through as best I could. I didn't want to raise you whipping post strict, the way I was brought up, and the way I suspect is more than a bit of Vickee's short past. So I played a pretty slack hand with you, thought I was doing you a favor letting you grow up on your own. Since you've lived here, I've spent a lot of time with books or with minding the store, but I wasn't meaning to ignore you. I wanted to give you the kind of space I wished for when I was a kid. Maybe I could have seemed to pay more attention to you, but I was encouraging you to be an independent thinker, not dependent on me for everything."

"Well, that part kinda worked."

"Maybe better than I expected. There are some things a person can only learn by experience, things that don't seem obvious at first, or what seems obvious is wrong. Let me give you three quick examples. If you ever happen to be climbing a mountain, don't hug the rock, but push yourself at arm's length from it. You'll have better balance and control. If someone's taking a punch at you, and the fist is headed for your face, move toward the blow, not from it. By shortening the distance you take a lot of the force out of the blow. And, if you're driving at night and a deer runs out in front of you and you can't possibly miss it, accelerate into it. Don't brake. If you brake, the nose of your car will tilt down and the plane of your front windshield will be vertical, and the snap of stopping will likely send the deer through the windshield directly at you, and you can get hurt. If you accelerate, there's a better chance the deer will be tossed away from you, and if it does hit the windshield, it'll be at an angle and the pitched glass will have a better chance of deflecting the deer."

"Well, thanks for all that. I can hardly wait to use it. But what's it have to do with Vickee? What should I do there?"

"That's one of those decisions you're old enough to make on your own. Let your heart be your guide. What's it say?"

"We weren't close at school. Kids a couple or three grades apart hardly ever are. But we did go to the same place, and I felt something awful about her death, especially the way she died. No matter what she was, Vickee was a human too, and one I knew. No one seems to be doing very much about her murder."

"People are doing something. Don't discount the sheriff and his staff because of your experience with him."

"You never said."

"Said what?"

"About TyTy. What should I do there?"

"I thought that's what I was illustrating in a way that showed instead of told, that way you get to make up your own mind. The Reader's Digest version is that he's a far better fellow than I was at that age. You'll have to allow him an awkward moment or two, especially until you two are more than just friends, though don't take that to mean I'm shoving you toward anything."

She tilted her head in thought. "I'll see how he does helping

East-odd BMS

Sarah S
Beth B

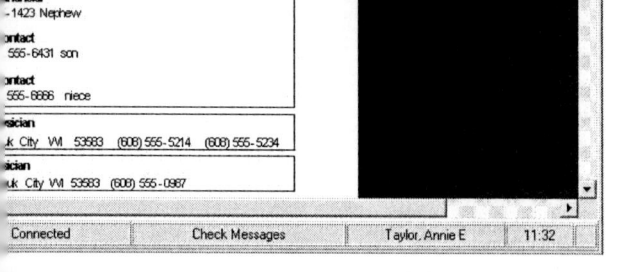

navigate to the Report Maker (**File > Setup >**
he report you are previewing.
nd click **Run**. The report is updated with the

me ask a few questions."

Giff looked at her. She might seem a young girl, but she was pretty grown up inside.

She nodded, her eyes fighting to keep open.

"You think you wore yourself out enough to sleep by now?"

"Oh." She jumped up. "I've got to check on Miss Dumpsie."

Giff was in his room and had his shirt half off when he heard Cory scream.

He tugged the shirt back on and ran out through the house and back into the barn.

Cory stood staring, her hands down at her sides clenched into small fists.

Across one of the wide wooden slats of Miss Dumpsie's stall someone had spray-painted a message in red letters that dripped like blood: "Lay off!"

CHAPTER THIRTEEN

"Cory, I've got to go check in at work, explain why I was in jail, and see if I still have a job. Okay? Do you understand?"

Cory looked up at TyTy. She stood huddled behind the counter, in Giff's usual spot. She felt scared, threatened, and small. Someone had invaded their house and had gotten near enough to Miss Dumpsie to do her harm. What had Cory done to rouse that kind of anger, whatever it took for someone to do . . . oh, sure, it was probably the person who had murdered Vickee. He. Cory could only see it as a he at this point. He had to be scared of getting caught and had to be more than a little panicked himself. TyTy was still looking down at her.

"Yeah, sure. I understand." Even her own voice sounded small, made tiny and scared.

The bruises were nearly faded into the tanned look of TyTy's face. He was one good-looking young man, and the concern for her was more obvious than it had ever been. Uncle Giff was always saying that no matter what bad thing happened, something good always came of it. Maybe there would be something from all this, but she felt too beaten to savor anything at the moment.

TyTy started to extend a hand.

"Better get going," Cory said.

TyTy spun and walked through the store, his back stiff and upright. When the screen closed behind him, Cory sighed to herself.

Sheriff Sparrow sat over by the stove in the chair Zoe usually occupied. Cory didn't know what fascination there was to sitting around a stove that wasn't even on and going, but men, the sheriff included, sure seemed to lap it up.

"You look pleased," Cory said.

Sheriff Sparrow looked up from his chair as if it was all he could do to keep from tilting back and looking smug. He said, "This is the first solid break I've had. Of course I'm pleased."

Giff was over at the coffee pot refilling their cups. The tall deputy with the strange eyes, Winslow, stood by Giff, putting extra cream and sugar in his cup. Giff looked stiff and upright compared to Sparrow's sprawl.

"Where're Zoe and Shimmy?" Sparrow called out.

"At work," Giff said without looking up from the cup he was filling. "They do have jobs. Zoe at the feed store, and Shim with that oil rig supply place. Why?"

"Oh, I don't know. I thought they were just loafers."

"This writing gives you a handwriting sample, and what else?" Giff said across the room.

"From what you've said before, you know police procedure about as well as the average lay person. We've been focusing on locals. Now we know the circle is tighter. This eliminates a lot of people—those who don't know your Cory was nosing and messing around—and it gives us another starting point. And those who didn't even know Cory had a horse. If Cory stirred up something, then we go back to those she saw."

"The only person I saw was Crystabelle, and she says you've already spoken with her several times," Cory said.

Sparrow ignored her. "And the other good thing is, now that TyTy is out on his own, your little part in this is over."

"What do you mean?" Cory said.

"Tell her, Giff," he said over his shoulder. "Anything more she does at this point is going to put her at greater risk."

145

"You can't just order me around that way. Even Uncle Giff can't."

"I see I may have to take back some of the positive things I said about the way you were raised."

"Tell her, Giff," the sheriff said again.

"You tell him, Uncle Giff." Cory folded her thin arms across her chest.

Giff brought his cup of coffee and walked over to stand in front of Cory. Sparrow looked on with pleased expectation. Giff said, "While I'm gone this morning and you're watching the store, think it over. On the one hand, TyTy is out, and that's what you said motivated you. If your conscience tells you to help in whatever other way you can, you might think about doing it in cooperation with the sheriff. He doesn't want vigilantism, but he shouldn't say no to support. You've heard me often enough say that Pericles said the good citizen doesn't just have a duty to participate in social issues, a person isn't even a citizen if he or she doesn't become involved. The choice is yours. No matter what you decide, just remember that people care about you. That means when you commit to something, you commit others with you."

Sparrow stood up from his chair and stared at Giff. "I've had double-talk gibbered at me from college lectures, pulpits, and political platforms, but I don't think I've ever heard it slip and slide better than that. Did you just tell her to quit messing around, like I asked, or not?"

Giff gave the sheriff an irritated glance. "You don't find it ironic that you're trying to share essentially the same message as we found spray-painted on the horse's stall?" He turned back to Cory, who still looked up at him. "You understood me, didn't you?" he asked her.

She said, "I'll let you know when you get back."

"Just tell her. Don't ask." Sparrow was frowning at Giff.

146

"Sheriff, you're a bright individual. I'd be careful of telling people how to raise kids. Talk like that might get you pigeonholed with the likes of Dewey and Louie."

The sheriff's car was pulling away out front when Giff went back into the store, called over to Cory, "Are you going to be all right handling the store while I'm gone?"

"I'll be fine." Now that Sparrow was gone, some of her former spirit was seeping back into place.

Giff pulled the big olive-drab canvas backpack from under the counter. He had gotten it half packed before Sparrow arrived. He moved about the store, gathering up goods. He put in bottled water and the kind of canned goods Saris usually bought. The radio was playing its scratchy classical music, something from Vivaldi's "The Four Seasons."

"He as much as said I was being some kind of Nosy Parker," Cory said.

"Try to understand his point of view." Giff straightened, closed the top of the pack, and hoisted it onto his shoulders with a grunt. Damned water was heavier than he remembered. "He's been getting a lot of pressure. Murder isn't as common out here as it is in the cities, and especially one with the frills this mess has. Sparrow's been getting nowhere. But now he knows something is stirring, though that means it could also be dangerous for you. He didn't do the best job of expressing it as a concern for your safety, but that's part of it, Cory."

"You're too generous with that man," Cory said. "His interest stops where his own reputation is concerned. That's the way I read him."

Giff admitted to himself that her take was more accurate than the one he had tried to hand her.

"What'd he say to you, when he whispered to you at the door before he left?"

"Just more of the same," Giff said. He looked at her, lean and attentive behind the counter, like some smaller blond version of himself. He felt a short spike of pain low in his chest, did not know what caused it. "He said that this is the defining point in the case. Things should move faster and more dangerously. Anything that happens to you after this point is on my head."

"And what did you think about that?"

"That it's been a while since he got out of Harvard, if he ever went. I wonder if that ring he wore wasn't his father's. He's a manipulative man who likes to be in control however he can get there. That makes him almost as dangerous as our killer."

Giff turned and started toward the front door. Over his shoulder he heard Cory call out, "Are you even sure you know where Saris lives? Is it within a walk of here?"

Without turning his head, he called back, "Well, he makes it in here by foot. If he can, I can. It's out a ways, but I went by the area once when I'd just moved here. I used to get out and around more."

"That's been a long while," Cory said. "You sure you're up to this?"

"We'll soon know," he said. He turned at the door, gave her a short wave and a forced smile. Then he went outside into a day that promised to be a scorcher. He could hear Cory changing the channel on the radio as soon as he was outside. Some rock and roller was belaboring the obvious, "You're gonna miss me when I'm gone."

Giff shifted the bag on his back until something with a sharp corner quit poking him in the shoulder blade. Then he started off toward the trail that led to Saris's place.

The morning air was still cool from the previous evening as he started out. No birds were stirring and the sky stretched in pale cloudless blue over him. He always wore running shoes in the store, so his feet gave him no trouble, though he felt his leg muscles resisting the early going, along with his back beneath the bag that was heavier than he should have packed.

But the hike felt good, like a pilgrimage or quest. It had been too long since he took any time off from the store to get outside. He felt himself warming against the cooler morning air as he walked. Behind the row of low buildings across the street he found the beginning of a path. It was not very worn; Saris was the only one who used it. The trail led off through low stands of mesquite trees, sage, prickly pear plants in sprawling small masses, sumac, yucca plants with towering spears of white blooming clusters, agarita, javelina bushes, and past other plants Giff could not name—almost every one with some kind of sticker, thorn, or poison berry. The fruits on the prickly pear cacti were red to purple, ready for eating. Each was about three times the size of a jumbo olive. Zoe had shown him how to hold the fruit in the palm of a hand, cut around it longways and pull off the skin. Inside was a pale oval of moist pulp that had seemed to have little taste to Giff. He'd heard that folks picked the young cactus leaves and cooked them up just like green beans, but it was too late in the year for that. He imagined that Saris had eaten his share of both.

The recent rain had washed away some of the dust, leaving the plants in their darkish flat green of late summer. The morning cool would keep any rattlesnakes and scorpions tucked back in their rocky nooks. High above him a bird of prey let out a shriek—looked like an eagle. The wingspread was wide and the wings formed a flat line across the top, not a "V" like buzzard. It was just as well. He could do without buzzards circling just now.

Cory looked up from the small file case she had open on the

counter when she heard the screen door slam. It was TyTy coming in.

"That was a short work day."

"They have enough hands on the job for the day. I caught some hard words from Fergus but suppose I still have a job. Anyway, I'm to show up tomorrow at a decent hour, so he said. They've been goin' at it since six out there." He stopped short of the counter by a few steps, hung back, and appeared to look at a display of blue and red handkerchiefs.

"You go to some college, and you won't be doing construction work that way."

"Oh, I don't mind. I kind of like the work, and when I'm done for the day I don't have to rush off and work out at a gym or nothin'."

"Let's see how you sing that tune when you're coming into your forties and don't know which to grab at first, your hernia or your bad back."

"I'm not smart like you, Cory, nor your uncle."

"Uncle Giff says that back before he used to jog he told someone he didn't because he didn't have a jogger's build. That person said, 'Jogging's how you get a jogger's build, Giff.' "

"See. You tell stories to make a point, just like he does."

Cory tried to imagine if she didn't know TyTy what her impression of him might be right now. He was a little uncertain, upset about missing work and trying hard not to show it, a little off-balance in general. She would try to take it easy on him until he got some of his old self back.

"What are you doing?" he asked. He saw the spread of file cards she had taken from the box and spread across the counter.

"Trying to think like a sheriff," she said. "I know a little about opportunity, motive, and all that. But he talks about that paint like it was the very first clue."

"It was, wasn't it?"

"Think, TyTy. What about the rope that was used? It looked fairly new to me."

"You can buy rope anywhere."

"Describe what you saw about this rope, TyTy."

"It was just like any rope you'd buy in a store."

"No, it wasn't. I know neither of us looked at it close when Vickee was tied the way she was. But I saw it closer at the sheriff's office. It was a nylon rope with little green threads woven into it."

"But what about it?"

"Nothing, if the sheriff thinks like you that it's rope that can be bought anywhere."

"But isn't rope pretty much rope?"

"Do ships use the same rope as mountain climbers?"

"No. I'm pretty sure not."

"Of course not. So, what do people do a lot around here?"

TyTy's forehead wrinkled. He frowned at her.

Cory caught herself making an exasperated little snort. It was harder to steer people than she thought. She began to appreciate for the first time the gentle nudges in conversation that her Uncle Giff used.

She said, "They ranch, TyTy, and they compete in rodeos, ride horses."

"Oh."

"You do know that there are different ropes for different jobs, don't you? It's why there are tack shops for horse owners."

"You'd know more about that than me. I haven't ridden in a long while."

Cory started to say something, but clamped her mouth closed. TyTy's dad had run off on them when TyTy was only eleven. He lived with his mom, the one with the Indian blood. TyTy was supporting them both now. They wouldn't have the money to own a horse anymore, though she knew TyTy had one

151

when he was a young boy, but they'd had to sell it.

"Look, I don't mean to be giving you a hard time. You really don't know the difference between a head rope and a heel rope, do you?"

"I'm gonna bet I'm not entirely alone there."

"Well, without getting too technical . . ."

"Thanks for that."

". . . they both come in several grades specific to what you use them for. A stiff head rope would be used by an experienced header; it can be swung harder and thrown harder without the loop closing. An expert'll want stiffness without the rope being wiry or bouncy. But it's got to be stiff enough to wave off the horns if the right loop doesn't land just so. Some like a head rope with more tip weight, which makes it easier to swing. A heel rope ranges from a stiff rope that'll stay open and catch to one you might use to force a throw in a tight situation, all the way to a soft or even a medium-soft one used by ropers who don't use a lot of power in their delivery. Novices most often go with the softer heel rope for their first rope."

"Cory," TyTy said. "Cory Lee."

"What?"

"You went way past what I can absorb or care about quite a while back. Isn't there a short version?"

"Okay," she said, "for you Reader's Digest subscribers. One company that makes these kind of ropes is Cactus Ropes. They put a small color of thread in to color code the stiffness and types. The reason I know about it's because I had Uncle Giff order me some to use with Miss Dumpsie when I was practicing lassoing barrels. I . . . I never told anyone, but I got the softer rope, 'cause I was really just getting going. I didn't want anyone to know because . . . well, you know how that is?"

"No. But I don't want to go there. Why does that have you looking through your uncle's sales records?"

"Uncle Giff had to order a half-dozen of the thirty-foot lengths to keep the shipping charges down on the one I wanted. See, over there in the hardware section, we still have four of 'em in stock. I thought if someone charged it, Uncle Giff might've written it down, and I'd have a lead."

"That you could pass on to the sheriff?"

"I'd have a lead." She looked back down at the cards to hide the small frown she felt form on her face.

"Cory. I hope you aren't going to do something really stupid."

She looked up at him. "Like go into a house I might think is haunted and find a body of a schoolmate? Like date one girl and squeeze another one on the side out of respect for the first one?"

TyTy reeled back a step. A whole range of emotions flickered for only a second across his face. Then it went back to the stony look that only he, with his Indian heritage, could achieve. He turned on a heel and started to walk toward the door.

"TyTy."

He didn't stop.

"TyTy. Come on. I didn't mean . . ."

He was halfway to the door. She pushed herself upright from the counter and raced around the end and ran the length of the store until she was ahead of him. She spun around and faced him.

He looked down at her but didn't smile. He put both hands on her shoulders to move her to the side. She reached up, grabbed both sides of his face and pulled it down to her until she could rise up on tiptoes and press her lips against his.

He pulled back, started to step aside again and say something at the same time. But he stopped and lowered his head again. They stayed that way for one long kiss, then pushed apart, only to lean together again for several small butterfly kisses before pushing apart again.

His dark eyes were all the way wide open, but there was a softness to the look he gave her. He walked sideways, leaned an arm against a counter, nearly missed it with his elbow and sort of fell, but righted himself.

Cory stood in the same place. Her head was filled with a rush of thoughts. The first kiss had been like it was electric. It may not have been the best one ever, but it was her first. After the rest, she felt giddy, so lightheaded she wanted to babble, say a hundred things. She forced herself to keep her mouth pressed shut to say nothing.

"Well," TyTy said. "Well, well, well, well, well." A light sweat had formed on his tanned forehead. He reached up to sweep a hand across it.

"So?" she said when she finally thought she could keep from sounding like an idiot.

"Is everything all right with us?" he said.

Everything was fine. It was wonderful, she wanted to say. But she said, "Will you help me look through those records?"

They divided the rest of the file cards in the middle of the remaining alphabet of those Cory hadn't gone through.

"What am I looking for?" he asked.

"Uncle Giff made the sale, so it'll be in his printed scribble, almost too tiny to read. It'll either say Cactus, or just rope. Let your eye track it that way."

TyTy spread his out across the counter and let his eye run through them that way. Cory started to say something to him, then stopped herself. She went through the cards she held one by one, sneaking a peek at him now and then, watching his forehead wrinkle in concentration as he scanned the cards far faster than she was going through them. Cory smiled to herself and went back to her own cards.

"Hey." TyTy sounded excited. "Could this be it?" He held out a card to her.

She reached for it. Yes, it looked right. Then she looked up at the name on the account. She gave a low whistle. "I think you found it, TyTy." She reached, without thinking, and gave him an excited hug around the shoulders. "But we've still got to check all the other cards to make sure this is it." She looked at him. He beamed at her.

"Cory, you are so smart." He pulled her face to his and kissed her square on the mouth again.

When they pulled apart, she said, "I hope that wasn't just an excuse to steal a kiss." But she didn't really care, didn't care the tiniest bit.

CHAPTER FOURTEEN

Sheriff Sparrow led the way down the hallway until they came to the door marked with its makeshift star. The sheriff's hand went up to rap on the door, then he paused and leaned closer. Winslow stepped closer too, until he could hear the scrambling around inside, the muttering. It sounded a lot like someone packing in a hurry or searching for something.

Sparrow looked up at him and gave a nod back toward the side door of GALS through which they'd entered.

Winslow slipped back out the door into the sun. He followed the faded chipped paint on the side of the warehouse-like building and then on around to the extension that had been added on for dressing rooms and storage. He was still being very quiet as he eased along the outside of the building, though he had to wade through a clump of beggar's tick plants that quickly covered his uniform pants with the little gray burrs that gave the plant its name.

He heard the sudden banging on the door and could make out the muffled shout of Sparrow's voice from inside. Then he heard the sound of the window he was nearing being unlatched. It slid slowly open. The glass had been painted black, no doubt to keep peepers willing to brave the thick weeds behind the honky-tonk from having a look into the dressing room.

There was a rustling thump as a small handbag fell down into the weeds, and that was followed by a bigger thump of a mid-sized pale blue suitcase landing on the weeds and smashing a small square of them flat. A leg came out the window, feeling around for something to step onto. It was a nice leg, with a small woman's sneaker on one end, and bare up to the shorts.

Winslow stepped closer and spoke softly into the open window. "You want me to hold my hands together so you can step into them and down?"

"Well, shit." The leg pulled back inside and Crystabelle's lightly made up face replaced it at the window. She stared at Winslow.

"Maybe you'd better go open the door and let the sheriff in," he said.

She let out her breath, and with the disgusted expression still on her face pulled back into the room. Winslow waited until he heard her unlock the door, and Sparrow's voice talking to her in an exaggerated conversational tone inside the room before he turned and waded back through the path he'd made through the weeds. At the side door, he paused, took out a pocket knife and used it to scrape the clumps of gray beggar's tick burrs off his pants. When he'd gotten all of them off that he could, he went back inside the cooler building.

The door to the dressing room was still open, and Crystabelle sat in a chair with her back to the sheriff. She was staring at herself in the mirror while Sparrow sat in a chair against the wall.

"Planning to take a little skip on us, were you?"

"I was just . . . oh, hell, you wouldn't understand."

"You're the one who doesn't understand. We're running a murder investigation here, and anyone who does something skittish is going to catch our eye. Why were you thinking of cutting out right now? That doesn't look good, does it, Winslow?"

"Oh, great. I'm the one who gets scared, and now I'm a suspect." There was a quiver in the singer's voice. Around her the room looked tossed, as if she'd been packing as fast as she could before being interrupted by the lawmen. She hadn't taken any of the gowns that hung on the rack made out of metal pipes that stood along one wall. But there was a gap where clothes had been removed, and empty hangers in litter on the floor. Several of the drawers on a small dresser were also open and partially emptied.

"Why were you scared?" The sheriff's head snapped to Winslow as soon as the deputy spoke and gave him an irritated frown. But Winslow's eyes stayed fixed on the girl in the mirror and watched her eyes swing toward him.

She kept her back to them both and fiddled with the brushes, combs, and makeup scattered in front of the mirror. "This is a tiny little place, and I live closer to Bent Bell than to Carnicius. Everyone's heard about someone threatening that little Purvis brat."

"How's that affect you?" Winslow asked. The sheriff's expression didn't look any more cheerful, but he let the deputy ask his questions.

"Look, everyone knows that cops out here in the sticks are fine for setting up a speed trap or intimidating drunks or little old ladies, maybe even breaking up a bar fight or a domestic quarrel. But when it comes to catching a murderer . . . Well, I was just gonna take my chances someplace else."

"That's a nice little vote of confidence," Sparrow said. His eyes had narrowed. "But if everyone opened up a bit on one or two things, it might be a safer place to live. You haven't been any real cornucopia of information yourself, you know, and there are one or two things you know and are just dying to share with is, aren't there?"

Her eyes were locked in the mirror with Winslow's. Her mouth opened, but the lower lip quivered too much to speak. Her eyes welled, and in one second she'd changed from the over-sophisticated performer to the twenty-year-old country girl she really was. She snatched angrily at a tissue out of a box and rubbed hard at the moist dark lines starting down from her mascara.

"I'm scared." It was a little girl's voice. "Just scared. Can you understand that?"

Sparrow rose and nodded to Winslow. "That's why we're going to take you in and ask a few questions."

She lowered the stained tissue and turned in the chair to glare directly at the sheriff. "Is that your plan? Lock everyone up until no one's left loose at all in the county?"

"Come on," Winslow said. "You'll be safer where we're taking you. We'll get your things too."

She sighed, stood up on legs that had a touch of wobble now, and reached for the tissue box, tucking it under her arm. "Let's go then."

Giff came around a thick stand of cactus and could see the green trailer sitting at a tilt up ahead. He tried to imagine living in there, with everything running off in the direction of the tilt. But then, Saris didn't have that much in the way of possessions anyway.

The day was heating up. That's what Giff really couldn't figure. A little trailer like that, with no electricity even for a fan, had to get like an oven every day out here. How did Saris stand it?

"Yo, Saris," he called out as he got closer. "It's me, Giff Purvis. You around?"

It was still out there in the middle of nowhere. The surrounding vegetation here was a pale brown and dusty green this late in the year. A light breeze swept through the opening, barely enough to rustle the leaves. Giff took another step, heard a rattle, and he froze where he stood.

His eyes swept the low cover near him, looking for a rocky

shelf or other place a rattlesnake could hide. He saw nothing. Then something brown shot out of the base of a clump of brown-eyed susans. Giff stumbled a step back before he saw it was a huge grasshopper flapping its wings in what sounded like a snake's rattle.

"Didn't know you come all the way out here to dance." The voice came from behind Giff. He turned, saw Saris's head poking out around the trunk of a mesquite tree.

"There you are," Giff said, then felt foolish for belaboring the obvious. "I'm alone," he added.

"I know. I back-tracked your trail."

Giff swung the heavy pack of his back and lowered it to the ground, felt the light breeze on the damp back of his shirt. He felt a sharp stab of pain in his lower back as he straightened.

"You crawl around diggin' under the trunks of trees or bent over a sifter going through creek bed rocks all day and you'll feel worse than that," Saris said. He stepped through a gap in the green and came out into the clearing to stand beside Giff. Sweat had poured through his safari shirt in several spots, and a white rime of crusty salt had formed at the edges of the damp spots.

"I brought you some stuff," Giff said. He tapped the bag with the toe of his sneaker.

"Can't pay for it just yet, like I said." Saris's face showed even more wrinkles past the whiskers out in the bright sunlight. His squinty eyes swept from Giff to the trail he had come along.

"Don't worry about that. I just don't want to carry it back."

"You come all the way out here to be some kinda Welcome Wagon? I don't know about that," Saris said.

"Sheriff told me he was out this way. I was afraid he'd given you a shock."

"Thought you'd changed your mind about that stuff you let me take and had sent the law after me."

"I wouldn't do that, Saris. My word is good."

"I guess I know that. But havin' the sheriff pop outta the woods and come at me took a year off my life. All I could think about was that gun on his hip, that I was gonna get shot to death over a few cans of beans."

"You should know you can trust me," Giff said.

"Oh, I do. I'm sorry to be so tetchy. It's just . . . well, you live out here too long like I have and you hear things, voices in the night, all manner of stuff. You start imaginin' all sorts of plots against you. You know how that is?"

"Not really. But I understand." He paused. "There was a girl killed, Saris, over at the Whalen place. It's a farmhouse about a four-mile hike from here."

"I know the one you're talkin' 'bout. But I never been inside. Never. A young girl?" His eyes snapped open wide. He tilted his head to peer up from under the shadow of his cap at Giff. "He don't think I had nothin' to do with it, does he?"

"The sheriff's asking everyone questions, anyone who might have seen anything. That's all. It's routine when there's been a murder."

"Well, I don't know nothin'."

"And that's what I'll tell him. That should save you a visit."

Saris's eyes went rheumy damp again. He said, "I try hard never to be a bother to no one. You know that."

Giff nodded. He remembered his own dream once of being alone.

"Fact is, you're just about the only person I do trust or have any truck with."

Giff nodded. The intense eyes were fixed on him, measuring him.

"I been wantin' to ask if you could do a favor my way."

"Sure," Giff said, a little too quickly. He should have asked what kind of favor.

"Wait here." Saris turned and clumped off.

Giff opened the pack, took out one of the bottles of water, and drank. Then he squatted down in the clearing and waited. It was almost ten minutes before Saris appeared again, shaking bits of dirt off a leather sack half the size of a basketball.

"What d'you have there? Your poke?" Giff struggled back upright.

Saris had narrowed one eye at him. "Yeah, how'd you know?"

"I was kidding. I didn't know people had pokes anymore."

Saris relaxed a bit. He brushed at the bag a couple more times, then held it abruptly toward Giff with both extended arms.

"What?"

"I'd like you to hang onto this for me."

"I told you before. When you've made money, pay me off then. I can stand the wait."

"It's not that. There's no banks out here, especially for this kind of thing. I just want you to hold it for me."

Giff took the bag. It was heavier than he expected, and his arms dropped down a few inches with it before he applied more muscle.

"What's in here?"

"Topaz," Saris said.

"The whole bag full?"

"Don't make no sense to keep nothin' else. Sure enough that's all that's in there. I said I trust you."

"You don't need to . . ." Giff stopped because Saris had frozen and was looking up over Giff's shoulder, a look of horror spreading across his dirty and tired face. He wheeled and ran.

Giff spun, saw Farley coming through the gap that marked the end of the trail. He was in street clothes but held his revolver pointed straight up in his right hand.

"Hey," Giff yelled, waving for Farley to go back. He turned

and saw McFeeney zip out of sight into the thick of the prickly brush.

Farley broke into a run. He ran across the clearing and tried to go around Giff and chase after Saris. Giff reached out and grabbed at him. Farley spun and lowered the gun until it pointed at Giff's stomach.

"What're you doing?" Giff said.

"Sheriff's tryin' to talk with that fella and couldn't get him. I'm gonna get him for Sparrow." His pig-like eyes were squeezed into a glare.

"Are you really as dense as all that?"

"Don't you talk like that to me! I'm doin' a job here."

"Everyone knows you were suspended. What're you trying to pull here? You think if you somehow drag in McFeeney that Sparrow's going to be pleased enough to put you back on the force? If you do, you're thicker than any of us even thought." Giff stared at the gun Farley held in an unshaking hand. The knuckles on three of the fingers were split open and covered in scab.

"Get . . . out . . . of . . . the . . . way." Farley pushed at Giff with one hand and tried to run past him.

Giff dove and tackled Farley at the knees. They crashed to the hard soil and rolled in a knot of flailing arms and wrapping legs. They stopped with Giff's back pressed against a cactus. But he had bigger worries. He could see that Farley was trying to twist the gun around to point it at Giff. The barrel was within a foot of Giff's head when Giff grabbed Farley's pistol hand with both his hands and twisted. Farley screamed and let go of the gun, but he used the moment to shift on top of Giff. For a grown man with rawhide lean strength, Giff had his hands full hanging onto Farley to keep him from getting up to run after Saris. Farley fought with the hysterical strength of a madman. Giff saw one of Farley's arms reach for a flat rock. He tried to block the arm, but the rock came through and clipped him along the side of his head. His vision faded, went to black.

When Giff's eyes opened, Farley was gone. The cool breeze was slapping at his face. Far away he heard the shriek of the bird of prey again. He rolled slowly away from the cactus, each point pulling away from his shirt with a small ripping pop. He reached up and felt a crust of dried blood along the side of his forehead. He thought of Saris and forced himself slowly upright. There was a dull throb along the side of his head, but it was no worse than hangovers he'd had back in the days when he drank.

He staggered over to the backpack that still sat where he'd dropped it. The leather sack Saris had given him was beside it. He took out the water bottle he'd opened earlier and drank all of it. The clearing was still, and he could see neither Farley nor Saris. When his head was as clear as he figured it would get, he crossed the clearing and started up the trail where he had last seen Saris.

Briars plucked at his clothes. This was a less used trail. It wandered through tighter and tighter squeezes of thick vegetation until it abruptly closed. A rocky cliff stood along one side, dense brush closed off the rest of the trail. There was no place for Giff to go. He looked around, could not see where either of the other two men could have gone or where they were now.

He trudged back to the clearing and looked all through the trailer. There was no sign that Saris had been in it for days. It was oven hot inside and had a dry dusty smell mixed in with the odor of an old man who didn't bathe regularly. But the insides had been dry-baked clean of the intensity of any smells. It didn't seem like Saris had cooked, eaten, or even slept in the trailer.

He must have been cowering out in the brush since the sheriff's first visit. Now Giff didn't know what to think. Either Farley had found him and dragged him in to talk to the sheriff, or Saris had hid even better and Farley had slipped away while Giff was unconscious. He had seen no sign of a struggle. That encouraged him that at least Saris had eluded Farley. In either case, Giff would have to go back to the store first. He didn't relish the idea of the long hike back.

Giff left the dim shadows of the trailer's inside and stepped out into the sun. It slammed into him. He felt himself take a sideways step without meaning to. He lifted a hand to his head. There was a slow pounding just back of his forehead, and his eyes were having trouble fixing on objects. He was no doctor but figured concussion. He could only hope it was a minor one.

He made it over to the pack and plopped down beside it. He squatted there, his head in his hands. He may have passed out again for a few moments. A voice seemed to be coming at him as if down a long tunnel. He blinked opened his eyes. He heard his name, lifted his head, and forced his eyes open. There was Cory coming into the clearing on the back of Miss Dumpsie. "Uncle Giff," she called out to him. "Are you okay?"

He nodded slowly, went to stand and tottered. He lowered himself back to the ground.

"Ohmigod." Cory jumped off the horse's back and came running to him, wrapped her arms around him. "Your head's all bloody. What happened?"

"Farley. Hit me with a rock." He looked up into her face, which was pressed almost up against his. *So this is what it takes to get a hug these days,* he thought. "Who's watching the store?"

"TyTy."

"Good," he said. "I'll probably need his help tracking Saris. If he's out here hiding after getting a scare from Farley, he might well die of exposure."

"Uncle Giff, what about yourself? Shouldn't we . . ."

"Let's get back to the store. I need to call the sheriff," he said. "That okay with you?"

She turned and whistled through her teeth. Miss Dumpsie whinnied and clopped over closer to them.

Giff looked up at the paint horse. "What is it, Dumpsie? What're you trying to tell us? Is Timmy in the well? Should we get help?"

"Uncle Giff!"

"Oh, I'm okay. I was just kidding. It's an old Lassie gag."

"Well, don't kid. I thought you'd gone spacey on me for a second. You know I didn't grow up with a TV in the house."

She helped him stand upright. When he tottered, he put a hand on her shoulder. In the other hand he held Saris's poke. "We'll leave the pack here with the supplies, in case Saris comes back. But I don't think he will for a while, if I know him."

It took a couple of tries to get him onto the horse, with Miss Dumpsie dancing a few steps sideways and Cory talking low to the horse. When he was upright and settled behind the saddle, Cory hopped up lightly into place. "Here, give me that." She tied Saris's bag onto the saddle horn with a leather thong. "Now hang on."

Giff put his hands on Cory's bony hips and they were off, bouncing and swaying to Miss Dumpsie's careful pace up the narrow trail.

Giff was muttering low, "Back in the saddle again. I'm . . ."

"Uncle Giff."

"What? It's an old Gene Autry song."

"Please don't do stuff like that. You've got me worried half sick about you. Start acting all light-headed like that, and I'll be thinking you're gonna die on me."

They went a few more feet before he spoke again.

"I'm just glad you care," he said.

CHAPTER FIFTEEN

They came in sight of town. Miss Dumpsie picked up her pace from the careful one she had used through the briars. The slightly more brisk gait rolled Giff from side to side. He could see the low line of buildings that looked a dull and dusty brown, weathered, and a bit out of kilter and perspective, like a bad oil painting.

Cory turned her head a quarter-turn back and said, "How would you mark a sales record on one of your file cards if Wesley bought something on his dad's credit sheet?"

"I'd put a W.H. beside the items. Why?"

"Just wondered." She was looking straight ahead again.

"You were going through the credit charges?"

"You carry a lot of people around here, Uncle Giff. And most of them don't hurry to pay you back. Why are you so nice to some people who aren't nice to you? We should send out some dun notices."

"We make enough profit to just get by," he said. "Some people have it hard. They don't need me riding them too when times are rough."

Cory just shook her head.

She tied up at the porch and helped Giff down from the horse. When they banged through the screen door, TyTy came rushing over to them.

"What happened?" He managed to sound excited without looking it.

Giff noticed that TyTy checked to see that Cory was not hurt too.

"I need to use the phone," Giff said.

"Not till we bathe that wound." Cory's voice was firm. "I'm going to call a doctor."

Giff wove through the store to the phone, managing to bump into two counters on the way. Everything seemed to be in slow motion and hazy. He glanced back at Cory and TyTy, saw them looking at him in an odd way.

He had to reach for the phone twice, and when he got it and opened the phone book he found his vision was so blurred he couldn't read the numbers.

"Cory, could you help me dial the sheriff? Please."

She came over and looked up the number and got it dialed for him. Her face was a wet sheen. In a choked voice, she said, "After this, the doctor. Okay?"

He nodded.

When he had Sparrow on the line, Giff said, "Did Farley bring in Saris McFeeney to your office?"

"Now why would he do that?"

"I don't know. Maybe he got the impression he'd be off the hook with you if he did."

"He didn't get that from me. Why are you asking?"

"Because Farley just tried to bring in Saris at gunpoint. He clipped me along the head with a rock in the process."

"Saris?"

"No. Farley got me with the rock when I tried to stop him. And, by the way, his knuckles were banged up before he started on me."

"So are Wesley's," Cory called across the room.

"Did you get that?" Giff said.

It was quiet on the other end of the line. Then Sparrow said, "I'll be right out there."

"It'd help if you stayed away from Saris's place. He's scared to death of your department right now. He's taken to the hills and I've got to go back out there and try to find him before he hurts himself from exposure."

"And I suppose you think this is somehow my fault."

"I don't give cow flop about fault," Giff said. "I'm worried about a man's life here."

He slammed the phone onto its hook.

"Mr. Purvis?"

Giff turned slowly. He saw TyTy standing there making a weaving motion from side to side. "I need your help tracking Saris, TyTy. Is that okay with you?"

"Sure. But can Cory call now? She's upset and wants to call a doctor."

"What's the matter with her?" Giff pushed away from the wall too quickly and took a spin that headed him for a counter. He fell against it, braced himself with his forearms, waited on the room to hold still before he tried again.

"It's not her." TyTy's voice was right beside him. Giff realized TyTy had a supporting arm around him and was helping hold him upright. "It's you."

Giff felt them both leading him across the store to sit him in one of the chairs beside the stove. He sat and leaned back in the chair the way he'd seen Zoe do so many times. The chair's back thumped against the wall and caught. He leaned there, let the side of his face rest against the cool wall. *It's not bad over here,* he thought. *No wonder the guys like to sit here so much.* Across the room Cory was speaking into the phone in a hushed and concerned tone.

The front screen banged. Giff's head swung slowly that way. It was Dewey and Lou.

"Good," Giff said. "You've come to help."

"Why, Giff Purvis, I might know I'd find you sittin' and lollin' while Rome is churnin'." Lou came closer until her face was at the same level and two inches from his. She peered into Giff's face. Usually her head came to the middle of his chest. Being face to face with her was no bargain. Up close he could see she was dressed in some kind of dark muu-muu, the way they used to say when someone's clothes fit them as loose as a saddle on a sow's back. She said, "You don't look so hot. We just come to tell you 'bout Cory runnin' loose half over the county. Do you hear what . . ."

"It's the early bird gets them firm," Giff said. "The stitched mime sounds about fine."

Lou stepped back, her head cocked to one side.

"You dare to mock us," Dewey said. He had crowded close beside Lou.

"Both of you, out," Cory yelled behind them.

They turned to her slowly. She stood with hands clenched, her face red in fury. "Go over to Carnicius and meddle where you buy your goods. Leave him alone. No. I mean it. Go."

They started to argue. TyTy came over and stood beside Cory and gave them his firmest stare. "Can't you see Mr. Purvis is hurt?"

Giff started abruptly, looked for Saris's leather bag. He saw it over on the counter by the register. He said, "Poke. I've got Saris's poke. 'The woman that kissed him, and pinched his poke, was the lady that's known as Lou.' "

"Well, we don't need this," Dewey said.

"You still owe for the last things you ever bought here," Cory said, "and that was three years ago. Come and pay that sometime if you want to do something around here besides hang like a pair of hyenas who bark here and shop in Carnicius."

"Take it easy, Cory," TyTy said.

Dewey and Lou clutched each other and didn't look back as

they left the store.

"Don't touch me," Cory snapped, and as quickly added, "Oh, please do. What made me act like that? I've never been so mean to two old people before."

Giff was aware of being helped out to TyTy's car, Cory locking up as they went out. It was his second ride to Carnicius in a short while. He started to watch the scenery go by, but his eyes closed. When he opened them next he was in a hospital bed, the room white and full of square edges. Cory was slumped over in a chair beside the bed. He watched her for a while and let her sleep. Then he drifted off again himself.

Cory woke. She looked around the room, got her bearings. Her Uncle Giff was asleep. Someone had put the spare blanket over her in the night. From the way his sheets were ruffled, she figured it was her uncle.

She stretched and stood. Then she folded the blanket and put it on the chair. There was a white bandage around his head. He seemed to be sleeping peacefully, and he was already getting breakfast through some tube dripping into his arm.

At first she was not sure what had drawn her out of the room. She was hungry but didn't dare make too big of a fuss. It was probably not visiting hours. She was not sure if she would be shown to the door if some nurse spotted her.

She could hear a couple of the nurses talking up around the corner, loud as if they didn't know people were sleeping all around them. From the distant clattering noise down the hall, along with the smells, Cory sensed that breakfast was being prepared. She slipped quietly up the hallway, peeking into open doorways until finally she saw what she was after. She glanced up and down the hall, then darted through the open door into the room and closed the door a few inches behind her.

Sherm Hargate lay in the bed nearest the door. The sheet was

171

drawn around the other bed in the room. She looked at him. He was sure a contrast to Uncle Giff laying there. Sherm's big paunch pushed the sheets up into a round mound. The bandages around his head did not cover the baldness, nor the expanses of face that had purplish skin. He had taken one sound thumping. But he still looked like some kind of white manatee under the sheets, hardly the lean figure that Giff cut.

One bloodshot eye blinked open. She realized he was looking at her and she started.

"You damn sure ain't the nurse." His voice was scratchy, as if little used.

"No," she admitted. "I'm Giff Purvis's niece, Cory."

"So it's little Cory, is it."

"Mr. Hargate." She nodded.

"Oh, you might as well call me Sherm. Most of the young fillies do. Surprised a thing as young as you'd take a fancy in me and pay a visit."

"Well, I . . ." She felt mad at her own sputtering. He seemed pleased that it had taken so little time to get her flustered. She should have been more surprised at the man's audacity. He lay there all bruised and lumpy, looking like something a truck had left behind, and he shifted right into his sweet-talking. The man was a compulsive Romeo who had problems she might want to know about, but she wasn't sure she wanted to deal with.

"Well, Cory. You got me at a disadvantage, not catchin' me at my best moment and all. But I'm sure it's not my charm brought you here."

"I'm the one who found Vickee. You know, out there at the Whalen place."

"Why's that bring you to my room, though heaven knows I could use visitors?"

Cory had noticed the absence of flowers or a bowl of fruit, anything that would have indicated that Sherm's wife or Crystabelle wanted to demonstrate missing him.

"I wanted to see how you were getting along," she said.

"I've had finer moments," he said. "But I mend well and quickly. I'll be out two-steppin' again quicker'n you can say, 'Gosh, you're gettin' fresh with me, Sherm.' " His eyes narrowed, watching her for a blush. He sure enjoyed rattling her.

But it had not taken Cory long to toughen to his jabber. What she felt for him now was closer to pity.

"I heard the men talking about what happened to you. I was sorry to hear about it."

"That's kind. I'm glad for a little comfort."

He was going to say more, but she interrupted to press on. "But I don't understand about you not being able to recognize who did it."

"It was very dark, and I have to confess that I'd had more than my share of the spirits that prevail in a place like GALS."

"Hmm." Cory said. She rubbed her chin with a hand.

"What is it?" He lay still, the tubes dripping with fluids to help heal him, the sheets covering him like something beached on Galveston Island sand. But his eyes glittered in a crafty, worldly-wise way that said he could out-fox any man he met, much less a little sprat of a girl.

"I heard that Bryce, the bouncer who found you, had it figured for two guys. He said you weren't all that drunk, and that you were more than a match for most men."

Sherm's chest swelled beneath the sheets. Was he trying to suck in his stomach and look more manly? Well, he wasn't succeeding.

"It's true enough I won my share of scraps out in that and other parking lots," he said. "But it was dark out there. I told you that."

"Because," she said, feeling herself edge a step back without meaning to, as if he could leap from the bed and grab at her,

173

"both Wesley and Farley have the kind of skinned knuckles you'd get in a brawl like that. I just wondered if you weren't being quiet to protect your son."

His eyes opened wider and for the first time looked mean. But the look faded. He was tired, and still beaten. He muttered, "Now ain't you the little Sherlock pigeon-toed Holmes."

"I'm confused," she admitted. "Why would any son be a part of beating on his own father?"

Hargate sighed. He looked up at the ceiling but still spoke to her. "I've done the best I could by that boy. But he ain't altogether right. He got confused. All youth are confused. You're just one of the first I've ever heard admit it."

"What was he confused about?"

"Bird-doggin'."

"I don't get it. What's . . ."

"Bird-doggin' is when one man plays sly on another, his friend or someone like that, and tries to steal the other guy's girl away behind his back."

Cory didn't need to know the origin of the phrase; she caught the principle. "You were hitting on girls Wesley dated?"

"He thought I was. Confused, that's what the boy was."

Cory tilted her head in thought.

"Why don't you just wait until I'm all patched up here and you can come by and sit on my lap some time?"

Cory looked back at the man. She had known his reputation, but even then could not believe his brass.

"I was just wondering," she said.

"What?"

"If Vickee was one of the girls you bird-dogged from Wesley?"

He tried to roll away from her, but something hurt and he gave it up. He stared back at the ceiling, then closed his eyes. "I'm feelin' poorly," he said. "Probably need to get some rest."

"Because if the sheriff starts looking in some of the right

places, instead of grabbing at each easy fall guy he thinks will keep the voting public calm, he might find out about the rope that was used being charged to you. And don't say it was just any rope. It was a soft grade of a known brand marked with light green threads all through it. There's only one place in this whole area you can buy rope like that, and the only missing length of it went to your charge account at our store."

He struggled to get upright, twitched in place, but was too sore and beat up to make it. He flopped back on the bed and turned his head to glare at her.

For a few moments he lay staring, started to say something a couple of times and stopped. At last he said, "What you say makes me sound kind of stupid, don't you think?"

"I'm not saying that. But there's only a few ways what happened to you makes sense. Let's say you get beat up by Wesley and Farley—your own son and his thug friend. Why? Then, you don't tell who thumped on you. Why? Now, I understand a father protecting a son, but what I don't understand is protecting one with enough motivation to beat you this way."

He glared at her, the purple of his face getting darker. Then he plopped back onto the pillow and stared straight up. "I think it's time you dusted your skinny little ass off and took it home, little girl."

"I'm sorry to bother you," she said, though she was not that sorry. "I've got to get back to . . . I've got to go as well."

She turned and was halfway to the door when he spoke.

"Missy. Stop a sec."

She didn't like to be called "missy." She turned back to him.

His head was lifted as painfully high as he could get it, which was just another inch off the pillow. "You be careful, you hear. You think this is a peaceful little chunk a' Texas. But it's the kind of place where you pull the skin back, you're gonna find violence. You just think about that before you poke at every scab

175

and boil you think you find."

She felt a small shiver, as if someone had cracked the freezer door open behind her. What he said could be taken as a caution or a threat. She did not believe he cared enough about her to caution her.

She spun and hurried out the door to head back to Uncle Giff's room and almost ran into the chest of Sheriff Michael Sparrow. He stood leaning against the wall outside Hargate's room. Behind him stood the taller deputy, Winslow. Both were in uniform and looked serious.

Sheriff Sparrow bent down closer, his eyes glittering until they nearly threw sparks from beneath the shaggy white eyebrows. "Very insightful. You'd make a good deputy if you weren't such a little pest."

He stood and nodded to Winslow. "Let's get in there while he's all warmed up for us."

The sheriff eased close to the bed while Winslow took up a position just inside the door. Sparrow was getting quite a kick out of the expression on Hargate's face. Sherm's eyes had narrowed to slits in the chubby folds of his face. As much as anything, it reminded Sparrow of a snake he'd seen cornered in the rocks once, except that the snake didn't have a shadow of fear flickering at the edges of its intent face.

"Think you might have been a little rough with her, Sherm? She's just a little girl," Sparrow said.

"You were hangin' outside my door, eavesdroppin'," Sherm said, on the offensive at once. He was reading something on Sparrow's face. "I want to know why."

Sparrow sat slowly on the edge of Hargate's hospital bed, watched Sherm respond to the affront he never would have stood for a few days back. Hargate's mouth merely tightened.

The sheriff stared at Sherm for a few minutes before he spoke again. It was quiet in the room; only the sound of nurses calling to each other and banging around in the hallway filtered through. When he spoke, there was snap in Sparrow's tone. "What makes you think you can talk to a sheriff that way, especially one who's investigating a murder?"

Sherm's eyes swung from Sparrow to Winslow, then back to Sparrow again.

"Oh, so it's like that, is it?" he said.

"Like what?" Sparrow snapped.

Sherm ignored him and talked instead to Winslow. "You're new here, ain't you?"

Winslow nodded slowly, staring back at Hargate, neither his brown eye nor his blue eye flinching, nor did he let his gaze be pulled to the white mound that was Hargate's prominent belly.

Sherm faltered when Winslow seemed as unimpressed as he did. He was used to people being more intimidated. He turned back to Sheriff Sparrow but spoke to Winslow.

"I don't know what our sheriff here's told you about himself, but I'm sure I could do a more thorough job if need be."

It was a threat, but Sparrow didn't rise to it. "Enlighten us, Sherm," he said.

"This really what you want?"

"Why not?"

Sherm turned his head to look right at Winslow. "He never told you why he isn't still sheriff over to some clam-suckin' county there on the East Coast somewheres, has he? You oughtta ask him about the Gilbert-Simmons case. That's gotta be a favorite yarn of his."

"Insufficient evidence," Sparrow said. "Everyone thought the little girl's parents killed her. But we didn't have anything hard. You making something of that?"

"I don't have to, Sparrow. Everyone there already did." His eyes had swung to the sheriff, but they went back to the deputy.

"Hell, everyone knew it was gonna cost Sparrow the next election. Even his wife was one of the rats leavin' the sinkin' ship. She woulda rathered he was a yuppie-type lawyer in the first place, not a second-rate lawman."

Sparrow's face gave a small jerk at the mention of his wife. That was low. His face ran to pink flickers of color along his temples, although his expression never changed.

Sherm shifted back to Sparrow, his mouth twisted in disdain. "I guess you were over your head when it came to real detection. All that fancy schooling didn't amount to a rat's fart, did it. But, hell, it was a win-win for this little county. We got us a slick talkin', highly educated sheriff—he got a county to watch he could handle, where watchin' paint dry is kind of a kick most days. It was all smooth sailin' as long as nothin' happened. But . . ."

Sparrow had had enough. His face was a warm flush of color when he interrupted. "Now I'll tell you something, you hard lump of cattle drop."

Sherm's eyes snapped open wide. "Now, you listen . . ."

Sparrow interrupted. "You just played a card you should have played when it was trump. As it is, your card isn't worth the cardboard it's printed on right now."

Hargate's mouth opened, then slowly closed.

"You know, Sherm," Sparrow said, "one of the non-charming aspects of rural sheriffing is dealing with all the large frogs in the small pond. And I don't mind saying that you, sir, have been one of the froggiest. In the course of the past year alone you've butted in and thrown your weight around at least fourteen times. But with this case, the most colorful we've had in a long spell, you haven't said a word. Now why do you suppose that is?"

Hargate glared, said nothing.

"It's not like I haven't had any calls. I've been damn near

swamped by them. I was even called in for a private meeting with a handful of the other large croakers from this county. Folks with a couple of bucks to rub together, and some that don't, feel something like this gives them a chance to call and do a bit of backseat driving, armchair coaching, call it what you like. It's been a whole lot of pressure I didn't need. Your name was dropped around a bit in all that, but you weren't present yourself. Maybe I should be thanking you for not bugging me, but it does call attention to you—that and this licking you took without swearing out a complaint."

"I've got nothin' to say."

"Did the young girl say it all?"

"That meddlesome little . . ."

"Let's look at what she said. Wesley and Farley beat you. Why? You won't say who did. Why? The rope used to tie up the dead girl may well be traced right to you. Sherm, I've got to tell you, I've been working with damn little. But all this is just starting to look like something."

Hargate tossed restlessly on the bed, caught himself and stopped, but not in time. "I . . . I got somethin' to say," he said.

"First, Winslow," Sparrow said, "read him his Miranda."

"Oh, come on. I waive the damn thing."

But Winslow went over and recited the whole thing, starting with, "You have the right to remain silent." When he was done, he stepped back and stood by the door.

Sparrow took out a small pocket tape recorder and turned in on in plain sight of Hargate. He held it out in one hand while he talked. "Tell me about it," he said.

Sherm Hargate turned his head away. Sparrow watched the emotions wrestle on his face. This wasn't the easiest thing for someone like him—well, for anyone.

"I was the one out there," he said, his face panned back to Sparrow.

179

"What?"

"I was the one out there that night, with Vickee. At the Whalen place. Are you deaf?"

Sparrow glanced at Winslow, then back to Hargate. "Go on," he told Hargate.

"That's it. Just that it was me."

"Why did you kill her?"

"I . . . I don't know. I was just out of my head, I guess."

"Where's the knife?"

"I threw it in the river."

"What river?"

"McConnell's Slough, the nearest one that runs by the Whalen place. You know it."

"What kind of knife was it?"

"It was . . . it was . . . Why are you askin' me? Why don't you just go find the damn thing?"

"Sherm, you are just about the worst liar I have ever heard spout. How do you get by cheating on your wife all these years if that's the best you can do?"

"What gives you the right to call me that?" Even more of Hargate's confidence oozed from his face.

"I know that McConnell's Slough is a dry river bed ninety percent of the year, although there was water in it after the storm, but there wouldn't have been at the time of the murder. It's only a puddle or two up and down its length now. But you wouldn't have been able to recognize the knife if I showed it to you because you've never seen it. All I have is a probable description from the autopsy report, but I can tell you more about the knife used than you can tell me."

Hargate stayed silent. He sulked and glowered at Sparrow.

"I wouldn't have expected anything half so noble from you, Sherm, even if it is your son you think you're sheltering here. What I want to know is, why do you think he and Farley beat you if Wesley was the one who killed her?"

"You can gibber all you want from here on out," Hargate snapped, his round cheeks pinched in anger, "but I'm done talkin' with the likes of you."

"You've said enough," Sparrow said. He turned off his recorder, slid it in his pocket, and nodded to Winslow to open the door.

"Sparrow."

The sheriff turned and looked back at the bed. Hargate said, "You just be careful you don't burn the bridge you're standin' on."

"You are sure one for threats today." Sparrow shook his head. "But you know, Sherm, you're not much of a bridge. After all," he patted the pocket that held the recorder, "you did just confess to murder. I'll always have that if I need it."

CHAPTER SIXTEEN

Giff looked up from the crossword puzzle he was fussing over and saw Sheriff Michael Sparrow standing in the hospital doorway. The tall deputy, Winslow, towered behind him.

"I've been hoping to talk with you," Giff said. "They say I could leave but that you asked them to hold me here until you could talk with me. I hope that's not just to save the taxpayers a few pennies on gas." Giff was more irritable and snappy than usual. He was anxious to get back to Bent Bell and head out to look for Saris.

"I had so hoped that you and I would get along," Sparrow said. He glanced over at Cory, who sat in the chair against the wall. She held the other section of the morning paper and had paused from reading it to watch him.

"I'd hate to think that you two had been withholding evidence."

"You do have a way of looking a gift horse in the mouth," Giff said.

Sparrow moved a step closer to the foot of Giff's bed. "For a man of your education, you seem to have picked up a dependence on clichés," he said.

Giff was tempted to say, "If the shoe fits, wear it," but instead said, "Cory just told me about the rope. It's the first I heard about it. I'm surprised your investigation didn't take you that far yet. Did she get a chance to tell you about the initials?"

"What initials?" Sparrow looked over at Cory.

"On Sherm Hargate's account card," Giff answered for her. "Where we record his charges. The rope purchase had the initials 'W.H.' beside it. I remembered putting them there when Cory showed me the card. It means Wesley was the one who bought the rope. It was a special kind of rope. I still have a few lengths if you want to buy them. But don't lay that withholding rap on us. You're the one, after all, who must have assumed the rope was the kind you could buy at any hardware store."

"Everyone seems to want to tell me how I ought to be doing my job."

"Might be you're just a little oversensitive about that." Giff met the sheriff's stare.

"Winslow," Sparrow snapped. "Get over to the jail and check with that boy. Now."

The tall deputy turned on one heel and shot out the door. While he was leaving, Sparrow said to Giff, "First I get Sherm confessing to the murder, now this." He paused. "Are you going to press assault charges against Farley?"

"No. I imagine he realizes by now that he did something wrong."

"You'd be surprised how little he realizes. Well, I guess I still have enough to hold him a bit until I straighten out a few loose ends."

"I didn't know there were any. Word around the county makes it sound like you'd already rounded up Vickee's killer. I was waiting for the story in the paper. Now with the bit about the rope to add to what you had, don't you have enough for a case? No one really likes Wesley, anyhow." Giff wasn't successful at keeping all the sarcasm out of his tone.

"Think about what I'd have to take to a grand jury," Sparrow said. "I don't have squat—just some circumstantial evidence and some pieces that don't hold together."

Sparrow said to Cory, "Why didn't you mention that bit

about the initials to Sherm?"

"I wanted to see how he'd react if it pointed right at him first," she said.

Sparrow sighed. "I guess that's what I'd have done too. But why did you?"

"Because there was the chance that Mr. Hargate was the one who took Vickee out there. Vickee might've stolen the rope from Wesley—everyone knows how light-fingered she tended to be." Cory kept her voice and posture demure, but Giff could see she got a kick from explaining her reasoning.

Sparrow looked at Giff. "She's a regular little prodigy, isn't she?"

"You can talk directly to her, Sheriff," Giff said. "She can take the big words and all."

"Something about me bugs you, doesn't it?" Sparrow said to Giff.

"I vote," Giff said, "just like the rich people around here."

Sparrow's face flushed. He took a moment or two, then asked Cory, "But if the rope purchase pointed to Wesley, why were you asking the kind of questions you were of Sherm Hargate?"

Cory kept her voice humble, "Because I couldn't explain Wesley beating up his father if Wesley was the one who killed Vickee."

"So you think that the evidence points to Sherm, do you?"

"I did," she said, "until you just told us he'd confessed."

"Come again." Sparrow's forehead was showing all the lines he'd gathered through the years now.

Cory said, "That means he's been thinking all along that Wesley was the one who killed her. I'd guess that Mr. Hargate was the one who took her out there. But I understand she liked to be left there sometimes, tied up. It added to the thrill, or something. What if he went back out to check on her and found her dead?"

"That doesn't fully jibe with Wesley beating him," Sparrow said.

Giff noticed that Sparrow's tone had changed. He was taking Cory seriously now, perhaps for the first time.

"No, it doesn't," Cory said. "But some of that is something you can straighten out. Wesley isn't handy for me to talk to, but he is for you. I'm just trying to help, not do your job for you."

Sparrow's face took on a bit of pink again. But before he could say anything, the walkie-talkie on his waist belt crackled. He snatched at it. "Go ahead," he said.

Winslow's voice came across, loud enough for Giff and Cory to hear, "The boy says the rope was stolen out of his truck a long time ago. He . . ."

Sparrow cut him off. "I'll be right over."

He shoved the walkie-talkie back into its leather holder.

"He could be lying," Giff said.

"Doesn't much matter as far as this case goes." Sparrow spun and started for the door.

"Did the boy say why he helped beat on his own father that way?" Giff called to him.

Sparrow spoke over his shoulder without looking back. "Not yet. But he will."

Giff lay across the back seat of the extended cab in Shimmy's truck. Cory sat up front, squeezed between Shimmy and Zoe.

Shimmy's lights were on and the black road came at them in on-and-off flashes of white and yellow in lines on the pavement.

"It's dark," Giff said. He watched the lit up front of GALS go by his window. It was the first bit of color he had seen in the night for a while.

"That's good, Einstein," Zoe said. "They really did a job on your head in there."

"I mean, I wanted to be out sooner to go and check on Saris."

185

"You'll have to talk to Cory about that," Zoe said. "She's the one upset the hornets' nest.

"It's not like I did anything just to upset people," she said in a small voice.

"Ol' Sparrow's got his britches all in a knot," Zoe said. "First he thinks it's TyTy. Then he has Wesley and Farley—only that's a problem because one of 'ems his deputy—and now he's rattling Sherm's cage like he don't know where to jump next. I don't know, Giff, about how smart this bird is supposed to be. Maybe Harvard's not the school I thought it was."

"He's plenty smart enough," Giff said. "He knows the public wants a quick solution more than it wants justice. Maybe he got that from Earl Warren."

"Wherever he got it, he oughta give it back. Imagine, Sherm Hargate a killer. The man's just so much wind; same goes for his son. Now, Farley, naw, even he don't have the sand. What about you, Shim? What d'you think? You haven't said a thing."

"I ain't got no opinion. It's all over my head."

Zoe said, "What I heard around Carnicius sure made it sound like he'd wrapped the case when he brought in Wesley. So whatcha think Sparrow will have for the papers tomorrow, Giff?"

"Sparrow never said Sherm's his man," Giff said. "He didn't say that about Farley or Wesley either. He's just holding those two. Things will sort themselves out. We can have a poke at Sparrow, but he's a professional. He's sorted through worse messes than this. He'll follow procedure, question people, revisit alibis. Before we know it he'll have everyone fighting with each other worse than they are."

"Seems like the only hard evidence, which Cory here dug up, points to Wesley. You're the one, Giff, said the initials on the charge mean he got the rope."

"Wesley claims the rope was stolen out of his truck," Giff said. "Who do we know who was light-fingered?"

"Vickee, with two Es," Cory said. "But if she took the rope and had it for someone to use, it puts everything all up in the air again. It could have been anyone."

"You sound like this is some board game, Cory," Zoe said. "It worries me some. Didn't the sheriff give you a little speech again? I mean, what's this girl Vickee to you anyway? You didn't even like her, did you?"

"Everyone acts like all this is a part of Vickee's life," Cory said. "Well, it's not. I hate to be hard, but she doesn't even have a life anymore. She was a part of my life, and until Sparrow is sure he's got the right person, TyTy could still be in hot water. I feel I have a right to help solve this, a duty."

"I just worry about you," Zoe said.

"I know this all seems like big people stuff. But I haven't seen much get done by all the so-called adults yet." Cory's voice was subdued enough to pull it off, not overconfident or an outright rebel. "I don't always get to do much good around here. I don't know why people resent it when I do."

"But the danger . . ." Zoe said.

"There can't be much danger if half the county is locked up or in the hospital, now can there?"

"So, Cory, I guess that means you're not going to stop?" Zoe persisted.

"What would Pericles say, Uncle Giff?"

"Who?" Shimmy asked.

"I guess I should have stressed Socrates's story too," Giff said. "His sense of playing by the rules of his society is why he, in the end, drank the hemlock."

"Everyone knows how and why Socrates died, Uncle Giff."

"I sure as hell didn't," Zoe said.

"Well, I think I mentioned you cooperating with the sheriff, didn't I?"

"I've never seen anyone who wants cooperation from others

less," Zoe said. "He wants folks serving him. Doesn't he know the sheriffing job's him serving his county? But all that aside, how about it Cory? You gonna stop?"

"Not unless somebody makes me."

Giff could see Zoe shaking his head. "You know what they say: what doesn't kill you makes you stronger. But I can't help worrying about you. I'm like your other uncle."

"Just what she always never wanted," Shimmy chuckled.

CHAPTER SEVENTEEN

"I appreciate your taking a day off to help me, TyTy. Your boss must be understanding." Giff led the way up the trail. He wasn't carrying a pack this time. TyTy was right on Giff's heels, but he would shift around to the lead when there was any tracking to be done.

"He's not. But maybe he'll fire me and that will force me to go off to college. Ain't you the one always saying that something good always comes of stuff, no matter how bad it is?"

"I've had my words come back and bite me like a rattlesnake I thought I'd harbored as a pet before, too." Giff looked up at the sky. It was a mottled gray, darkened to black in some spots. "Does it look like it might rain to you?"

TyTy looked up. "I can't say. I've seen worse skies pass right over."

Giff said, "You know, when you work inside the place you live all the time, weather is, at best, something of minor interest, a conversation piece. It's of far more interest to those who have to work outside."

"I hear you on that. But we're outside today, and if it rains hard we're not gonna have anythin' to track."

"I hope I don't sound like I'm on an ethnic jag when I ask you about the weather or to help track. It's just that I've heard people say you can track like nobody's business."

"Maybe some of the stuff they say has a little weight. I can see sign on the ground and through the brush just like you read

189

through books. If my mom was with us, she could tell you whether it was going to rain or not, and when, and how much."

Giff heard a mockingbird crying off in the distance. He looked to the tips of trees, knew they liked to sit high with their tail feathers at a tilt. "You know what it is about the end of summer, TyTy?"

"No."

"There's a sadness. Each day begins to feel more precious. You want to hoard them, savor them, have them to enjoy when the weather gets nasty later."

"You are talkin' 'bout the seasons, aren't you?"

"Why?"

" 'Cause Cory says that most of the time there are at least two meanings to everything you say."

"I'm glad we had this little time to spend together," Giff said. "I can learn a lot."

"I don't know. Cory doesn't think I'm much of a communicator."

"Oh, you do fine. There comes a point later on for lots of folks when it's easier not to say stuff than it is to say it. To just go along not making waves, even if they're unhappy."

"Can violence be a form of communication?"

"Too often it is."

They were quiet the rest of the way to the trailer. The pack still sat out in the middle of the clearing, untouched. Giff sighed. "Well, TyTy, the trail starts here. When I last saw Saris he was off like a shot through there." He pointed to the spot where Saris had disappeared in the brush.

TyTy went over to the spot. He bent low and looked around. "Two other fellas were through here too. One of these sets of prints is yours, isn't it?"

"Yeah. Farley chased him, then maybe came back that way. Then I went all the way back and couldn't find Saris."

"I could tell the order from the way your prints comin' and goin' are on top."

"You see, TyTy, you do read that sort of thing better than I read books."

"It just seems obvious to me."

Giff came over to follow TyTy. "That the trail isn't as clear to me and most of the rest of people is all the difference between us, TyTy."

He stayed back and let TyTy move ahead on the trail. When they were almost to the end of the trail, TyTy looked up at Giff. "He's back-tracked on you here."

"What's that mean?"

"He went up there somewhere, then came back this way trying not to leave any prints."

"But you found something, didn't you."

"There's sign." TyTy pointed over the top of a jumble of prickly briars. "He's skirted this close and gone off that way."

TyTy shot around the stickers in relative ease. It took Giff longer. He had to stop and pull himself loose from the clinging strands of brush a couple of times. Then the going was thick for twenty or thirty feet on the other side.

Up ahead Giff heard shouting. He hurried, felt the stickers rip at his jeans. But he ignored them as best he could and rushed until he could see TyTy bent over a body.

"Is he . . ."

"He's alive," TyTy called over to him. "But barely."

When Giff got all the way up to them, he bent closer. Saris was curled up against the trunk of a mesquite tree, huddled like he had been keeping as warm as he could against the cool evening. He was more frail than Giff had ever seen him. Saris's skin was a pasty gray, wrinkled and drawn, stretched across the unbearded part of his face like drying elephant skin on a skull. Giff felt for a pulse. It was low and weak.

"Let's go," he said. "We've got to get him back to town."

Giff scooped him up. Saris seemed light, but after only a couple of steps Giff felt woozy and dizzy. "TyTy."

"Yeah?"

"You better take him. I'm not all the way right yet."

TyTy carried McFeeney and led the way back to the clearing. They lowered him next to the backpack. Giff took out a water bottle and wet McFeeney's lips. TyTy helped him open the mouth, and they were trickling some water down into him when they heard the clopping.

Giff looked up, saw Cory come through on the trail on the back of Miss Dumpsie. "I knew you'd find him," she said. "But then I started to wonder at how you'd carry him out."

"It's getting so you're always one step ahead of me, Cory." Giff smiled at her.

She hopped off Miss Dumpsie and rushed over to help TyTy and Giff lift him up onto the horse, too caught up in concern for Saris to savor the moment.

Saris opened his eyes, and his bony shoulders gave a small startled jerk. The movement woke Giff, who had been dozing by the bed in one of the straight-backed chairs. The room was dim, just a night light and another small lamp they had rigged to help watch.

"Where am I?"

"In bed, here at my place, Saris. It's me, Giff." He didn't add that it was his own bed Saris was occupying.

"I can make you out. How did I get here?"

"We brought you in. You were pretty dried out. Don't you remember kicking up a fuss with the doctor about not wanting to go to the hospital?"

"Don't like 'em. Almost everyone I ever cared for died in one."

"You made it clear at the time that we couldn't drag you into one."

"What's this thing?" He rattled at the I.V. tube that ran to his arm on one end and up to a bag on the other.

"Doctor rigged that up for you to put some liquid back in you."

"I'm glad I wasn't around to see that. I'd have fought it."

"Oh, you did. Trust me on that."

"What happened to you?"

Giff reached up, felt the white bandage still wrapped around his head. "That kid with the gun that burst in on us when I was talking to you at your place did this."

"Thank goodness. Thought I might've done it."

"You?"

"Don't scoff. I was a violent one once. You'd be surprised what'll set a man off. He can go along peaceful as anything, and then some buncha little stuff'll pile up and he'll snap as violent as any wolf. I know. I hurt a woman, one I cared about. It's why I live out there all alone."

"Some kind of penance?"

"No. To protect the world from a worthless old scoundrel like me. I shoulda been drowned like an unwanted kitten at birth."

"No one deserves that."

"Well, I did. I don't know if you get it from your pa, but I hear the old man ripped and tore, beat on women too before he left us when I was a kid."

"You beat on several women?"

"No. Just the one—Betsy. It wasn't no beatin' really either. I just slapped her the once. But if you'd seen her face. Oh, the dreams I've had 'bout that."

"I used to keep a dream journal. I don't anymore. Cory, my niece, keeps one I think. She has quite a few of those Indian dream-catchers in her room. Have you ever seen one of . . ."

"I've seen some," Saris said. He was feeling around at the quilt and the sheets. "This your bed?"

"Yeah."

"It's a fine one. I appreciate your givin' it up for the likes of me. I never could've hoped to die in a finer bed than this."

"Oh, come on, Saris. You've had a shock, but you're as tough an old bird as I've ever seen."

"Giff, I won't lie to you. I'm a cat with eight lives spent, and spent loose, like chips fallin' in a Vegas game a' chance."

"You might surprise yourself."

"No I won't." Giff was surprised at the raspy finality in Saris's tone.

"I've still got your poke. It's safe. I'm holding it here for you."

"I never thought different. You wouldn't rob me, Giff Purvis. You're 'bout all the family I got. Sad, ain't it."

Giff went and brought the bag in, held it out to Saris, helped him lower it to his chest when he reached for it. Saris clutched it like it was a teddy bear. His eyes sparkled in watery brightness even in the dim light. "Wouldn't it just be the greatest," he said, "if you could buy back just a few seconds of time when you did the wrong thing?"

Giff nodded.

A small head stuck out around the door frame. Cory's blond hair looked tousled and her eyes bleary. "I thought I heard voices." She looked at Saris. "Do you need anything?"

He had at first recoiled at another person. Giff said, "My niece, Cory Lee."

"Am I in trouble?" she said.

"No, why?" Giff said.

"That's usually the only time you add the Lee anymore."

Saris clutched his bag and watched them, calming a bit in the banter of two people as relaxed as these two were around each other.

"You must be a great comfort to your uncle," Saris managed.

Cory's mouth lifted at a corner. "He knows I won't be around forever. One of these days . . ."

"What?" Saris asked.

"Tell him about the eaglet, Cory." Giff watched her, all gawky and awkward with being a near adult, but pushing constantly to be considered a full one.

She gave a short huff, looked at Saris. "This is one of his favorite stories. There was this eagle's nest . . ."

"An aerie." Giff caught the look from her and shut up.

"An aerie high on this mountain," she said. "One of the eaglets got restless and was tossing around in the nest. While the mother eagle's attention was turned, the eaglet tumbled out of the nest and started down the steep side of the mountain. It rolled and bounced all the way down until at last it was all the way at the bottom, where it rolled into the farm yard and came to rest in among the chickens. The mother hen swept it in with a wing, and it went with the other chicks, learned to peck at the ground and eat seeds. In time, the other chicks grew up into chickens and roosters and found their place on the farm. The eagle had grown to full size but still pecked at the ground for its seeds just like them. Then one day, the young eagle saw a shadow cross the ground and looked up. High in some thermal in the sky an eagle soared, swept, and glided with a grace only it could have. The bird looking up said, 'Ah, if only I'd been born an eagle.' "

Saris's eyes had threatened to close, but he forced them open. "That's a nice story," he said. His voice sounded more tired. He looked over at Giff. "You're right proud of her, ain't ya?"

"I am," Giff admitted.

"If you two don't need anything, I'm going to go back to

bed," Cory said.

"It was nice meetin' you," Saris said, with more sincerity than Giff expected from a loner like him.

Cory left the room. When she was gone, Saris said, "You're missin' her already, and she ain't gone yet. That's a shame."

Giff watched Saris clutch the bag, his eyes struggling to close again.

"Will you be able to sleep a while?" he asked Saris.

"I can try."

Giff leaned back in his chair, let his head tilt back against the wall.

He dreamed of an earthquake. The shaking woke him. It was Cory, tugging and pushing at his shoulder. Light was coming in the cracks around the pulled window shade. Her face looked distraught.

"Uncle Giff, wake up. Saris has died on us in the night."

CHAPTER EIGHTEEN

Cory stayed at the store to help Giff that afternoon, even though she had promised to be at the feed store and help Zoe with the inventory. Giff was a zombie; she watched him move around with stiff steps and in a staring state. He had recovered from getting hit on the head with a rock, she figured, but having Saris die on him had been a blow she couldn't figure. Since the funeral home's wagon had come and taken Saris's body to town, Giff had been like this—restlessly moping around the store, straightening a row of cans only to have it fall into a pile as soon as he turned from it. About an hour, ago he had walked over and snapped off the dial on the scratchy radio, right in the middle of Dvořák's New World Symphony, which he usually enjoyed, tapping along with a finger and wearing a half smile behind the counter. Now the music seemed to get on his nerves.

It was as quiet in the store as she had ever experienced it. A wind whipped along outside, blew dust and loose branches against the building. Cory ached inside; there was nothing she could think of to say to him.

They had the regular straggle of customers, folks coming in for a quick loaf of bread or milk. Half the time Giff didn't look up. Cory had to ring up the sales, chatter as best she could with the locals and one trucker who said he was passing through. On any other day Giff would have been on point to probe for a story. But he sat in one of the chairs by the stove with his wrists lying loose across his knees, and he never looked up.

197

Late in the afternoon a woman came through the front door and looked around. She seemed uncertain, a bit afraid.

Cory went up to where she stood. The woman looked to be in her thirties, wore a dark blue business dress, and had very red hair in a fluffy bush that came down in bangs. The skin of her face was pale, with just a hint of tasteful make-up. She had green eyes, and a dimple, but she did not look happy.

"Ma'am?" Cory said, though she hated that word and never used it. Some of Giff's awkwardness must be rubbing off on her today.

"Is there a Mr. Giff Purvis here?"

Giff looked up slowly as she spoke. Cory nodded back to him. He stood with one arm on the unlit stove, staring out through the store.

She walked back to him. "You don't know me," she said. "The sheriff sent me here. He said you knew Saris. I'm . . ." she choked, but forced herself to go on, "Betsy McFeeney."

"Are you . . . are you his daughter?"

"No, his wife. He was barely forty himself. Maybe you didn't know that."

"No, I didn't." Giff had always talked to Cory about him as if he was quite a bit older than himself. Being outside, doing that kind of work can take a toll. But Giff must have had no idea. His eyes opened with even more shock than he had been showing all morning. Cory moved closer, fascinated. She wanted to hear everything that was said.

"I don't know how well you knew him," the woman said. "Sheriff Sparrow says you're about the only one around here who knew him at all. I've been trying to find Saris for fifteen years. I even hired a detective once, but he never got anything. It was all my fault. I've been . . . I've been trying for so long just to find him and say I was sorry." Her head bobbed down, and her shoulders shook.

Giff's eyes cleared, but he stood awkwardly with arms half lifted, not knowing how to reach out and comfort the woman.

Cory went back into the house and got an open box of tissues. She brought it out and went over and held it out to the woman. Betsy looked up, her eyes all puffy now, and reached for a tissue. "Thanks," she said.

Cory set the box down on one of the chairs and eased away.

When the woman's crying slowed, she glanced around, saw the chairs. She said to Giff, "Do you mind?"

"No, please. Where are my manners? Sit down."

She sat, and he lowered himself into the nearest chair and sat on its edge. His forearms rested on his knees and he leaned closer.

"So, you're his wife."

She nodded.

"Ever remarry?"

"No. We're . . . still married." She hesitated. "I won't lie and say I didn't have any comfort from other . . . men during the past fifteen years. But I've always waited to find Saris or have him come back."

"What happened?"

"It's a long . . . well, not so long story. But it's so ordinary, so stupid, and wrong."

"Did he ever slap you?"

"I don't know," she said, and reached for another tissue. "If he did, I deserved it. He caught me cold with another man. Saris and I had been married only two years then. He was delicate, an artist. I never meant to hurt him. The look on his face . . . oh, that look."

"I'm sorry you had to finally find him this way," Giff said.

"The sheriff called. Saris even had me listed as next of kin on things found at his trailer. He had no driver's license. He'd been hiding out here all these years, within a drive from Austin where I've been living, or half-living, and waiting."

Giff was watching her.

Her head raised. "Oh, if only there could have been a way to reach him, talk to him."

"Saris told me," Giff said, his words slow and careful, "almost the same thing. He said if there had only been a way to buy things back like they were, he would have."

She nodded. "That sounds like him. Oh, if only . . ."

Giff stood. "I'll be right back."

When he came back into the store from the house he was carrying Saris's leather bag.

He held out the bag, lowered it slowly to her lap. She looked surprised at the weight of it. "What is it?"

He said, "Saris would have wanted you to have it."

"What's in it?" she repeated.

"Topaz. That's what he's been doing out here all these years, digging at the packed dirt beneath tree trunks in the hills and sifting the streams when there's water. All to stockpile what you have there. And I doubt if there was an hour of any day he didn't think about you while he was doing it."

"Do you think I . . . no, he gave it to you, didn't he?"

"Keep it."

"Do you . . . oh, I will. But I . . ." She stood, barely able to hold the bag. She turned, hesitated, but then kept moving all the way through the store and out the door.

Cory waited until she was gone and there was the sound of a car pulling out. She had heard Giff on the phone earlier agree to pay for Saris's funeral at a cost she knew they couldn't easily afford. She asked Giff, "After all he went through, you think she had that coming?"

"It was none of mine, Cory. It was his, and she was closer to him than I was. What drove him wasn't me; it was thinking about her. Sure, she has it coming."

Chapter Nineteen

Wesley Hargate sat at the table in the interrogation room. There was nothing wrong with his chair, but he didn't look comfortable. Sheriff Michael Sparrow stood looking through the two-way mirror at him, watching Wesley squirm every now and then. Deputy Winslow had taken Wesley in an hour ago. Now Sparrow was letting him stew. The sheriff glanced at his watch, then moved away from the window and went around to the interrogation room door. He pushed it open and went inside.

"How're you doing?" he said. Sparrow pulled the yellow chair away from the steel table and sat in it.

Wesley glared. His hands were in cuffs fastened to the ring. He lifted his arms and jiggled his handcuffed wrists and hands at Sparrow. "Just what the hell is this? You have me picked up like some common thug and then you . . ."

"Shut up," Sparrow said. He did not raise his voice, but the words were clipped and acted like scissors on Wesley's flow of words.

Sparrow leaned back in his chair, narrowed his eyes and looked at Wesley. The boy had a medium long and square face, clean complexion but the lip looked ever poised to curl, and not in the way that made female Elvis fans coo. He was looking at Sparrow now with distaste that matched Sparrow's own thoughts that some kids ought to be left out in the woods for a couple of weeks after birth.

"Why do you think I had you two brought in here? You and

Farley." Sparrow was looking down at Wesley's knuckles.

Wesley shifted in his seat, looked away, then appeared to remember that he should maintain eye contact. His stare was insolent enough for Sparrow to think longingly back to the days when you could rattle a witness like a maraca if it helped get him started talking. But he had something as good.

"You're not a very popular fellow. Did you know that?" Sparrow said. Wesley's mouth dropped open a half inch, but before he could get a word out, the sheriff said, "Best friends with a fellow like Farley, too. That tells a whole story."

"What's wrong with . . . He works for you."

"You know I started with him first since he's a deputy. He told me quite a bit."

Wesley started to say something but forced his mouth closed. Sparrow waited. It would be impossible for someone like Wesley to stay clammed. Sparrow tapped a foot slowly and stared at the boy. It was like watching a clock and Old Faithful. Wesley stewed and boiled inside, exploded suddenly with, "Where do you get off dragging me in and talking to me like this? You know who I am."

"If you mean to throw the weight of your father's ranches around and all the acreage he owns in the county, try not to forget what charge you might be facing. It was him, after all, who took the licking. Are you convinced to the bone that he wouldn't ever press charges on you?"

He watched the boy thinking. It was a struggle.

"Now, we went around about that rope earlier. You claim it was stolen out of your truck, which is pretty lame and convenient. I get from Farley that the two of you went after your old man because you think he was the one that spent time with Vickee the night she died. Then I talk to your father himself. He's willing to go along that it's your rope and you never lost it, kind of sly like, the way he can be. Trouble is, I have a hard time believing him, since it looks like you and Farley had just given him a thrashing and a half. I distrust Sherm's motives. You figure he might just say, 'What the hell?' and let you take a fall for him? I don't know. You tell me."

Sparrow stopped and watched Wesley. The boy was probably rotten at poker as a whole wrestling match was happening behind Wesley's effort to maintain a stone face. The room was still. Outside they could hear the screaming and kicking of someone being brought in. Sparrow glanced at his watch. A bit early for a DWI.

Jerry Plattern, the turnkey, stuck his head in the door. Sparrow glared at him. Jerry knew better than to interrupt an interrogation.

"Sorry, Sheriff, but the DWI's Clayton Falcone. Thought sure you'd want to know."

That did pop Sparrow's eyebrows. But he waved Jerry back out the door. He'd go out in a minute and see what was up. The boy was due to pop at any second.

A crafty look stole over the boy's face. It was the same "fox in the chicken yard" look Sparrow had seen Sherm Hargate use. Wesley said low, "Farley never said nothin'."

"Think about it, son. Which do you think he values more: the job or your friendship? Think hard on that."

Had Wesley been a hardened criminal, or if he had the intellect of a more mature adult, Sparrow would not have been as optimistic as he was. He tapped one boot toe, waiting. There was this little wait on top of the longer one earlier while Wesley sat and wondered what was going to happen. He watched the boy's face tie into an emotional knot like a baby's clenching fist.

Wesley looked down at the table, then looked back up. His eyes were watering with tears he wasn't able to stop. "He took her out there. Dad did. We all know that. We know how she was, and we know it was him with her that night. Hell, we saw her get into his truck. We beat on him for that. It was all the justice that's needed, and it's done. I mean, the girl's dead. I know you can't just drop it, but . . ."

Sparrow said, "That's why Farley went after Saris McFeeney, then. You two thought if I had a fall guy the whole thing would wrap itself up. You thought that I'm the kind of guy takes the easiest way out. All I need is a body. It doesn't even have to be the right one, eh?" Sparrow fought for control of himself. He realized his voice was booming in the room, that he was losing it. He remembered the tape rolling, catching the whole thing.

He rose and called for a deputy. He followed as Wesley was led back to his holding cell. He listened, heard Wesley call out, "Farley, you rotten S.O.B. of a rat. When I get outta here . . ."

Farley interrupted, his voice coming back the length of the row of cells, "You want to see a rat, find a mirror to look in sometime. If you'd have thought half a second, you'd know I'd never talk. This'll cost me my job sure."

Deputy Winslow pushed Wesley into one of the cells, where he plopped down onto the hard bed. Sparrow watched with satisfaction, knew it was going to cost Wesley a hell of a lot more than that.

He could hear the steady thumping all the way down at the end of the hallway, and as they walked past the bars of other cell doors, Sparrow glanced over at Winslow, who worked a momentary shrug into his stride.

They came to the cell door they called "the presidential suite" since it was once of the few private holding cells in the jail. It was where they put the occasional well-off inebriate or housed more famous criminals being routed through the area for one reason or another.

Sparrow looked in. The thumping became clear now. Clayton Falcone lay across the length of the metal cot and was tied in place with heavy nylon straps. His arms were tied at his sides, and his ankles were strapped to the lower end of the bed. But he could still move his head a bit and, by stretching, he could bang his head steadily against the rounded metal tube at the head of the cot. His eyes were closed tight, and the steady thump echoed down the hallway, where it was unusually quiet in the other cells.

His head had already been wrapped with gauze, but one end of that was coming loose and flapping as his head swung repeatedly toward the end of the cot.

Clayton wore a suit, but the tie was missing, and there were smears of blood on the collar. A bruise was beginning to darken one cheekbone.

"You get anything out of him?" Sparrow asked.

Winslow shook his head. "He's been pretty much like that since he was brought in. What I did get sounded like Bible gibberish, some sort of talking in tongues, maybe, but not the inspired type."

"He was tied then?"

"No. We did that when he was really slamming himself around in there on his own."

"Wouldn't do to have a clergyman come out of jail looking like he'd been beat up, now would it?"

"Nope. Some of his congregation's already been around ready to bail him out, tarnished halo and all."

"You'd better have Jerry tie the man's head down, too."

"I already told him, and he's gone to get some extra pillows and more strapping. Usually what he used is enough, he told me. But you can see this old boy's wired for the moment."

"Any idea what set him off?"

"Nope. Just drink, I guess, and he was pretty forlorn-looking at the funeral home. You figure guilt?"

"About something, but not the death itself. You checked the

alibis too, didn't you?"

Winslow nodded.

"Oh, he feels something. He and the niece had some history, the way I figure."

"That's what I thought."

"Tell you what. When he's fit to turn loose, you let them bail him out, then you follow him."

"What if he goes to the church?"

"That should be all right. In the meantime, get in there and hold his head until Jerry gets more strapping."

"You afraid he's really going to hurt himself?"

"No. I just think a fellow like him might be enjoying that too much."

Giff sat in the back seat of TyTy's car coming back from the memorial service. Betsy McFeeny had been there, wearing a simple navy blue dress. She, Cory, TyTy, and Giff were the only ones at the service, although Sheriff Sparrow showed up before the last amen. Giff's insides felt hollow, scooped out by the flurry of recent events. He had been back and forth across the road to Carnicius more times than he could remember ever having made the trip. The dusty trees and struggling scrub bush all passed his window in a blur now. He was bone weary of everything.

"You okay, Mr. Purvis?" TyTy glanced back at him. Halfway on the ride back, Cory had slid across the seat to him, within distance to hold his hand.

"I feel like a part of myself has fallen into the ocean," Giff said, not sure if he made a lot of sense, or whether that even mattered.

As soon as the store was opened and the lights on, Giff gravitated to his spot behind the counter next to the register. He touched each familiar object there in an unfamiliar way, seeking something—comfort, reassurance, who knew?

TyTy lingered behind in the store, looking awkward. Cory shot into the back, headed for the stable to check on Miss Dumpsie.

Giff leaned forward, settling into his traditional pose. TyTy ran a finger through the thin film of dust on a humane armadillo trap. He eased closer to the back counter.

"Mr. Purvis?"

"Yeah, Tracker?"

"Tracker? That's new." Lines showed on his forehead.

"Aren't you just a bit tired of being called TyTy?"

"Yeah. I guess I was. Tracker's fine. Real good, in fact." He paused. "There's something I've been wanting to ask you."

"You should know that the hand comes with the rest of her."

"It's not that," he said, more embarrassed than before. "We both know she's a little young yet."

"She doesn't," Giff said.

"It's about college."

"What about it?"

"How do I get fixed up to get in one, to improve myself?"

"I thought you weren't too keen about going on for more school?"

"I did okay in high school, and if I applied myself . . ."

"Cory have anything to do with this?"

"Well, she likes the idea. And I find that when she likes an idea it kind of grows on me. Besides, I need to keep busy while I'm waiting for her to get a bit older. And, truth is, it kinda bugs me that she's so much smarter'n me."

Giff's head moved back an inch as he looked at TyTy. The usual serious look was on his face. A lot was sure happening lately, and fast. The two had been just pals for so long it was hard to imagine them anything other than that.

Giff heard the scream and spun toward the house door. Cory

came running through into the store, her face red and twisted in grief and rage. She ran right at Giff. He held his arms out for a hug, but she stopped in front of him, pounded on his chest with her small fists and screamed, "You told me this would happen."

"What?" Giff said. "Calm down and tell me. You're not making sense yet." His arms and hands were useless in stopping the blows without hurting her.

"It's Miss Dumpsie," she sobbed. "Something's wrong. Really, really wrong."

Sparrow left a deputy out in the hallway watching the door he closed behind himself as he entered the hospital room.

Sherm Hargate looked up at him. He used the remote to turn off the television.

"How come you don't get flowers from anyone, Sherm? Seems like someone ought to care enough to send along some cheer. Or did someone send some and you had the nurse get rid of them so the wife wouldn't wonder?" A pile of rumpled magazines littered the stand beside the bed.

"So you're talking to the nurses now. What else do they say? They describe my colon, or any other part of me to you?" The earlier harshness in Hargate's tone was gone now. He had swapped his sarcastic manner for one of reconciliation.

"That must have been what they meant when they called you one real asshole," Sparrow said. They both chuckled softly. You could call another man an asshole, if you smiled. Sparrow eyed the chair near the bed, but he stayed standing.

Before Sparrow could speak again, Hargate's eyes lowered and raised. He said, "I guess I was a ways out of line earlier reamin' you 'bout what went on back there in a part of the States I don't know all that much about. I spoke a mite out of turn and didn't have all the facts. What really did happen back there?"

"That's all pretty stale news, Sherm."

"I'm still interested to learn."

Sparrow looked down at the fingernails of one hand before he glanced back at Hargate and said, "A young girl was molested. That was established. She was only eleven, and she knew who'd done it, though she was slow coming forward with that. Before she could say anything, she was murdered. The prime suspect was her father, the son of an influential . . . well, a damned wealthy man. Where we're talking about big spreads out here, we were talking about billions back there. Chances were, nothing would have landed on the boy no matter what I did."

"But the case hung fire?"

What did not need saying was that the case had cost Sparrow his patronage in a place where one phone call from the right person weighed more than hundreds of calls from other people. It had popped any bubble he'd had about how the system worked, or didn't work, and was why he was here now, repairing damage with the likes of Hargate.

Sparrow nodded slowly. "Like I said before, not enough hard evidence. But I do hope the parallel of the rich son wasn't lost on you."

"Where's that takin' you?"

"There're a couple of new wrinkles, Sherm."

"Why don't you set a spell, and we'll iron them out?"

"Shouldn't take all that long."

"Well, get to it, then," Sherm said. The bandages were still around his face, but much of the swelling had gone down. The skin that showed was bright pink, no longer purple except for a small spot here and there. His stomach still raised a bulge under the sheets. "It's just us, after all." He was someone who liked to get about, be visible in one place or another all day. Being confined to a hospital bed was starting to wear on him.

"You recall us talking earlier about that rope, the kind was used to tie the girl?" Sparrow said.

Hargate said nothing. The patient look on his face reflected the small-town craftiness that was his reputation. Sparrow had seen an imitation of the look on Wesley's face only a short while ago.

"Looks like I might even be able to pin the whole thing on Wesley," Sparrow said.

"What?"

"He bought the rope that was used. That girl, Cory, put us onto that."

"It's a sad day when a man of your years has to lean on words from the mouths of babes."

"Why, that's almost biblical, Sherm. The other babe, then, would be your son. He and Farley are the eyeball witnesses that put you with Vickee the night she died."

"I confessed to that, to the whole thing—killing her and all."

"Yeah, but I didn't believe you then. I do now believe, at least, that you were the one with the girl. There're even eyeball witnesses saw you leave with the girl." He didn't mention that one of them was Crystabelle now, that they'd gotten that much from her. "I thought you were covering up for Wesley. I still do think you're trying to protect him."

"You just make sure this doesn't land on him."

"Sherm, Sherm, Sherm. That's the old Sherm Hargate talking, the richest man in the county who throws in his two cents whether asked or not."

"I'm just telling you . . ."

"Shut up and listen, Hargate. You're in deeper shit than you've ever waded out of before. Even without you on the kibitz crew I'm getting more pressure than ever before to wrap up this case as quickly and tightly as possible. And I'm going to crack this thing just as sure as you're going to quit adding to the confusion and start helping."

"What are you accusing me of now?"

"I had a good talk with Wesley, although he might not think so. What's making you so damned squirrelly is that you're afraid he killed her. You'd have never done anything as stupid as confess unless you thought you were saving him. And Wesley, hell, he thinks you killed her. I mean, wasn't Wesley telling you the whole time he was helping beat you to the ground that that was your medicine? Now here's what I think: neither of you killed her. I was just rattling your chain about pinning it on the boy. Now, think carefully. Are you sure you want to take the fall for the whole thing, for murder? Her clothes, after all, were torn, but she was killed with a knife. Why would someone tear her clothes when they had a knife to cut them. That opens a possibility for there to have been more than one person with her that night. Come on, talk to me, Sherm. Tell me what really happened, all of it."

There was a long pause. Sparrow watched Sherm think. At least the clever eyes flicked about in rapid permutations of possibilities. After a minute or two, Sherm spoke.

"You're right," Hargate said, "I was with her. But not all night. You don't know how she was. But ask anyone. When we were . . . When I was done . . . She wanted to be left tied up there, have me come back later and go at her again. She liked to hang there all night, even think about who might walk in on her and find her naked."

"All the way out there?"

"It'd happened before. She talked 'em into jumping her too. This time I came back expecting her to be there. She was. But she was dead. I cut out. What would you have done? But she wasn't dead when I left her the first time, Sparrow. I swear that."

"Trouble is, I believe you."

"That's a problem because you need a solution."

"Right."

"You dropped that Purvis girl's name pretty handily. What's she, the bait?"

"She is the big cheese," Sparrow admitted. "She's making the killer more nervous than anything I'm doing. She's been warned to quit meddling twice, and that's the only active part of the case right now. But don't get too comfy. Until something else breaks, you're it, big fellow."

"Have you thought of looking into my alibi?"

"I have. I have indeed."

Dr. Heck Thomas came out of the barn into the house. "That's one sick horse you got there," he said. "She's over most of the convulsions. But it's fifty-fifty whether she makes it. I pumped the old gal's stomach. God knows, there have been higher moments after veterinarian school at A & M than that."

"What caused it?" Giff asked.

"Plants. Could be Jimpsonweed, locoweed. I've got to have someone else check. Whatever it was, she ate the whole mess. What I have is from the gastric lavage—the stomach pumping. I'll have to have someone else look at what I have and let you know. She didn't get them from your pasture. I'd guess the mare got them out of the feeding tray. There's indication some fresh greenery was in there. Someone put it there. Go figure. You or Cory wouldn't do anything foolish like that, would you?"

"Of course not."

Deputy Winslow held a cup of coffee but still followed the doctor out to talk. Giff turned and went back to the stove where the sheriff sat tilted back in one of the chairs.

"Lord knows, I tried to get along with you from the first, Giff," he said.

"Well, you won't accomplish that by trying to dredge up my academic past and make me an outsider to my own established circle of friends. What Zoe, Shimmy, and the rest of these dusty pals of mine think far outweighs anyone who wants to claim my attention by waving school flags."

"I don't know why that bothers you as much as it does. When I checked on your background I found you had wonderful grades—you even turned down Phi Beta Kappa, which I would have loved to have been offered if my grades had been up to it."

"Your checking's what bothers me," Giff said.

"That's misguided. I checked on everyone. That's standard procedure, and you know that. Don't fault me for doing my job."

"That's with the premise that we all have something to hide, even you."

Sparrow frowned. "I guess you could say that. Everyone who voluntarily came out to this out-of-the-way place just might have some dark secret—real or imagined. But I couldn't find anything on you. What was it brought you out here?"

"Maybe society'd had enough of my company."

"I do think you took Saris's death harder than anyone. Maybe you related more. You're not the hermit recluse he was . . .'"

"I probably have Cory to thank for that."

". . . but you aren't living up to your potential."

It was Giff's turn to frown. "Even I can't be the judge of that."

Sparrow stared at him, a pensive, sort of expectant look across his mug.

Giff didn't have any dark secrets, and if he did he wouldn't have shared them with the likes of Sparrow. What Giff had were everyday ordinary secrets, the kind that get swept out of every barroom at closing time and show up on the blotter of the most boring divorces, except that he'd never been married. He had gotten to the point where he'd been disgusted with himself, had told some fine and attractive women that he had nothing to offer them. His head had become an emotional wasteland by then, and it wasn't all that much better now. He had one thing going for him, and that was Cory, and she would be leaving the nest soon enough. He figured a lot of women he'd known would have gotten a good laugh out of the broken glass that was rattling around inside him these days. A few men might chuckle too, but Sparrow wasn't going to be one of them.

Sparrow finally gave up waiting and said, "Zoe was easy because he's always lived around here. Shimmy is Zoe's cousin. He moved here about the time you came to Bent Bell. Shimmy was an outstanding high school footballer, but he couldn't last the academics at Penn State, even if he hadn't been caught painting tiger stripes on the bronze Nittany Lion on the campus up there. He set new academic lows when he flunked out and got into a brawl or two near the end. And though we'll never be able to prove it, we think he's the one moved a couple of real estate signs around here over onto the city park. We had people calling the agents trying to buy the land before we got that mess straightened out."

"That's some real detecting, finding that out about Shimmy."

"That he's a prankster? Not the brightest bulb on the Christmas tree?"

"No, that he's Zoe's cousin."

"All right. You want detecting. I'll give you some." There was snap in Sparrow's voice now, and none of the congeniality of before. "We just had us a suicide this afternoon. Clayton Falcone, the deceased girl's uncle, got bailed out on a DWI charge and went and hung himself right in the church where he preaches. We tried to talk to him while he was in the holding cell but got nothing. We checked the suicide scene already and I can tell you this too, the rope wasn't the same kind used on Vic-kee Allen."

"Good lord. Did he . . ."

"Have an alibi? Of course, he did, the best kind." Sparrow's voice had risen to a near shout. "He was preaching to his congregation the night she died, and stayed the night in a visita-tion praying with an older couple. They had him sleep on the couch. So he's clear on the murder."

"Why would Clayton kill himself?"

"Now that comes under the heading of another unsolved mystery, though I have ideas." Some of the steam seemed to have eased out with the shouting. His words trailed off to a normal tone, though each word still seemed laden with purpose.

"I've a few ideas myself," Giff said.

A short silence settled in the store. If Sparrow reacted right away, Giff didn't catch it. He'd been pretty worked up there, Giff figured, so he gave him a few minutes to get back in control. He thought about Clayton, a preacher, who'd hung himself. Things seemed to be happening fast and at a tilt. He watched the front door, occasionally glancing to the back where Cory was nursing her sick horse. When he glanced back at Sparrow, he was startled for a second.

What was in Sparrow's face, no longer lurking but blazing now, was an intense fever, not just to succeed, but at all costs to avoid failure. It wasn't just the calls from the busybody locals that drove him. Something deep inside, some inner personal history was at work. It was what drove him deep into the background of others but would have made him violently defend anyone looking into his own.

"Someone did that to the horse, Giff," Sparrow said, his voice like a rusty gate being opened, "just as sure as they wrote those spray paint letters on the stall earlier."

"You ever get anywhere with that handwriting?"

"Not yet." Sparrow crossed his legs and picked at a bit of mud by the heel of one boot. "What we do have is that Sherm Hargate was the one with Vickee in the first place. He's the one who took her out there and tied her up."

"And left her?"

"He said she wanted it that way. He was supposed to come back later. It was all part of the fantasy it took to get her rockets lit, apparently. But when Sherm went back, she was a bloody mess, and dead. Someone had cut her good. He was gone for four hours, from ten P.M. until two A.M. So I have a window of time unaccounted for, and, if he's telling the truth, a clean slate as far as knowing who killed her. Don't think we didn't run every forensic test we could, either."

"You missed the rope business on the first go around, didn't you?"

"We did at that." Sparrow's eyes narrowed. He looked up at Giff. "I have to admit that every successful step of this case has been because of Cory—one way or another."

"I don't like that idea," Giff said.

"You did damn little to shut her down in the early going," Sparrow said. "Now all I need is another little jump start from her to wrap this up and we can get this community back to normal."

"What are you asking for, to make her a target?" Giff's hands clenched, and he stood up stiffer.

"I think I know who killed Vickee," Sparrow said. "I just have no proof, nothing I could take to a grand jury. Things haven't changed much from before. The only thing that's happened at all has involved Cory—these threats."

"I say no." Giff found he was speaking through his teeth. "Don't you under any circumstances stake her out."

Sparrow didn't laugh or even grin. He let the chair rock down to the floor and stood slowly. He tapped the edge of his hat on his holster and looked over at Giff. "Why don't you knock off all the sugar coating and tell me what you really think, Giff?"

Giff tilted his head at him. "I think you're the most dangerous kind of man there can be—one who will do anything and everything to favorably affect the impressions others have of you. It's not solving the case that drives you, but what the public thinks of you. You did your early law enforcement work somewhere else. Did you make a mistake there, misjudge the community and have to leave?"

Sparrow brushed some imaginary dust from the front of his uniform slacks and then looked up at Giff. "If the person who killed Vickee does come around here, you can always try out one of your stories on him. And the odds are about even that he will come back. With the spray-painted warning and the kind of things whoever it is has done to Cory, I'm inclined to think it's one of the area young ones. That's why I liked Wesley for it until it turned out it wasn't him. But keep your eyes open. She's your responsibility, you know."

"You want a story," Giff said. "I'll give you one."

"Spare me." Sparrow turned and started for the door.

"The last time Cory acted as screwy as she has lately was just before my birthday a couple years ago," Giff said.

Sparrow stopped, whether from politeness or something else Giff couldn't tell. But he pivoted and stood waiting until Giff could finish.

"She was wound tighter than a spring and was snappy, had a short attention span. I tried a lot of things, couldn't get through to find out what was bugging her. Then on my birthday she came to me, all coy, and handed me a package. I opened it, and I didn't know what to think. It was this pen you see in my pocket."

"Pretty expensive."

"That's what I thought. I couldn't imagine where she'd got the money. I've got to confess that my first thought was that she'd filched it out of the register, or someplace. I thought that's what'd been bugging her, and I snapped at her. She shot off to her room and after a few minutes I went to talk to her."

"Kids. You can't . . ."

"Let me finish," Giff interrupted. "I thought myself that I was going in that room to give her a lecture. But I'll tell you, when Cory came to me she had one possession, one thing in the world that she had left from her life before that mattered to her. It was the wedding picture of her parents in an antique mahogany frame. Cory was on her stomach across the bed crying. What caught my eye was the picture of her parents, propped up on her dresser without its frame."

"She'd hocked the frame?"

"She sold it on consignment at Nellie Mae's Antiques down the street to get the pen she'd spotted earlier. What had been bugging her was that we don't get all that much traffic going through town, and she was afraid the frame wouldn't sell in time to buy the present."

"It's a nice sentiment."

"The point is," Giff said, "I wouldn't part with the pen for anything. But even harder for me is that Cory's going to be leaving here one day herself. That alone is going to be as big a leap for me as for her. But I won't. I absolutely refuse to let you do anything that will imperil her. Do you hear me?" He realized his voice had risen higher than he usually ever let it. Sparrow's eyes widened, then narrowed.

"You don't need to appreciate that I have a job to do, but catching a killer is my top priority."

"I have no beef with that. Just be careful how you do it."

"I never had kids myself," Sparrow said to him as he turned and started up through the store. "I was just lucky that way."

"There are folks'd argue that one with you," Giff said.

Sparrow spun and went on out of the store. Giff watched his back fade and disappear. There still seemed to be more concern for public opinion than individual rights to Sparrow. He shook himself, tried to pull away from harshly judging the man who might only be doing his job with a touch more misguided zeal than was needed.

Zoe was coming in as Sparrow went out. They nodded, and Zoe headed toward the back of the store, straight for the chair Sparrow had been warming.

"How's Miss Dumspie?"

"Too soon to tell."

"What's put a burr under Sparrow's saddle?"

"Hard to say."

"Well, you're damn sure chatty today," Zoe said.

Giff didn't say anything.

"You hear about Clayton Falcone, the preacher?"

Giff nodded slowly.

"Oh, don't worry about Sparrow. He's just never become one of us, probably never will. But you have." He saw a question in Giff's expression.

Zoe settled slowly into the chair, tilted it back, and gave a small sigh.

"Why wasn't he let in?" Giff asked.

Zoe said, "Sparrow's always holdin' something back."

CHAPTER TWENTY

The store got wind-creaky quiet as the day ground slowly along. Giff eased over to his spot by the register and lowered himself to his forearms on the counter top. The scratchy radio was wrestling through Suppé's "Poet and Peasant" overture.

The past few days were a jagged blur to Giff: Cory coming home with the sheriff, Saris dying, all the other stuff. But the swirling ghosts of memories clouding his head at the moment had nothing to do with any of that. That's what puzzled him. All his life's regrets centered on the ones where he had turned down opportunities to get closer to women, to mate, to settle down and have children. Seen clear and detached in his hindsight now, the wreck of each possibility had come from a twist of communication. Why in creation all that came back to him now, he had no idea. He shook his head.

"Hello, in there," Zoe called over.

"What?" Giff looked up at Zoe, who still leaned back in his chair by the stove.

"You were about two-and-a-half light years from here. What were you thinking about?"

"You know how when you clip off the top of a wildflower, it'll scramble and bloom even from its shortened stem?"

"What the hell?"

"I mean, it's a defensive reaction. Its job is to put out seeds and by damn it's going to do that, even after a setback. I mean, the thought of death always stirs up a thirst for life, doesn't it?"

"Giff, sometimes you're as strange as a left-handed armadillo egg-beater."

Giff shrugged. He said, "Sometimes I try to imagine what it'll be like come the day Cory's not around here anymore. I guess I can see you, Shimmy, and me in our usual places, but I can't picture much more than that."

"Do we have gray hair and false teeth?"

"It wasn't in that kind of detail, thank goodness. Where is the Shimster, anyway?"

"Haven't seen him. Heard he wasn't at GALS last night either."

"That's something." Giff stood up straighter. "Zoe, did you go by his place and check?"

"You know, I did. Nothing."

"It's really not like him to miss a night at GALS."

"Maybe he's saving his beer money, heard about your expenses buying Saris's funeral—and the vet bill for Miss Dumpsie on top of that. Man, that's running into some serious coin. How're you gonna handle that, Giff? Didn't that just about ruin you? I'll help you all I can, but you're the first to know . . ."

"I'll work something out, and it won't mean taking it from Cory's college fund."

The screen door opened and two people came in. Giff looked up and saw Dewey and Lou, their arms linked, coming toward him. He sighed without showing it.

"What brings you two here?"

"A couple of things," Dewey said. His chest was puffed out, and his back looked stiff. "But first I want to say that your little girl . . ."

"Niece."

"Cory . . ."

Giff nodded.

"Yelled at us the other day."

"I'm sorry about that."

"Well, don't be. We could'a stood it. She was right, you know. So that's what the two things are. We came in to apologize and to pay up our account." He held out a scrap of paper and some bills and change, plopped them on the counter in front of Giff.

Giff looked at the money and the wrinkled old invoice. "I hope this doesn't mean you're not going to shop here anymore." The invoice went back three years.

"It means we're gonna shop more," Dewey snapped. His eyes sparkled. "I told you the little girl was right. Got us to thinkin'. Here we're supposed to be good examples of Christians, and we ain't always doing right by our own. We'll get all the others we can here too, Giff."

Zoe's chair dropped to the floor, and he stood to look over at the money on the counter and then at them. "Well, I'll be . . ."

Lou glanced at him, then at Giff. She huffed. "A couple a' bees in the sod," she said.

They turned and started up to the front of the store. After only a few steps, Lou stopped and Dewey was yanked back by the arm that looped through hers. Lou turned back and puckered her brow at Giff. "The early bird gets them firm. My stars," she humphed. They spun slowly and went on and out of the store.

Another couple came in while Dewey and Lou were going out. They held out a checkbook and a paper slip of a bill for goods bought long ago at Giff's store. Behind them came in Sherrie Easton. She winked at Giff, but got out of the way of Frank Murray, who came in and started pulling goods off the shelves and putting them in a basket. Giff hadn't seen Frank inside the store in a year.

Sherrie sidled up to the counter. From the side of his mouth, Giff asked her, "Any idea what's going on here?"

She leaned closer, let him get a whiff of her perfume. "Word's all over the town and area about what you did for Saris and about little Cory's horse. Folks got talking and decided you're a better man than they should ignore. I could have told them that, though I hope it doesn't turn into more competition for me." Giff didn't let his inner smile show. He was not sure why what she said pleased him, but it had in some strange way. He hadn't changed his thinking about married women; it was just that he found the aura of sexual tension that surrounded her like a cloud of her perfume to be more playful and comforting now than threatening. She moved away when half-a-dozen more people crowded to the counter wanting to pay up old accounts.

Giff looked past them to Zoe, who could only shrug back. He came around the counter and started to help Giff look up accounts in the file as people held out cash.

Giff could see out the front screen door that what had been a sun-washed oven of a day was beginning to fade to dusk. But more people were pulling up and getting out to come in. Word must have gone to every door in all of tiny Bent Bell and the surrounding area.

In the first lull they had, which did not come for a long while, Zoe looked over at Giff. Both of them looked a little haggard after the flurry. "Well, ol' pard," Zoe said, "it looks like your problem next week's gonna be restocking. You sure got a lot of old accounts settled, and more than half of the folks stayed to buy new stuff, which they paid for in cash."

"As the problems in life go," Giff said, "I think I'm prepared to wrestle with that one."

The flow of traffic in the store of people paying their bills surged and waned through the rest of the afternoon, but didn't slow to a trickle and stop until after the usual closing time. Giff and Zoe looked at each other, then Zoe slumped off toward a chair by the stove while Giff leaned in a tired droop across the pad in his comfort zone by the register. The gravity of everything else that'd gone on settled over them again. Zoe took special care as he tilted back until the chair touched the wall.

In a few minutes Giff would go back and see how Cory's horse was doing, or, more importantly, how Cory was doing. But TyTy was back there, and Giff wanted to give Cory a bit of space, if that's what she needed right now. It was a good ten minutes of solid quiet before he spoke.

"You know, you've been quiet as damn all about some aspects of this whole murder thing, Zoe. For you, I mean. You're usually the one who really likes to poke into the details of every little thing. But not this time. A couple of times when folks have started in on the details, especially anything about ropes, or being tied up, you've gotten up and taken a hike. Is something here hitting you on a tender spot?"

Zoe kept his chair tilted back against the wall, but Giff could tell he was far from comfortable. He started to speak a couple times before he finally succeeded. "You know how it is, don't you, that there are some people who you're drawn to . . . magnetically?"

"Irrevocably. Yeah."

"I mean, we've all had a few of these five-minute romances, someone we see on a bus, or in a store."

"Speak for yourself."

"You know what I mean. The person can even be married, or the wrong age. None of that matters. You're just drawn by some . . ."

"Inexplicable chemical or pherenomal force."

"Look, you want to tell this, or me?"

"Go ahead." Giff was getting a comfort out of Zoe's awkwardness in sharing this particular tale.

"Anyway, it ties to why I don't go to GALS anymore."

Giff's mouth opened and closed. He gave a nod and hoped

he looked encouraging.

Zoe rubbed a finger along one eyebrow and looked off about a foot to the left of where Giff stood. "What I'm going to tell you about took place about a year or two before you arrived on the scene here. I didn't get out on the town much even back then. When I did, I was the kind of emotional time bomb we can all be when we're young and spending too much time alone." His eyes lifted for the barest flicker at Giff.

"I had slicked up as much as I ever do, or did. Since I was no dance-hall regular I stood around and watched others dance, link up in whatever mating ritual was working for them."

"You were the fish on the bicycle, eh?"

"Yeah. But then I looked through the solid mat of faces and got my first glimpse of Ilsa, the dark angel of my life."

"You never told us about any Ilsa."

Zoe held up a hand. This wasn't an easy story to share and was going to be impossible with Giff butting in.

"I couldn't believe, in the first place, that anyone who looked as innocent as that would be in a place like GALS. She had the kind of raw curiosity on her face you might see on a fifteen-year-old. Then I couldn't believe she was staring at me. I did one of those look-behind-me moves, to see if she was really looking at someone behind me. But it was me she was interested in, even though I made pretty quick work of demonstrating that I danced like someone on bent stilts. But it was the attraction—the raw pull toward her that hit me. That and the fact that she seemed to be as drawn to me. I was enough younger then to believe I could attract someone.

"I'm gonna fast forward a bit here, 'cause I can see you're on a short attention span leash today. I drove over to her place two days later. It's way out in the middle of nowhere—an older house, hardwood floors, the breeze whipping through the place lifting gauzy white curtains. She opened the door wearing a white nightgown that was just sheer enough to yank me through the doorway."

"Like a hooked speckled trout," Giff said.

"Yeah, but I was blinder than all three mice right then. You've got to understand that."

Giff nodded.

"Otherwise I might've thought something was odd, would have kicked a bit more when she suggested tying me up."

Giff had been bent over the counter, but now he snapped upright.

Zoe went on as if he hadn't noticed, having built up momentum by now. "I mean, she had these old sets of nylon panty-hose right under the bed all ready, and she whipped them out, and I didn't make anything of that, I just went along. You've got to remember, she was looking more Sunnybrook than Sunnybrook itself, and was naked besides. So, I let her tie me up, wrists and ankles to the oak posts of her bed. They were strong, too—don't think I didn't find out later. I don't remember now her exact words, just that I didn't hesitate nearly long enough. I was tied up there like that for three days."

"Three days?"

"And nights."

"Good lord."

"I thought of that too. But even praying didn't help. First it was fun, I have to admit, but then it went too long, and finally I was mad. I struggled, but those damn oak posts, and the hose. Hell, if I could have gotten to a wrist I might have chewed at it."

"But didn't you have to . . ."

"The bathroom stuff? Well, she was a nurse. She took care of everything: feeding me, all the bathroom stuff, sponge baths. Oh, I raged at first, and I tried to resist her, not respond, you know. But I was young and that was impossible. She'd come in with feathers and ice cubes, that hot tongue of hers . . . oh, it was no use. I tried with everything I had to ignore her. But instead, I was there for her every time, ready until I hurt, until I wondered how she could stand it because I couldn't anymore."

Zoe paused, but there was nothing for Giff to say, though he was starting to think Zoe might have some special understanding here. Zoe began to speak again.

"I'd wake up and start screaming all over again. I even tried to bite her, but she was quick. After a while I quit that. I wasn't even sure if I was going to die there. I ate. I slept. I was used. It got surreal. No, I take that back. It started there, and went way beyond that. When she finally untied me, she jumped back, like she expected me to spring up and beat her. But I could barely drag myself into my clothes and get myself out of there. When I got home, Biff was there from the feed store, checking on me. He said, 'Where the hell were you? You've missed three days of work.' I told him, 'I was tied up.' "

"So, in your case it didn't have anything to do with the way you were brought up, or any kind of guilt you felt."

"Dammit, Giff. None of it was my idea at all. It's nothing like whatever Vickee needed."

"And that was the end of that?"

"I wish."

"You didn't go back and see her again, did you?"

"No. She tracked me down, told me she was pregnant, that I was the father."

"So what?"

"She didn't want to marry me, or anything like that. She wanted an abortion, and for me to pay for it."

"You were set up."

"Don't I know that? Of course I was. I knew that even then, though there wasn't a whole lot else I did know. I even went to my doctor, found out I was sterile, that it couldn't have been me. I could never have kids. That's when I found out about that."

"But you paid anyway."

"Yeah, I paid for it, took her to the clinic too—all the way in to Austin."

"Why?"

"I don't know what to say about how my head was then. I was still in a bit of shock, I guess."

"Whew. You never mentioned any of this before."

"Why would I?"

"Why did you now?"

"I don't know. It was heavy, and a bit of baggage I guess I was ready to toss out. But you can see why this business about Vickee got me stirred up a bit, then on top of that you sharing your thoughts about having a family and children of your own."

"Wow."

"Hell, I'm just glad you've let me be a kind of honorary uncle to Cory."

"She did that," Giff said.

"I don't know if that was what you were fishing for." Zoe looked around the room as if getting his bearings. "It's the first time I've ever told anyone about all that. Thought I might feel better if I did, but now I don't know."

"I think I was just trying to see how much you knew."

"Why? You think you know more about who killed Vickee than the rest of us?"

"I have an idea I've been kicking around, though I don't like it much. I'm hoping I'm wrong."

"Why don't you tell the sheriff, then? He's sure in a lather to know."

"I think he suspects the same thing I do."

"Which is?"

Giff gave a nervous shake of his head.

"You know, it just might be you're not getting enough sleep, up prowling around like the ghost of Hamlet's father, as you used to say. Only time you've took a rest is when someone's knocking you out or you're in a hospital bed."

Giff did not respond. In a few minutes, Zoe had to ask, "You really think you know?"

Giff shared a reluctant nod.

"Then why don't you tell the sheriff?"

"I'll tell you something about Mr. Michael Sparrow, the main arm of the law out in these parts. First of all, it turns out he did go to Harvard."

"I thought we knew that."

"People can say anything. I checked."

"How'd you find out, confirm it, so to speak."

"There's hardly one of those Crimson-bleeding yahoos who doesn't keep in touch with the alumni office. They never know when they'll want to wrangle a ticket to the annual Harvard-Yale game, though I doubt either team would fare well against, say, the University of Texas. You can damn well bet that the college's development people keep an eye on all those Crimson grads in case any of them get the notion to share endowment money. I made a call, that's all."

"You made several calls, back there before Saris's death knocked you for a loop. Is that what those were about?"

"Yeah."

"And found out what? You gonna make me drag this outta you?"

"Turns out we were right that being sheriff here's his third time, and perhaps his last chance to make it."

"You can't hold that against the man. We've all bounced once or twice."

"Sparrow makes an interesting study, though. If you took the average of all Ivy League grads who were ever drawn into criminal justice fields, with the exception of lawyers, you get a pretty low tick. But Sparrow's folks being killed by a burglar must have set a hook. I called a few newspapers at the places where Sparrow's had an address over the years. It's stuff other people must already know, but he started as a cop in a small New England town, worked his way up to chief. He bounced out of that the hard way when an investigation of his came up a goose egg and he landed in Ohio as a sheriff. The curtain of that job was just about to come down on him in an ugly way when a handful of those-who-would-control from around here got wind of him and hired him to ride the range down here. He could talk real pretty, and they figured they had his high-credential but low-performance ass in their pockets."

"You mean there were people here who wanted a sheriff with luggage, one they could squeeze a bit if there was something they wanted to keep quiet? I'm talkin' here about whatever went on between that Vickee and her uncle, and whatever else goes on around here that folks'd like to keep swept under the carpet."

"Exactly."

"Was Sherm Hargate one of those movers and shakers?"

"Certainly, and Spencer Allen, too."

Chapter Twenty-One

"What's with you? You're squirming enough for half a dozen deputies." Sparrow frowned over at Winslow. The man was almost too tall for the inside of the patrol car. Maybe sitting behind the steering wheel this long made him a little claustrophobic. It was dim inside the car, with only the dash lights to give their faces an eerie and sinister greenish red tint.

"I don't care much for stake-outs," Winslow said. "Especially this one."

"You've seen all the local big frogs in the pond coming and going from my office. What do you think they've been pounding the table about? They want results."

That damned Giff Purvis had been closer to the mark than he could have known. Giff's guessing right stung more than Sherm Hargate knowing. But no matter what had happened back in that county full of fish nets, crab pots, and the ocean stink, he was paying for it now by being in this little fleabite of a county. He hadn't been in a position to say no when those dirty-fingernail rich bastards from here had come to him and offered him the job then, nor was he in a position now not to get the job done as quickly as they wanted. At times it made him feel his soul was no longer his own.

"You said you know who it is. Why don't we just bring him in?"

"We've got nothing but some good ideas. I told you that."

"I just wonder if there isn't a better way."

"Your job isn't to . . ."

The radio interrupted with a squawk as Moll back at the dispatch desk keyed the mike. "Got a domestic in progress over to the Wood Shadows Trailer Park."

"Can it wait?"

"Jeb Garland's slapping Elsie up and down their place like her head's a handball's what I was told."

"Moll," Sparrow cautioned. He'd warned her enough times about too much detail over the air. There were folks with gnawing interest and little enough color in their lives that they did nothing but scan the police bands for juicy information, the kind Moll was too prone to share.

"Guess we'd better look into it, and be quick" Sparrow said. He let Moll know they were en route.

Winslow started up the car, hit the lights and pulled out. Once they were going he didn't feel so good about leaving the stake-out either.

"We'll get back as soon as we can," Sparrow assured him. "Damn trailer courts. Hurricanes and tornadoes have the right idea about what to do with them."

Cory stood beside the opened end of the horse stall. Miss Dumpsie lay on her side in the middle of the stall, too exhausted to get up. Her side rose and fell in jerky breaths. Her nose looked crusty to Cory, and her big eye was foggy and uncertain. She lifted her head an inch and seemed to search the barn for Cory's voice. TyTy was sitting on a bale of straw across room.

"Don't you die on me, Miss Dumpsie," Cory said. She felt her own voice quiver with emotion, part fear, part anger.

The stall was still a mess. She took the pitchfork down from the wall and went to fork some more straw and spread it out in the stall around Miss Dumpsie.

TyTy hopped off the bale of straw and got out of her way. He said, "I can help with that."

Cory shook her head as she carried the extended pitchfork into the stall. "No. I need something to do. I can't hold her head or make her drink." Her throat knotted, and she choked off the last word. A bit of hay and some of the good oats was in Miss Dumpsie's trough, and a bucket of water was beside her stretched head. But the horse just lay there, tired and still sick from whatever she had eaten. And the vet's stomach pumping.

Cory had to look away, the lump in her throat about to strangle her every time she thought of losing Miss Dumpsie. Doc Thomas said it would just take time to see, but that was so hard. Everything in life was take time and wait and see. She could barely stand it.

"Do you think I was being a busybody too?" she said. She leaned on the pitchfork and looked at TyTy.

"Nobody thinks that."

"A lot do, and especially whoever poisoned Miss Dumpsie. I've been . . . I've been such a fool. I thought I needed to do something. I should have just stuck my head in the sand like everyone else around here."

"Don't be so hard on yourself."

"If I'm not, who will be? I'm just starting to realize how spoiled rotten I am."

"You're not. Now someone like Wesley Hargate is. But not you."

"Oh, his dad has money and lets Wesley have plenty of it. But look how Uncle Giff treats me, and I've been such a little turd lately. Now someone has tried to poison Miss Dumpsie too because of it."

TyTy's expression said he was awakening to the idea that this was an argument he shouldn't be in, that he had no way of coming out ahead. "Look at it this way. Wesley's in jail, and you're not."

Cory took the pitchfork over and hung it back on the wall. She went close to Miss Dumpsie and bent over. She couldn't see any improvement, but the horse was breathing more regularly, not as jagged as she had after having her stomach pumped. It had been a rough day for the old girl. Cory tried hard not to think of the possibility of her not being around. She pushed herself to her feet and started back across the open space.

TyTy came over and stood in her path. She stopped and looked up at him. He put his hands on her shoulders and looked into her face. It was exactly what she had been wanting him to do. "What's the matter with you, Cory?"

"I used to feel good about myself. Now I'm starting to wonder."

"You're so good you don't even know how good you are. Now lay off. I'm here because I believe in you. Isn't that worth anything?"

"It's worth a lot." She laid her head on his shoulder. It was the first time since she had found Miss Dumpsie floundering and in convulsions that she had relaxed.

"Your uncle's calling me Tracker now," he said.

She tilted her head back to look up at him. "Tracker. I like that."

"Better than TyTy?"

"A lot. Oh, what the hell. I like you, no matter what you're called. But Tracker is an improvement."

"Did you hear something?" TyTy said.

Cory looked to the door outside, where he was staring. "No, but your ears are better than mine."

He went over to the door. It had gotten darker out. He pressed himself against the barn's inside wall just by the door and held up the flat of his hand to Cory. Then Cory could hear the soft steps too.

Cory cringed, not knowing whether she should get behind something or stay where she was. A large body filled the doorway, came the rest of the way inside. It was Shimmy.

"There you are, Cory. I heard about what happened. I came to see how you were."

"You nearly scared me to death, Shimmy. Why'd you come around the back way instead of coming through the house? Haven't you been to see Uncle Giff in the store yet?"

Shimmy wore his usual bib coveralls. He grinned, reached into his pocket for the round can of snuff. But when he glanced at the horse the grin faded. "That's a damn shame," he said. "Is she going to die?"

"I hope not." Cory could barely choke out the words.

There was a soft noise behind him. Shimmy looked back, saw TyTy step away from the wall. " 'Lo, TyTy," he said.

TyTy nodded. He moved around cautiously until he was beside Cory.

Shimmy's face held nothing but concern. His tongue tucked the snuff into place and he put the can back. "You been cryin', Cory. Are you okay now?"

"No, Shimmy, I'm not okay." Cory's voice still had a quiver to it she didn't like. "I've been having a kind of rotten day."

The phone rang. Giff tried to discourage people from calling in orders or checking to see if he had Prince Albert in a can, but after the flurry of store traffic earlier he figured it was one more well-wisher getting into the community spirit of things. But it was the veterinarian.

"How are you doing, Heck? Learn anything?"

"I did," he said, "I just got off the phone with the sheriff's department. Sparrow wasn't there, but I passed along that it was water hemlock. You all are just lucky it wasn't poison hemlock. The two look near enough alike. If someone had put

235

that in your mare's trough we'd be digging a big hole about now. It's just lucky we pumped her out when we did. If she's gets to where she can stand on her own, she's probably around the corner and gonna make it."

"You think someone meant to put poison hemlock in there but didn't know the difference?" Giff asked.

"Exactly. Though I can't tell you what the person was thinking—anyone'd do a thing like that to a horse oughta be strung up."

Giff put the receiver back on its hook in stunned slow motion. He looked over. Zoe was staring at him.

"You didn't happen to mention Socrates drinking the hemlock to anyone but those of us who were in the truck the other day, did you?" Zoe said.

"No."

"I was just hoping."

"Me too," Giff said.

"That poor, sorry ol' S.O.B.," Zoe said. He was tilted back in his chair by the stove; but he did not look comfortable. He looked too pole-axed to move. "That's who you were thinking it was earlier, wasn't it?"

"We don't know," Giff insisted. He stood upright now, though still at his usual post behind the counter by the register.

"You just said there wasn't no one else you mentioned hemlock to."

"You didn't see him all day?" Giff asked.

"No. And he didn't show at his job either. I checked with GALS, and no one there saw him, and he's hard to miss." Zoe glanced at the empty chair beside him. "Where's Cory?"

"Out sitting with Miss Dumpsie. TyTy's with her."

"Is the horse gonna make it?"

"We don't know. The doctor said fifty/fifty, but that was in front of Cory."

"What was the point, of that and the spray-painted message? To warn little Cory off? Don't he know that'd just egg a kid like that on?"

"I don't know what the hell the damned point was, Zoe," Giff snapped. He had just figured something else out and was already moving fast away from the phone.

Zoe dropped his chair to the floor, started to rise but dropped back onto the seat. "Giff, I'm just sick. I mean it. I could hurl any second about all this."

"Well, try to buck up for Cory's sake." Giff raced into the back through the house. Zoe got up and staggered after him.

Giff burst through the doorway into the barn and stopped. Zoe was running close behind and slammed into Giff's back, almost knocking him over. When they got their balance and straightened, they stared at Shimmy.

Cory saw something in their faces. Her head swung slowly back to Shimmy, her eyes opened wide. "It was you, wasn't it?"

"What?" Shimmy's big head moved from Giff and Zoe back to her.

"You were the one that came in after Sherm Hargate left and . . . and . . ."

"Now that's wild talk."

". . . and you're hiding. I know. Sherm was your alibi; you were his. All that's out the window now that the sheriff and everyone else knows he was the one with Vickee first. But then Sherm left her, like she asked. You were the one with her before Sherm came back and found her dead, weren't you?"

Cory's face was flushed, and she leaned forward, her small hands clenched into fists.

Shimmy was fixed on Giff and Zoe. "Come on, you guys, tell her . . ."

"Heck Thomas just called," Giff said in a flat voice, "the vet. He says that what someone fed to Miss Dumpsie was water hemlock. It's not quite as likely to kill her as poison hemlock would've been, if someone knew the difference."

Cory leaped forward at Shimmy, but TyTy's arms were around her holding her back. She screamed, "You tried to kill Miss Dumpsie." Veins stuck out along her neck, and TyTy did all he could do to hold her back.

"No, I never . . ." Shimmy's face looked hurt. He looked at her, then at Zoe and Giff.

Zoe was still too stunned to speak. Giff's voice was soft, patient. "How did it happen, Shim?"

Shimmy's head hung, then he looked up. His eyes were watering, reliving something they hadn't seen. "I only went out there to help her, honest. I . . . I . . . I couldn't figure on her wantin' to be left there. I thought Sherm was bein' mean. I saw them leave GALS together. Hell, I knew where they might go. Sherm was leavin' the Whalen place 'bout the time I got there. I went in, and the girl was all tied up. Her clothes were torn from her. I knew . . . well, I thought she wouldn't have wanted that. I was just gonna cut her loose."

"You spray-painted that warning, and you tried to kill Miss Dumpsie," Cory yelled. She swung an elbow back into TyTy's stomach, but he managed to hang onto her.

"That's not all of it," Giff said. "What happened next? How did she end up dead like that?"

"I . . . I can't tell you."

"You mean you don't know, or you don't want to?" Giff's voice stayed low and comforting.

"It's too . . . too . . ."

"You're gonna have to say it sometime," Zoe said. "Might as well be to us."

Shimmy was looking at Cory. The guys he could have handled, but it was Cory's presence that made it hard for him.

"Go on," Giff said.

Shimmy hung his head, reached in and took out his snuff with a hooked finger. He let it drop. When he looked up his face was covered with tears, and his huge shoulders shook with sobs. "Everybody only knows I'm big, that I make jokes, but . . . but . . ."

"Go on," Giff coaxed.

"That Vickee got to taunting me, called me stupid for trying to help and cut her down. She shouted at me, yelled that I oughta take my clothes off, do somethin' about . . . about the way she was hangin' there a waitin'."

"What'd you do?" Zoe said, caught up in what he was saying. Even Cory had quit struggling and listened.

"Well, I . . . I got undressed. That's the thing, you see. When I turned to her, she laughed. I know I'm big on the outside, but . . ." He paused and glanced at Cory. "But I'm not big all over. I'm kinda tiny, in fact. It's why I don't usually mess around or nothin', just watch at GALS."

"And Vickee?" Giff said.

"She laughed," Shimmy said, his voice pinched with hurt. "She laughed hard at me, and she wouldn't quit. I was standin' there, naked and she laughed, me with the knife I was gonna use to cut her loose hangin' there in my hand. I don't know what happened then. It was all red in my mind. I just know I stopped and realized I'd quit cuttin' on her, and that she was dead, wasn't never gonna breathe again. And it was me done it. You can't believe how that feels. Me, who wouldn't hurt a bug."

TyTy's grip relaxed as he stared with the others at Shimmy. But something must have made Cory think of the harm done to Miss Dumpsie. She surged loose from TyTy's hold and raced across the distance to Shimmy. She leaped at him, pounded on him. He towered over her. His huge arms reached and held her at arm's length, as gently as he could. But she swung her thin arms at him with all she had.

His hurt eyes were fixed on Giff and Zoe. He still sobbed, "I just wanted her to stop, to stop laughing."

TyTy darted forward, his arms reaching to pry Cory loose. Shimmy missed the motive, only caught the sudden movement. His eyes snapped away from Zoe and Giff. A big arm swept at TyTy, who was lifted and flew backwards through the air and slammed against the wall. Cory screamed.

It looked like a mother bear defending a cub. TyTy slid down the wall and rushed back at Shimmy, who looked confused.

Something snapped in Zoe. He ran forward.

"Now, guys," Shimmy said. He gave Cory a shove to buy a moment, smashed his club of an arm on TyTy.

Once up to Shimmy, Zoe looked uncertain about what he was going to do. Shimmy's backswing caught him and sent him tumbling into a heap. "Stop it," Shimmy shouted. His voice was at full boom now and filled the barn.

TyTy lay where he had fallen. Zoe stirred in an effort to rise. Shimmy rushed over to him.

Giff could not figure out what was happening by now. He ran over and pulled at the back of Shimmy's coveralls, trying to yank him away from Zoe. It was a futile effort. Shimmy was way too strong. He looked back at Giff, though, and reached with a big paw to shove at Giff's chest. Giff leaped back, and the change in direction caused Shimmy to fall toward Giff. But he caught himself before his weight could land on Giff and crush him.

Cory screamed again and again. Giff looked up and saw her rush to the wall and grab the pitchfork off its hook. He looked up, and Shimmy was grinning at him, tears streaking his face, glad he hadn't hurt his friend.

"No," Giff shouted.

Cory lowered the tines of the pitchfork and ran across the room. TyTy's eyes had opened, but he was only able to pull himself into a sitting position against the wall. "No, Cory," he shouted too.

But she continued to run across at Shimmy. Giff pushed up with both hands on Shimmy's shoulder, knocking him onto his side. Giff scrambled and was half to his feet. Cory was nearly to Shimmy. The only thing Giff could do was throw himself in her path, and he did. A tine of the pitchfork entered his side and ran all the way through, tearing a bloody ring in the denim shirt on the other side and sticking out three inches.

Cory stopped, let go of the pitchfork and reeled back. But the weight of the loose handle brought Giff tumbling forward in a bolt of pain.

"Oh, my God," Cory shouted, her hands up to her face. She spun and ran over to TyTy's side. "What have I done?"

Giff tumbled to his side, grabbed at the pitchfork handle just after it had banged against the packed dirt floor once. The pain shot through him like a bolt. His head was full of a jumble of irrational thoughts, among them that the fork had been used in the stable, he would almost certainly need a tetanus shot. He saw Shimmy scramble to his feet and rush over to help. His face was full of hurt and concern. One big hand pressed against Giff's chest, the other pulled at the handle of the pitchfork.

Giff heard a shout, his head still a twirl of confused thought. He could see TyTy and Cory huddled against the wall. Through the door from the outside he saw the khaki uniforms as Sheriff Sparrow and Deputy Winslow burst into the room with drawn guns. Giff saw Sparrow raise his revolver.

"No," Giff shouted and felt a pain from shouting as well as another as Shimmy pulled the pitchfork free from where Giff had been stabbed.

The blast of the shot filled the room, seemed to take forever to quit echoing.

Giff stared up into Shimmy's face, saw the surprise and the

pain. Shimmy slowly rolled away from Giff, being careful to drop the pitchfork away from him and roll so that he didn't land on Giff.

Zoe was up. "Hold on there, Mr. Harvard," he shouted at the sheriff. He ran forward. Giff was watching Sparrow's face, the pleased expression that flickered across it before the mask fell back into place. Sparrow's gun swung up again, took steady aim at Shimmy. Giff could see the finger tightening for another shot. Giff looked at Winslow, who looked puzzled. Giff used all his strength to push with the flat of his hands to get himself to his knees and then work to stand up. Zoe helped him stand up, then bent over Shimmy.

"He's alive," Zoe shouted. "Hit in the shoulder. Call an ambulance, someone."

Giff was only just able to stand, the room oozed around. But he took halting steps, limped as rapidly as he could and barely stepped between Sparrow and Shimmy in time, spoiling the sheriff's clear shot at him.

"He'll have plenty of time to heal," Sparrow said, the finger lifting from the trigger and his gun hand slowly lowering to his side. He put his revolver back in his holster. His angry eyes fixed on Giff. "He's looking at murder in the second, easy."

Cory jumped up and rushed over to help hold Giff upright. He put an arm over her bony shoulder, let her support him a little.

Sparrow went over and reached behind the stack of hay bales. He pulled out a tape recorder; hit a button to stop it. "Voice activated," he said. "Left it here after the horse was poisoned, figured our killer had a fix on little Cory there."

He looked at Winslow, didn't like what he saw on his deputy's face. He looked at Giff, who was hobbling slowly toward him. "I told you I knew who it was, Giff, that I just didn't have enough to take it to trial yet. Now I do. What?"

"I thought we spoke about using Cory as bait," Giff shouted.

"Oh, calm down. From what I'm getting now it looks like we've a lot of confusion to sort through."

"If you were watching this place like some damned mousetrap, what took you so long to get in here?" Giff sidled closer to Sparrow, each step painful.

"Put some ice in your shorts. I've got a whole county to run, after all."

Sparrow watched Giff seem to topple forward, reached as if to help him. But Giff was dipping his shoulder and loading up. His uppercut sliced up, and his bony fist smashed into Sparrow's chin with a satisfying and painful crunch.

Sparrow lifted up off his feet, sailed back and landed flat on the floor. The recorder lay beside him. Neither moved after that.

Zoe looked up at the sound. He was bent over Shimmy, getting his head to rest against a clump of straw, while pressing a handkerchief against where the bullet had exited.

His eyes took in Winslow looking stunned, Giff rocking back upright, Cory struggling to hold him that way, then to Sparrow stretched out and unconscious. "Well," Zoe said, "it looks like Yale beat Harvard this year."

Giff looked into Winslow's eyes. He held out his wrists, though Cory still had to work to hold him upright. "Do what you have to do," he said.

Winslow's eyes narrowed to slits in the shadow cast by his hat brim. Giff looked up at him. The deputy slowly shook his head. "No. No sir. I got a daughter myself. But you better set a bit."

He helped Cory and Zoe stretch Giff out beside Shimmy. A splash of blood covered the flannel of Shimmy's shirt where he'd been shot, but the bleeding had slowed after Zoe had stanched it with his handkerchief and a piece torn off his own shirt. TyTy stood and tottered forward to help ease Giff down.

"Ain't one of you isn't banged up back here," Winslow said. "I'll go call for an ambulance."

"Better make it two," Giff said, "if Sparrow needs one. I'll ride with Shimmy, but I won't ride with him." He nodded toward Sparrow.

"I understand," Winslow said. He reached up and undid his badge, tossed it in a glittering spin over onto the sheriff. "I can't say as I want to ride with him again myself."

Giff felt giddy. "You know Sparrow's never even done anything about Farley killing Saris. He might say it was accidental or something, but Farley can't get away with what he done. I didn't press charges, but I still can if Farley gets off scot-free."

"I'll make sure Farley gets charges, Mr. Purvis," Winslow said. "I'll keep my badge long enough to take care of that." He picked up his badge and put it in his pocket.

Giff looked over at Shimmy.

The big face winced when he looked back at Giff, but then he grinned. "I'm just damned relieved all this is over. I'm gonna miss you guys, but I did catch myself up in somethin' that was way wrong. It made me crazier tryin' to sweep it under the rug than it would've to just come clean." It was hard for Shimmy to move his head, but he made the effort. He looked over at Cory. "I'm real sorry about what happened to Vickee. But I'm even more sorry about what I did to you. I never meant to kill your horse, little Cory, just make her sick so you'd quit doin' more than the sheriff ever could. I know the difference between water hemlock and poison hemlock; I just didn't know it'd make her as sick as it did. Can you ever forgive me?"

"It would take time," Cory said. She paused and gave it thought for a moment. "But I have plenty of that. We'll have to see."

Giff realized his head lay in Cory's lap. He looked up at her, but the back of TyTy's head was blocking the view.

"I was about to say," Giff said to Zoe, "that I couldn't remember when I got this much attention from Cory."

"I swear, Giff Purvis. You'll flop right through the gates of hell some day and be lookin' for the silver lining to that cloud." Zoe rose and went up into the store. He came back with gauze and a roll of tape.

"Let me look at that wound. You're making a mess of your shirt."

Cory helped tear away the shirt and dress the wound. "I'm so sorry I stabbed you, Uncle Giff."

"Paramedics'll just want to do all this over again," Zoe beefed as he worked on Shimmy.

"They can always work on Sparrow. He's still out like last Christmas's lights."

Shimmy said, "Man, you hit him, Giff. I didn't know you had that in you."

"The medics might get to work on my Joe Louis hand if it's broken," Giff said. "And it feels like it is."

"You know you're lookin' at some hard prison time, don't you, Shim?" Zoe said.

Shimmy nodded as best he could. "I already faced up to that. It's what I come to tell Cory, and apologize, before everyone went loopy on me. I never done such mean stuff in my life. I got a lot to stew over. But it was Cory there who scared me, little girl like that and all. It's just she's smarter'n Sparrow'll ever be. I'm so sorry."

In the distance they could hear a siren approaching. Miss Dumpsie stirred in her stall and struggled to get up. She tossed her neck and worked to get her legs under her. Her eyes were wide open.

"Oh, gosh." Cory jumped up and dashed over. Giff's head

fell back to the dirt floor with a soft thud.

Giff felt a slam of pain through his side, decided to lie where he'd fallen without moving. He said, "I think I know what was bugging me before, Zoe. Back when my head was screwed up."

"That's since I've known you."

"I mean earlier today. My head was some kind of tangled mess."

"Oh, and I suppose it's all better now."

Cory called over, "She's going to make it. I think she's going to be just fine."

He looked over to where Cory had her arms around Miss Dumpsie's neck. TyTy was close but stood back to let her have her moment with the horse.

Zoe said, "Maybe you've got to worry less about losing Cory and enjoy her more while she's still around."

"You're so right," Giff admitted.

"Even if I stab you now and then?" Cory's voice was choked—whether from remorse or with the tears of joy on her face about her horse, Giff couldn't tell.

"I'm no parent," Zoe said, "but I guess you just needed to feel needed."

"Well, I'm okay on that now." He was watching Cory clinging to the neck of her horse.

"Wiggle over here and give me a hand with Shimmy, then," Zoe said. "God knows, I need you for that."

ABOUT THE AUTHOR

Jan Grape's *Austin City Blue* was nominated for an Anthony for Best First Novel, and she received a special Shamus Award from the Private-Eye Writers of America in 2002. Other awards include an Anthony for Best Short Story and a McCavity for Best Nonfiction. Jan has also published a short-story collection, *Found Dead In Texas* (2003) and *Dark Blue Death*, the second in the Austin policewoman series (2005). Along with Barri Flowers, Jan co-edited an anthology of original stories by members of the American Crime Writers League, of which she currently serves as president. Jan lives in the Texas Hill Country with her black cats, Nick and Nora, and travels whenever possible.